THE
COUGAR
CANDIDATE

THE COUGAR CANDIDATE

WILL WORSLEY

HEDGELAND PRESS

Cover design: Peri Gabriel Book Design
Interior design: Alt 19 Creative
Author photo credit: Aaron Clamage Photography

ISBN 978-1-7356652-0-7 (tradepaper)
ISBN 978-1-7356652-1-4 (e-book)

Published by:
Hedgeland Press
4314 35th Street South
Arlington, Virginia 22206
www.hedgelandpress.com

For my sister Diana,
the best storyteller I know.

CHAPTER 1

Clement's Lament

UNTIL EIGHT THIRTY, when her unexpected visitor appeared, the weightiest things on the ex-governor's mind were the pink curlers in her hair.

Patty sipped her mimosa, gazing in frustration through the veranda's windows. Last night's rainstorm had stopped, and while she was glad for that, an impenetrable mist still hovered over the beach. If there were any surfer boys out there, she couldn't see them through her binoculars.

As if to make amends, the fog parted like a stage curtain over the indoor pool's glass roof, allowing her a clear view of Mylo instead. Strutting in a navy-blue swimsuit along the edge of the water, the new pool boy skimmed the surface with his long-handled net, wielding his tool with the practiced grace of an Olympic athlete. Patty focused her spyglass on the youth's nicely rounded buttocks, scanning his bare shoulders and toned biceps, lingering on his outstanding pectorals. A chest like that could be dangerous. Letting out a sigh, she imagined squeezing all of Mylo's muscles as eagerly as she ogled them, all the way down to his toes.

Looking up, he caught her gaze and grinned at her. Patty froze for a second before shifting her binoculars innocently back to the fog. *Oh, what the heck, he's eighteen. Wait, what's this?*

Something solid and blurry blocked her binoculars. Patty looked up, startled to see the lanky Englishman standing three feet before her.

"Nigel! How long have you been lurking there?"

The man, dressed in a gray business suit with a blue polka-dot tie, shook his head in disapproval. "That will be enough of that, Governor. Eyes off the pool boy. I texted and emailed you last night. Didn't you get my messages? I left a call on your phone too."

"I just got up. You know I never look at my messages before ten."

"We have to talk—it's urgent."

Nigel said he'd rushed there to discuss the bombshell story that broke overnight. As her former chief of staff, he thought it only fitting he should be the first to discuss the matter with her.

He drove twenty-five miles to Durango Beach to inform her about some political news? He must have more to tell her than that. Patty was not a huge fan of Senator Harry Clement, but the news about him couldn't be true. "Blackface? Harry Clement?"

"See for yourself." Nigel grabbed the remote off her side table and turned on her television.

The talking heads on CNN were buzzing about a grainy old photograph. It showed a little white boy with a big grin, sitting astride an enormous pumpkin, a cardboard box covering him from his chin to his knees. Sticking out of the box, his face, arms, and legs were stained dark brown.

Patty squinted at the screen. "That's Clement?"

"A disturbing photograph of Democratic front-runner Senator Harry Clement in blackface has been discovered," the news anchor said. "This highly disturbing image was the subject of a front-page article in this morning's *New York Times*. The Clement campaign has not yet responded to our reporter with an explanation, despite our many attempts to get through."

"But that's ridiculous."

"No, it's not," Nigel replied. "For Clement, it's curtains. He'll never survive this."

The butler, clad in livery, entered the veranda and set Patty's breakfast before her. She took a bite of bacon and bent her neck forward.

Maybe it was Clement. Nigel Windborne, an astute political operative, took such pride in getting his facts straight he was considered an insufferable know-it-all. He was almost always right, and even when he wasn't, he was awfully convincing.

"He looks like he's six years old."

Nigel pulled a note out of his coat pocket. "Five years, two months, and three days. Clement was rather large for his age. They found the photograph in his kindergarten yearbook. Happy Trails Kindergarten, Topeka, Kansas."

"Who found it?"

"Nobody knows. A reporter at *The New York Times* got hold of it somehow. Anyway, who cares how? It's explosive news all the same. That's the end for Clement. It's tits up for his campaign."

"You keep saying that. Please stop saying that."

Nigel clicked through the cable news channels. All of them were discussing the Clement photograph. "I thought you ought to know straightaway, Governor. You need to get ready. It's only two months until the Iowa caucus. We have a million things to do."

"What?"

"The party is bound to draft you to run in Clement's place. Somebody electable has to take on Diebold. That would be you."

She sniffed at him. "I'm sorry you bothered to drive down here to tell me about this. I've told you a dozen times: I'm done with politics. John Fist has seen to that. I'm not running for president, ever."

"And why not, if I may ask?"

She stared through the windows, into the fog. "It was so hard at first. I cried my eyes out for months after the election, but I made my peace with it. Nobody in the world wants me to run for president anymore, not after all this time. Nobody."

Her former aide stood erect, as if about to salute. "I do. I want to join your campaign."

"Well, that's sweet, Nigel. Nobody but you."

"You're selling yourself short. Five years ago you were the odds-on favorite. Everyone said so. And you were so keen to run."

That was before arch-conservative state senator John Fist had defeated her, making California's financial woes and Patty's role in causing them the focus of his campaign. *That damned Fist.*

She flung her head back and bit her lip, gathering the shards of her self-respect. "I have accepted the verdict of the voters. My political career is over. The party will never forgive me for losing to Fist. 'If she couldn't even win re-election in California, she can't win the country.' That's what they'll say. So what if they don't have Pitypander to kick around anymore? Who cares?"

"That's just hurt feelings talking."

She picked up her mimosa and clutched it with both hands. "I have a perfect right to my hurt feelings. I've earned them fair and square. I may as well enjoy them in my forced retirement."

Nigel leaned his long arms against the back of an overstuffed chair. "Hurt feelings are no excuse for abandoning your dreams. Get over it. You nearly won. With a couple thousand more votes, you'd still be in the governor's mansion and Harry Clement would be eating your dust in the primaries. Time to get back on the old horse, Patty."

"It's already November. It's six months too late to launch a presidential campaign."

"No, it's *almost* too late. We still have time, if you act now."

"I'm too old."

"Don't be ridiculous. You're only fifty-five. Clement is ten years older."

"Benny won't let me."

Nigel rolled his eyes. "Have you actually asked Benito?"

"Not directly," she said. "But I know he's tired of my politicking. The very mention of it seems to give him gas. He's made more than enough money off me already. He lives his life in Vegas, I live mine here, and we get along fine that way."

He sat down in front of her. "What the deuce has got into you? You're the former governor of California for goodness' sake. You're a modern woman. It isn't 1954. You don't need your husband's approval to run for office."

The Diva of the Downtrodden they used to call her in Sacramento. Heroine of the Hopeless. A first-rank leader of the feminist movement. But she was a wife, too, if only in name. At least she still did a good imitation of one.

Her eyes settled on a Renoir on the wall. A young bride, decked out in a wedding gown, danced joyfully with a man in a flower garden. "No, I don't need Benny's okay, but I wouldn't feel right running without it. He's still my husband."

"Well, things are coming your way, Patty. Like it or not, the whole world is coming your way, and fast. Mark my words, you will be running for president. America needs Patty Pitypander. No, America demands Patty Pitypander!"

"It's out of the question."

Nigel threw up his hands. "You'll see—within a fortnight. They're already talking about you out there. Won't you at least think about it?"

"All right, I'll humor you and think about it, but don't expect me to change my mind, because I won't."

"In a fortnight you'll be calling me for help." Nigel stood up, turned, and left.

Patty shuffled across the veranda in her slippers and peered out the window at the ocean. Shivering, she pulled her bathrobe around her shoulders. She hadn't asked for this. She wasn't ready to run for president. She hadn't even put on her makeup.

The fog began to lift. Looking down at the beach, she spied a surfer paddling frantically toward a wave. It crested and passed him by an instant too soon. But right behind it a much bigger and better wave was surging. He could catch this one if he got back on his surfboard now. Right now.

Patty reached for her binoculars. The surfer was handsome, broad-shouldered, and about twenty years old, his eyes blazing with determination. He recognized his opportunity, clambered back onto his surfboard, paddled toward the new wave, and caught it just in time.

They were already talking about her, according to Nigel. Was this her fresh new wave approaching?

She padded back to her lounge chair, where a paperback book with a bare-chested man on its cover lay on a side table next to a tall stack of similar works. Jenessa Fuller, the heroine of *In Love We Tryst,* had trysted entirely too much for her own good and found herself in the throes of a terrible heartache. Patty would learn Jenessa's fate within the next hundred pages, perhaps by lunchtime. She picked up the book and read from where she'd left off the night before:

> And in the dense and dying twilight, Jenessa imagined she saw his manly form lying upon the pearly white sand, his steely arms beckoning to her, his ruby lips breathing her name into the ether: "Come to me, Jenessa." But every thought of him was an illusion, a mere trick of her febrile imagination. For he was not there. Jenessa had been abandoned.

Patty laid the book down, too perturbed to read further. Jenessa Fuller's world was a thousand times simpler than hers. The sultry heroine had only to figure out how to bed the shirtless studs on the covers of Marjorie Mickle's one hundred romance novels. She never aged a day or needed Botox to disguise her accumulating wrinkles. Former staffers did not come barging into her home to disturb her breakfast, encouraging her to embark on such an arduous quest as running for the presidency of the United States.

After a few seconds Patty lifted her eyes once more to look at the little brown boy on the television screen. No, this time Nigel Windborne was wrong. Harry Clement surely had the political savvy to wriggle out of this.

AS A PHALANX of reporters armed with cameras and microphones shoved their way into his campaign headquarters, the leading Democratic contender for the presidency regarded his uninvited guests with grim resolve. "I was a fudge brownie," he thundered. "Yes, a fudge brownie!"

The media wasn't buying it. Harry Clement could tell from their faces. A fudge brownie? Looks of amused disbelief filled the room.

"Goddamit, I was five years old," the senator said. "It was a Halloween party sixty years ago. I'm sure the other kids must have been dressed up as something similar."

Clement's left hand trembled. His right swept the sweat from his forehead. For decades he had prepared for this: the campaign of his life. All those years of backroom deals, clawing his way to the chairmanship of powerful committees in the House and Senate, kissing colicky babies, begging donors for contributions, and now it was going to end like this? His lifelong struggle for power was to be undone by an ancient photograph that came out of nowhere?

"How do you know you were a fudge brownie? What corroborating evidence can you give us?" asked one reporter.

"It's obvious! Look at the damn photo!"

"Could be a Fig Newton," said a female Associated Press reporter in the front row. "They're square too."

As anyone who knew anything about classic American cookies could plainly see, the boy in the photograph looked nothing like a Fig Newton. Clement stared the woman down. *You brainless nincompoop, you're just trying to get my goat.* "Take my word for it. I was a brownie."

But how could the senator be sure, much less prove it? After six decades, who could know what kind of high-calorie pastry he might have impersonated in his formative years, long before posing as an upstanding politician had become his vocation? The only clue was the rectangular shape of the cardboard box around his middle.

Screw the truth. Full speed ahead. Clement puffed out his chest. No way these jackals were going to tear him to pieces.

A reporter from ABC News waved his arm. "Senator! Senator!" Clement called on him.

The reporter, a man with a well-coifed hairdo, was exactly the kind of airhead journalist the senator despised. He held up a copy of the photo like it was a smoking gun. "Senator, you initially denied the allegation it was you in the picture. Then two days later you admitted it was you. Why did you lie before about being a fudge brownie, or are you lying now?"

"I didn't lie." Clement sighed. "I didn't think it was me, okay? Well, I wasn't sure it was me. For Christ's sake, how could I know who was under all that, that—brown stuff?"

"You don't know what you looked like at five? You don't have other childhood photos of yourself? Really?"

Clement clutched his forehead, as if that would stop the throbbing. "Of course I know what I looked like, but not in blackface—I mean in brownie face, I mean as a brownie, dammit, because that's what I was, yes, a brownie, and nothing but a brownie, so help me God, I swear."

The senator didn't even recall until yesterday what the name of his kindergarten was. His staff had spent all last night scrambling to find out. Alas, they discovered the Happy Trails Kindergarten had closed down forty years ago. Clement couldn't remember the names of his classmates or teachers, and it seemed unlikely they would risk revealing themselves to an unforgiving world to bail him out now, as he might soon be *persona non grata*. Radioactive, even.

The biggest mystery was how such a rare photograph had fallen into the hands of *The New York Times* just as Clement had emerged as the Democratic front-runner. The timing was no coincidence. Who was sabotaging his campaign?

"What do you know about the photo, and how do you know it?" asked a reporter from NBC News.

"I found a copy of it in our family scrapbook after the story broke. I don't remember ever seeing it there before. I assume my mother must have saved it. On the back she wrote, 'Harry at his first Halloween party.' That's all I know."

"Was this your mother's bright idea? Are you blaming her for this, Senator?"

"Blame? There's no one to blame here. I was a fudge brownie, a perfectly innocent fudge brownie, I tell you!"

"So you deny any responsibility for your actions?"

"I'm sure it wasn't my idea. Dammit, what five-year-old boy decides to dress up as anything, much less a fudge brownie? I must have been pressured or bullied into it by some grownup. They made me do it."

The silver-haired Senate majority leader had been a victim of bullying in his childhood. It was a plausible excuse, even for a man at the highest rungs of national power. Wasn't everyone a victim these days? Overcoming adversity in his early years might even elicit admiration. But Clement knew this alibi was risky. It sealed off one hole in his defense only to open a bigger one: If little Harry had been the victim of bullying, his mother must have been the bully.

Clement's mother—what about her? Like baying hounds, following the scent of an even deeper scandal, the reporters took off in hot pursuit.

"Why did your mother think dressing you up in blackface was acceptable?" asked one of them. "What about the Black kids in your kindergarten class? Didn't she have any regard for their feelings before packing you off to school as a fudge brownie to offend them?"

"There weren't any Black kids to offend, dammit! My school was all white!"

All white. It just slipped out of him. The room fell silent.

"Oh? Was that your mother's idea too? To send you to a segregated kindergarten? What was her purpose in doing that? Did that make it more comfortable for you to wear blackface?"

Bluish veins, taut and angry, stood out on Clement's neck. He hadn't meant to throw his ninety-six-year-old mother to the wolves, not that she would ever know in her addled condition. To fend them off, he would appeal to their common decency.

"Could we leave my poor old mother out of this, please?"

"Isn't your upbringing a relevant issue for the voters, Senator Clement? Don't they have a right to know how their candidates for president were raised and what values their parents instilled in them?"

Clement wiped his brow again as he glanced at the front window. A separate commotion was building on the sidewalk outside the campaign headquarters. Protesters were marching in a circle, waving signs printed with the words "No Blackface in the White House, No Clemency for Clement."

"I was a fudge brownie, dammit," said the senator. "Really."

THE MAN IN the baggy brown suit had just rolled his luggage through the jet bridge when his phone buzzed.

Damn, can't Laprinsky wait until I get into town? I'll be there in an hour. No, Lieutenant Colonel Laprinsky would not wait. His supervisor was like an expectant father when doing assignments for Bludinov.

After scanning the gate area, the man merged into the river of people rolling their suitcases down the terminal. The next gate was just as crowded. He continued on, passing ten more gates before spotting an empty seating area in a corner. With his back to the wall, he laid his coat over his phone to shield it from airport security cameras and reached under the lapel to enter his fifteen-digit security code.

"Congratulations, Krok," the text message from Laprinsky read. "I see phase one of mission is accomplished."

Krok punched in his reply. "Have arrived in Las Vegas, going next to Pitypander Palace to investigate."

"One more thing," Laprinsky's next message read. "Destroy all remaining copies of Clement photo."

"Will do." Krok opened his briefcase and looked at the little brown boy on the pumpkin, still grinning up at him. The photo was incriminating evidence, to be sure, but to destroy such a fine piece of artwork would be a shame. Someone must have spent weeks on it, getting the details of the face just right. The eyes must have been the hardest part. They glowed with the wonder and joy of a five-year-old. Could a politician of such importance as Clement ever have had such innocent eyes?

Oh, well, I'm sure they have extra copies in Moscow. Krok tore the photo to pieces.

CHAPTER 2

The Trojan Horse

AT THE APPOINTED time, there was a knock at the front door. When the butler opened it, revealing the young man who had come to interview her, Patty did a double take.

He stood before her like a god. Jack Snap had a chiseled, muscular build, sandy-blond hair, and a boyish smile. He could have been a surfer who had walked up from the beach below the mansion—or if he weren't so real, right off the cover of one of her romance novels.

"Governor Pitypander?"

"Yes, come in, Jack," Patty said, her heart thumping. "Do come in."

He touched a marble column with his fingertips, tilted his head back, and gawked at the twenty-foot ceiling. For half a minute he stood against the massive Palladian windows, marveling at the spectacular ocean view, taking in the blue expanse all the way to the horizon. He spun around, his sparkling azure eyes appealing to her for guidance.

Patty motioned to a sofa by the windows. "Have a seat."

"Governor Pitypander, thanks…thanks so much for agreeing to see me." Jack opened his notebook and fumbled in his coat pocket for his pen, but dropped it on the floor.

Patty watched intently as he bent over to pick it up, her eyes fixed on the enormous biceps bulging beneath his shirtsleeves.

"Sorry, I'm a little nervous. I don't get to interview a real governor every day. It's such an honor to meet you. Mom's told me so much about you."

Such a well-mannered boy. Mimi had raised him right. "Not at all, Jack. Your mother and I were best buddies in college. I would do anything for her."

He checked his watch. "I know you don't do many interviews, Governor. I won't take up much of your time."

"Oh, pish posh." Patty giggled like a schoolgirl. "Don't worry. I have a lot of time on my hands these days."

"Well, I'm real grateful, all the same."

The butler returned to the living room, bringing coffee on a silver tray. Patty put her finger to her chin. "Now let's see. Mimi told me you want to be a reporter when you graduate. Is that right?"

Jack's eyes lit up. "Oh, yes, ma'am. I've always wanted to be one, ever since I was a kid. When I was seven, I even started my own little neighborhood newspaper. I didn't have any money to make photocopies, so I wrote out each copy by hand on notebook paper."

"Really? Notebook paper?"

"Yes, ma'am. I used to run up and down our country road selling it for a quarter to our neighbors. That was back in Nebraska, before we moved out here." He looked at the four Raphaels on the wall behind her. "Well, I don't mean here, like Durango Beach—I mean Burbank."

She knew what he meant. Durango Beach and Burbank were more than sixty miles apart—they existed in separate universes. One was the province of oceanfront mansions and the ultra-rich, the other a middle-class suburb where regular people like Jack lived.

"Oh, so you wrote your newspaper by hand, at seven years old. How cute. What about lately?"

"I covered sports at Clark High. At UCLA I've mostly done current events on campus. I majored in journalism, you know."

She sat back in her chair with a doleful look, distressed for his sake. It was one thing to dabble in journalism as a hobby, but to major in it defied common sense. What a terrible waste of a college education. He might as well have majored in art history. "Well, I admire your courage."

The young man cocked his head. "What do you mean?"

"Oh, nothing really. I only meant you're a little late to the party. Journalism isn't the noble profession it used to be, what's left of it. Your professors must have told you how hard it is to get a job. Not to mention the starvation wages. These days a reporter's life is tough."

Jack smiled, undaunted, as if he hadn't the slightest appreciation of what life after college was like. "Oh, yes, ma'am. I know, but I don't care. Even with all the newspapers shutting down, somebody still has to mind the store. It's a super important job, being a reporter. You know, a reporter can change the world."

Patty suppressed her urge to laugh. Young people had always wanted to change the world, but this generation was different—so moral and earnest. "How do you want to change the world?"

He looked straight into her eyes. "I want to tell the public what's going on, so they know who and what they're voting for. Journalists keep the government honest." He spoke without the slightest affectation.

Patty sat back, amazed. He was Mimi's son, all right, a throwback from an earlier era like his mother. His attitude was both disarmingly wholesome and hopelessly disconnected from reality. She didn't have the heart to tell him reporters weren't idealists seeking the truth. They were propagandists and smear merchants, a politician's natural enemies. They might even be a different humanoid species—a lower one, surely.

"I don't think people are well informed these days, do you, Governor?"

How could they be? Honest journalism was dying, and people only wanted news confirming their beliefs. Journalism catered to them.

With the electorate so divided, there was no middle ground anymore, nor any centrist politicians left to represent it.

"No, you have a point there."

"And, besides, I almost have a job lined up."

"Almost?"

"Yes, they were impressed I could get in to see you. I told them I have a special connection to you. I didn't tell them my connection was just Mom."

"Good for you, Jack. Your mom is good enough for me. It's none of their business anyway. But who is they?"

"*The Burbank Bee.*"

Patty stifled her amusement. *The Burbank Bee* was the perfect fit for Jack, an anachronism like himself. The local rag, among the last of its kind, was owned by a reclusive movie mogul in his nineties who had inherited it from his father and kept it going for sentimental reasons, unconcerned whether the tiny newspaper made money or not. It would die when he did.

"Ah, yes, the *Bee.* Gus Masterson's paper. That's a good place for you to start. Gus always played it straight with me. He's one of the last of the old-time journalists. What will you be doing for him?"

"Covering the presidential campaign. Starting in January, right after I graduate."

Patty arched an eyebrow. "Gus is giving you the political beat? Right out of school? To handle by yourself?"

"Yeah, pretty much."

She raised her hand to her forehead. "What happened to—let me see, what was the *Bee* guy's name? Mort? Mort Sheimer. Yes, that was him. A big bald guy with BO. Always wore the same striped yellow tie with a ketchup stain on it."

"Oh, Mort was laid off last year, they told me," Jack said.

"Laid off?"

"That's it, Thelma, way to whack it." Olympia clapped her free hand against the clipboard, her white hair blowing in the breeze. "Knock it down his throat, aim at the baseline. Make George scramble for it."

"Hello, Mama," Patty said.

Olympia didn't move.

"Hello there, Mama!" Patty bellowed.

Olympia turned around with a start and grabbed Patty by the arm. "Oh, hey, baby. Look who's here, everybody, it's my little girl Patty, here for a little visit. Louise, can you take over for me?"

The four men and eight women seated around the court smiled and waved. Olympia handed her clipboard to Louise and led Patty to the bleachers.

"So, Mama, how are you doing? You're looking good."

"Just fine, baby." Olympia rubbed her hands together. "We're getting ready for the National Senior Games. They're in New Mexico this year. I can't wait."

"Oh, that's nice."

"We lost last year, you know," Olympia said. "But we're going all the way this time. We've got two hot new players: Sammy and Jill over there. A bronze trophy won't do. We're going for the gold."

"And how's everything else?"

Again, Olympia didn't move.

"Mama?" Patty shouted.

Olympia cupped her hand to her ear. "What's that?"

"Mama, you don't have your hearing aids in, do you?"

Olympia made a face, reached into her purse, and dug around for her hearing aids. "Oh, I hate these things. They don't sound at all natural and they make me look so old." She slipped them into her ears.

"Are you still running?" Patty asked.

"Oh, my, yes. The half-marathon is in February. I've been out training every other day. When I'm not running, I'm volunteering for the county."

"Yeah, the *Bee* had to cut back hard. With old Mort gone they're using wire services a lot more now, but Gus still wants somebody at the paper to cover the campaign. He takes a special interest in politics."

Patty chuckled. "And he can afford you."

"Yeah, I guess that's it."

"Then I guess you'll have to do, Jack."

Poor old Mort, he must have been in his fifties, too old to start over but not old enough to retire. Sort of like her. The smelly veteran with the spot on his tie had been unceremoniously dumped for a complete novice. Jack was too green to appreciate what a plum job the political beat used to be at newspapers, even at the lowly *Bee*. But, being green, he was easy on Patty's eyes. Very easy.

"So what can I tell you about me?"

He shifted in his chair. "The same thing everybody else wants to know."

"Which is?"

"Well, like, with the Clement blackface thing going on and getting worse every day, whether you're gonna run for president."

She folded her arms. So young Jack wasn't as innocent as he appeared. He hadn't come for a softball interview about what it was like being California's first female governor. He was a Trojan horse, sent by a veteran newspaperman to ask barbed questions about her political ambitions. Shields up!

"The truth is, I haven't given it any thought."

"They say you're the only one who can beat Diebold."

His flattery, whether intended as such or not, brought a smile to her face. "They do? What do you think?"

Jack's eyes brimmed with certainty. "I think you can take him by twenty points. So does Mom. What with the women's vote and all behind you. Why not?"

It was all so simple to this boy. Why not, indeed?

Because P. Trayson Diebold, president of the United States, was a formidable opponent with his hands on the levers of national power. Because Patty had lost the governorship of California to a deranged gun rights proponent named John Fist, a Republican. For such grievous incompetence the ungrateful party for which she had worked so hard had not forgiven her. Because the world no longer hungered for the wise leadership of Patty Pitypander, deposed Heroine of the Hopeless. *That damned Fist.*

"That's nice of you, Jack."

"So is the rumor true?"

"Rumor?"

"The rumor that you're gonna run," he said.

The corners of Patty's mouth turned up. Jack was attempting to float a rumor to see if she would confirm it. Only a rookie would try such an obvious ploy on an experienced pol like her. She would have found his little gambit insulting if it—and he—weren't so darn cute.

Patty's forehead wrinkled with concern. "Who is this person spreading rumors about me?"

"Well, does it matter whose rumor it is, as long as there is one?"

Now Jack was straying into impertinence. In Patty's days as a high school guidance counselor, she would have scolded a boy for getting out of line like this.

"A rumor is not a story, and when all you have to go on is a rumor, you have nothing," she replied. "If you're going to be a real reporter, the first thing you'll have to learn is you never put any faith in rumors. Facts are what matter. I'm sure Gus would agree."

Jack shrank in his chair, paused a moment, and jotted down something on his notepad. "I guess that's a 'no.' Should I put you down for a 'no'?"

"Not even that. There's been no decision."

Jack's eyes brightened. "Ah, so there is a decision to make? You are at least thinking about running?"

"I didn't say that either. You're trying to put words in my mouth."

The young man's chin slumped to his chest. "I can't go back to the *Bee* with nothing. Gus will never hire me if I come back empty-handed."

Poor Jack, exposing his neediness like that, practically begging her to hand him a story. Old Mort would never have whimpered. But Jack wasn't a real reporter. The kid had so much to learn. Still, he was Mimi's kid, and so adorable.

"Tell you what. I've known Gus for many years. If you'll get off this silly topic and stick to the one we agreed on, I'll send him a note and put in a good word for you."

"Would you do that for me?"

Patty smiled. "Of course, any favors for a friend. You will be my friend, won't you?"

He pledged to be her friend.

Patty spent the rest of the interview telling him what a special privilege it had been to break the glass ceiling to become California's first female governor and how deeply she treasured her four wonderful years serving the homeless, the poor, the uneducated, the sick, and each and every oppressed minority in the state without exception.

When Jack had gone, Patty sat down at her desk and jotted down a brief letter to the editor of *The Burbank Bee*:

Dear Gus,

So sorry to learn about the *Bee's* recent downsizing and the unfortunate departure of Mort Sheimer, but I had the great pleasure of meeting your fine young intern, Jack Snap, at my home today and am quite sure that with his energy, dedication, and drive, he would make a splendid addition to your regular staff. Sorry I couldn't give him more information about my plans.

Best wishes,
Patty Pitypander

She handed off the letter to her social secretary to mail and walked downstairs to the indoor pool. Mylo was on his knees, his arm muscles taut and sinewy as he reached out to scoop up some water in a vial to test the chlorine level. He smiled across the pool at her as she sat down.

Patty opened her latest Jenessa Fuller novel, *All His Charms*, to the bookmark she had placed in it an hour ago. She began to read:

> If it had been her wish to have him that night, Jenessa should have uttered the words roiling within the darkest recesses of her soul, but the words she needed did not come. No, not the right words, the ones that could capture all his charms.

After another page Patty found herself stealing another furtive glance across the pool. It would be enough of an accomplishment for one morning to resist Mylo's charms. Jack Snap's were in another league entirely. For behaving herself in the face of them for a full hour—without flirting even once—she surely deserved a medal.

CHAPTER 3

Family Ties

THERE WERE SOME questions in life—like whether one should run for president of the United States—only a mother could answer. Patty went to the airport, boarded one of her husband's Gulfstream jets, and flew to South Florida to see Mama.

It worried Patty to no end that the people at the front desk of the Horizons House continuing care retirement community could never seem to keep track of her mother. Every time she would visit and ask for Olympia Ingratelli, they would shrug their shoulders and tell her that for all they knew, the eighty-seven-year-old might be beating the tar out of someone on the pickleball court, or pumping iron in the weight room, or jogging around Fort Lauderdale to prepare for her next half-marathon. They would tactfully remind Patty that Olympia was still in the best shape of anyone who had ever lived at the Horizons House; she was in the independent living unit, not assisted living; and it wasn't their job to know her whereabouts around the clock.

This time Patty found her mama on the pickleball court, clipboard in hand, shouting at the players from her chair beside the net.

Patty regarded her mother with amazement. "I don't know how you do it, Mama. You never stop."

"No trick to it, sweetheart. I just keep moving. So what about you, baby? Are you staying busy?"

"Uh, that's what I came to talk to you about." Patty placed her hand on Olympia's. "Mama, I need your advice. I'm thinking of running for president."

Olympia drew back. "President? Good Lord."

"Do you think I should?"

"Oh, baby, I don't know. That's so much to take on." Olympia's face darkened with concern, her eyes lifting to the sky. "Your father, God rest his soul, was afraid of this. He said so, when you were elected governor. He said to me, Luigi did, 'That girl's got a bee in her bonnet. She'll run for president someday, you watch.'"

"What do you think Papa would say now?"

Olympia patted her hand. "Oh, he'd want you to stay a million miles away from it."

Patty looked up. Clouds were rolling in from the west. Lightning illuminated the sky, as if her father were confirming Olympia's words. "Why was Papa always that way?"

Olympia frowned. "Your father didn't like the idea of women in politics. He thought it was beneath them and would only hurt them and bring them down to the level of men."

"I was only following in his footsteps, Mama."

Olympia gave her a knowing look. "Yes, that's exactly what he was afraid of. He didn't want that for you. You know, Luigi didn't always like being mayor. To you kids it may have looked glamorous, but he knew better. Of course he would never tell you how rough things got sometimes at city hall."

Patty remembered the sad look her father came home with on occasion. "I could tell anyway. So could Marco."

"He tried to protect you two from it, but sometimes his anger got all bottled up inside. One night he just had to let it out, and he told me what he was dealing with. It knocked me over. Some of the things the mob bosses wanted him to do for them, well, those things took a toll on him, baby. Killed him, in the end."

"Never mind what Papa would say. What do you think about me running, Mama?"

Olympia peered into her eyes, the way she used to do when Patty and her problems were small. "That depends. Why do you want to be president, Patricia?"

Patty had asked herself that all the way across the country. It was a bad sign when a simple question needed multiple complicated answers, a dead giveaway that no one answer was good enough by itself. Did a dozen weak reasons ever add up to a strong one, like the twisted strands of a rope?

Patty struggled to get the words out, to form a thought that made sense. "I, I, I want to help people. I want to be big, like Papa was. I want my chance. I don't see why a woman shouldn't have her chance. Didn't you ever want a chance to be big, Mama?"

The corners of Olympia's mouth lifted gently. "You don't have to be a politician to be big, baby. Lots of big people work in small jobs, and the world couldn't survive without them. As for me, I never wanted to be a politician, but there's no reason you shouldn't be one. You don't have children. The only person you have to worry about is Benny. What does Benny think, by the way? Is he on board with this?"

THE BEST TIME to catch Benny Pitypander was always lunchtime. Patty flew to Sin City to have lunch with him at the original Pitypander Pleasure Palace, where he had founded his empire.

Patty walked through the lobby, flanked by rows of fluted columns stretching thirty-five feet to the coffered ceiling. The labyrinthine hallways in the complex converged at an atrium, where the midday sun bathed a fifteen-foot statue of Benny in a shaft of light. The white marble figure of her husband towered like Zeus over a fake Trevi fountain, water spouts dancing obediently at his feet.

Marble Benny, as Patty called him, was a useful landmark if one got lost in the maze of corridors—and not just at this Palace. A Marble Benny guarded the center of every Pitypander Palace in the world.

In colonnaded courtyards to Patty's left, endless rows of slot machines rioted with flashing lights and ringing noises. To her right, croupiers supervised the drunks waging bets at the roulette and blackjack tables. Waiters in white togas and sandals floated between the gaming areas, offering customers complimentary platefuls of grapes and hors d'oeuvres.

Patty found the real Benny in his office on the sixtieth floor. With his deep-set brown eyes and stocky frame, he resembled an overstuffed owl, perched at his desk in his shirtsleeves, laughing into a speakerphone as a busty blonde in a low-cut dress stood by his elbow. Framed photographs on the wall behind them featured Benny embracing movie stars, glad-handing politicians, and back-slapping sports heroes. Patty waved at him from his doorway and took a seat outside in the waiting area.

Several minutes later Benny appeared, tugging his coat jacket over his shoulder. "Sorry, babe. It's the Gametime Hotels merger again. I had to straighten some things out so the lawyers could close the deal."

She gave him a long stare. "Who was that young woman in your office?"

"Oh, that's Gina, one of the lawyers," he replied with a grin. "She's lending me a hand with the negotiation."

Patty held her tongue. Every woman in Benny's Palace, even the lawyers and accountants, looked like a Playboy bunny, probably according to Benny's orders. None of them could be over thirty-five.

Patty and Benny rode the elevator down to Chez Raoul. When the waiter arrived, Benny ordered ravioli.

"Why don't you have something French for once?" she asked.

He frowned as he always did when she made this suggestion. "You know I hate French food."

Could Patty ever reform Benito Pitypander of Jersey City? He had never stopped missing his Italian mother's home cooking. All Pitypander restaurants around the world, even in Macau, stood ready to make at least three Italian dishes using Mama Pitypander's recipes, in case the big boss from Las Vegas ever dropped in.

Patty, twice as Italian as Benny, had been fed pasta up to her ears by the time she was twelve. The sight of spaghetti made her eyes bleed. She knew better than to insult the chef of a fancy French restaurant with an order of common pasta. Out of respect for Raoul, she chose the foie gras.

"Thanks for fitting me in today, Benny. There's something urgent I need to discuss with you."

He nibbled on a cracker and looked her squarely in the eye. "Go ahead, shoot. Anything for my girl."

"Have you been following the news about Harry Clement?"

"Yeah, a little," he said with indifference. "I saw something on the news about Clement wearing blackface. What about it?"

"Clement denied everything at first. Then he claimed he was only a fudge brownie and swore up and down he did it against his will."

Benny chuckled. "Ha! They forced him to be a brownie. The old victim routine. Yeah, that'll work. Everybody's a victim these days, even politicians and billionaires."

Patty wasn't sure what he meant by that remark, but decided to ignore it. She tore open two packets of Sweet'N Low and dumped their contents into her tea. "No, Benny, it's not working. There's blood in the water and the sharks are circling Clement. The party donors are getting antsy about giving him any more money. That's what Nigel says."

Benny frowned, laid his right hand on the table, and made a fist. "Nigel Windborne! Oh, crap, not again. I thought you were rid of that idiot."

"Nigel's back at his old law firm. But he's still involved with the party."

"No business like show business, right? Divorce lawyer to the stars. Now there's an easy living. What a shyster."

"Actors need lawyers too, Benny." She took a sip of her tea. "Well, anyway, Nigel called yesterday to tell me what's happening to Clement's poll numbers."

"And?"

"They're in free fall. He's lost twenty points in a week."

Benny's eyes bore in on her. "So why did Windborne call to tell you?"

"To let me in on the political gossip." She buttered a piece of bread.

"Hmm, he's got something up his sleeve, the bastard."

Patty leaned forward. "Nigel is convinced Clement will be forced out of the race."

"That's the big news? Who cares? So somebody else will take the lead. Brown or Krieger or what's-his-name. The guy with the big nose." Benny snapped his fingers to jog his memory.

"Sartini."

"Yeah, that's him. So who needs Clement?"

"The party does. He's electable, or he was before this blackface thing came out. Nigel doesn't think any of the others stand a chance against Diebold."

"Why?"

"Because Brown is an unlikeable turd, Krieger can't think on his feet without making a big gaffe, and nobody outside Ohio knows who Sartini is."

"Okay, so they're all mental midgets—prime candidates to lead the free world." Benny took a swig of his beer.

"This is important, Benny."

"Pffft!" he said, nearly spitting. "So what if all the Democrats have is a pack of losers? What do I care? I like President Diebold well enough. 'Be safe with Diebold,' isn't that what his bumper stickers say?"

Patty resisted the urge to slap him. "Benny, you're kidding. No one on the planet is safe with Diebold. The man's a total fraud, a charlatan. How can you believe a word he says?"

"Hey, fraud or not, he's cut my tax rates, like he promised he would. He's always pushing to slash regulations. What's not to like about Diebold?"

There wasn't anything to like, she thought. "For starters, he doesn't care anything about minorities, or the poor."

Benny shook his head. "There you go again—always the bleeding heart. See, that's where you're wrong, babe. Diebold cares about one oppressed group—us taxpayers. He cared enough about me last year to lower my taxes. That's the kind of caring I want from a politician. Any more caring gets expensive for me."

"You don't mean it, Benny. You aren't that heartless."

Patty thought back to the days when he wasn't so heartless, before he became a self-made man. When they were married, Benny had whisked her away to the Italian Alps for their honeymoon. They picnicked along the water's edge at Lake Como, two lovers locked in a romantic embrace, lobbing bread crumbs at the ducks paddling up to them.

And now? Patty raised a forkful of foie gras to her mouth and a revolting thought occurred to her: Their roles had changed. Benny now owned all the ducks. She had flown to him for crumbs, and his ducks were feeding her.

He took another swig of beer. "I'm serious. I'm not into politics, sweetheart. It's not my thing. The truth is, it bores me to death, like the way you feel about football. Politics is nothing but a bunch of useless yahoos buying votes from any fools who will believe them and vote them into office. The yahoos change and so does the score, but the game never does. Just like football."

She straightened up in her chair. "You think I'm a useless yahoo?"

Silence.

"I didn't mean you, babe. I think you're useful."

"Thanks."

He picked up his fork and stabbed his salad. "Look, power is your game, doll. Mine is making money. I couldn't play your game well if I tried, and you couldn't play mine. But that's why we've made such good partners. We're, what's the word?"

"Complementary," she answered.

"Yeah, that's it."

Partners. At least she had made partner in Benny Pitypander's world. Was she a general partner, or a limited partner? Patty wasn't sure, and their marriage certificate didn't say. Limited, she guessed. There was no Marble Patty—not yet.

Her eyes narrowed. "Well, partner, I've had enough of sitting around. I'd like to play my game again."

"What do you mean?"

"I want to explore running for president, Benny. I want ten million dollars to get started, to set up my campaign office."

His face contorted like he'd bitten into a lemon. "Why do you want to go back into politics? After you crashed and burned last time? What makes you think you could get enough support to take on Diebold?"

Crashed and burned? She had lost by the narrowest of margins. "I beg your pardon. I still have a lot of support in the party."

"Pffft! You lost the California governor's race, for crying out loud. You were in meltdown for three months afterwards. Why risk that again?"

"I want a do-over. I'll win this time."

Benny munched on his salad. "I don't think so. You'll lose again. You're not a good loser. You get super-bitchy when you don't get your way."

She crossed her arms. "Men always say that about powerful women, don't they? Powerful men are forceful, powerful women are bitchy. That's misogyny, you know."

"Yeah? Call it what you like. I call it reality." Benny pointed his fork at her. "You can't stand losing. You get meaner than a snake. You get like your father was."

She grabbed his hand. "Listen to me, Benny, I can win this thing. Clement is imploding, and the nomination is up for grabs. Nigel says nobody else can beat me for the Democratic nomination."

"Him again. Why does he care?"

"Because he wants to manage my campaign."

Benny looked at her with contempt. "Yeah, of course he does. Windborne is one of the useless yahoos. He's getting in on the ground floor. The bastard just wants to ride your coattails to power, yours or anybody's."

When would Benny stop blaming Nigel for everything that had gone wrong with her re-election campaign? It was all Fist's fault.

"Nigel Windborne has never lied to me."

Benny sneered. "He's a slimeball, I tell you. If you don't make it to the nomination, what do you think Windborne loses? He'll just jump on the horse that does get the nomination. As long as he ends up in the White House, it's all the same to him who gets him there."

Patty's former aide's transparent ambitions to rise in the Democratic Party weren't the point. She was lucky to have him on her team. "I need Nigel as much as he needs me. No one in Sacramento was more loyal to me. I can trust him."

"Ha! He's a damn Limey know-it-all. An Oxford smarty-pants."

"Maybe, but he's good at this. He knows his way around politics."

"Oh, sure. Then why is Fist in the governor's mansion? That's how good your Nigel is. He's leading you straight to the dumpster again."

She tapped her finger on the table. "I was hoping you would help me, Benny. I only need a lousy ten million, to prime the pump. That's chump change to you, but it would mean everything to me."

"I want to help you, babe." Benny reached over and patted her on the hand. "And the best way to do that is to keep you out of trouble."

"What trouble?"

He leaned forward and whispered, "The media exposure. You have secrets. Your years in therapy? The fantasies you were having?"

Her face tightened. "Who doesn't have secrets? I'm willing to take the risk."

"I'm not."

In the courtyard outside the restaurant window a woman was yanking down the handle of a slot machine. "Benny, you own the world's biggest casinos, but you won't gamble on your own wife?"

He pointed to the slot machines. "If you look around my casinos, sweetie, you'll notice the odds are heavily stacked in my favor. In your case, they're not."

"And why not?"

"Because you're not qualified, that's why not. Everybody can see that. You're a guidance counselor, not a politician. You aren't cut out for politics. This is just another little fantasy of yours."

"I don't have fantasies anymore. I'm cured."

"Ha! You have some big idea about being a big politician like your daddy, and you won't grow up and let go of it. Face it, you don't know the first thing about foreign policy or business or how the world really works. You don't know jack."

She didn't know jack? Patty's nostrils flared. "What did you say?"

He retreated immediately. "Okay, I'll admit that's a little harsh, but somebody's gotta tell you the truth. Your creepy friend Nigel won't because he wants to use you. You aren't qualified to be governor of California, much less president."

"But you supported me for governor!"

"Yeah, twice. My mistake—I wasted twenty-five million. California was one thing. I figured you couldn't screw up California any worse than it already was, but you did. You'll make a damn fool of yourself in a presidential race. This is not a good idea."

"For you or for me?"

"That's not fair, doll. I'm looking out for you."

Patty threw down her napkin. "Thanks for looking out for me, Benny." She stood up and walked out.

On the flight home Patty stared into the clouds until her anger subsided, and concluded Benny was right about one thing: she couldn't stand losing. She didn't need to, either. A former governor of California, with her name recognition, had a million ways to get ten million dollars.

Patty's eyes turned to the Gulfstream's cockpit and fastened on the square-jawed co-pilot radioing the tower. He hadn't been on the flight to Las Vegas. She reckoned he was in his mid-twenties, about Benny's age when the two of them had met. He had a nice smile. She craned her neck to see around his seat and caught a glimpse of the wedding ring on his left hand. She sighed, fell back into her seat, and closed her eyes.

As the jet descended toward the airport, Patty wondered what had happened to her and the young man at Lake Como in the past thirty years. Or was that a fantasy too?

CHAPTER 4

The Ladybugs

THE INTERNATIONAL LADYBUGS had turned the convention center into a sea of pink hats, each bearing the image of a beetle. A long banner strung across the upper concourse exhorted women to "Be a Ladybug! Join the Infestation!"

"Ah, the pink hats. These are your people, Patty," Nigel said with calm assurance. "Pitypander Power, that's what these women represent. On this rock you will build your church."

And yet the women perusing pamphlets at the information booths seemed so young. The tiny feminist organization Patty helped found thirty years ago had evolved during the Diebold presidency from a fringe group into a movement of two million vocal activists. Energized by twentysomethings in a rising tide of cultural protest, the Ladybugs set up chapters of volunteers in every city and state. They clamored for their rights in huge demonstrations and turned out in droves to vote.

The very sight of pink hats filled male politicians with dread. The general who could command this leaderless army could conquer the world.

Of course Patty should speak here. This was the ideal place to test her grassroots appeal. Lacking Benny's financial support, she had to find a base of supporters somewhere. But would these new Ladybugs, many of whom knew nothing about her, respond to her call?

"We'll see how well they remember me," Patty said. "I practically had to beg them to get fifteen minutes. If I was still governor, they would have offered me an hour."

"Ah, but they did make time for you, didn't they?" Nigel replied with his customary certainty. "That's because they want you. America wants Patty Pitypander. You'll see."

The convention organizers escorted Patty into the arena and asked her to wait at the bottom of the stage. Within seconds someone in the front row of the audience pointed at her. Heads began to turn.

At the podium above her stood a tall thin woman with straight pink hair down to her shoulders. "And so we fight, my fellow Ladybugs." The woman thrust her fist in the air. "We commit ourselves to struggle on together, to overcome every obstacle men set in front of us, to build on our gains until no sister suffers at the hands of the global patriarchy! Bug the patriarchy! Bug it until it falls!"

"Bug the patriarchy!" the ten thousand women repeated in unison. The Ladybugs' famous Five-Bug Chant rained down from the gallery: "Bug, bug, bug, bug, bug!"

The emcee scrambled up to the podium and took over the microphone. "And now, my dear sisters, it is my distinct honor to welcome an old friend of ours, a trailblazer for women's rights, the first female governor of California, a charter member of the International Ladybug movement, and an indefatigable supporter of our cause: Patty Pitypander!"

Nigel touched her lightly on the shoulder. "Knock 'em dead. You can do this."

Patty stepped up to the podium, waving back at the sea of pink hats. She pulled the microphone down to her chin and looked out at the television cameras at the back of the auditorium. Thanking the convention organizers for squeezing her into the program, she promised to keep her remarks brief.

Patty glanced at her notes, thrust her nose up into the lights, and assumed a regal pose. Her voice rang out, shrill as a whistle. "We've come a long way, ladies, but we have so many more miles to go! Since the glory days of the suffragettes, those fearless women who wrested the right to vote from men more than a century ago, our mission has never been clearer. Our goal is unchanged: To smash the last bastions of male dominance and privilege wherever they still exist, and right the wrongs of inequality and sexism imposed upon our gender from the dawn of time by the global patriarchy."

Applause broke out across the arena.

Patty pounded her fist on the lectern. "But this is a new day. The time has come to focus our efforts! Who, I ask you, is the current head of the patriarchy? Who sits at the pinnacle of the male power structure? P. Trayson Diebold, that's who! And what has the president done to include more women in his administration? What steps has Diebold taken to crack the glass ceiling? Has his party proposed a single piece of legislation to ensure women earn equal pay for equal work? I ask you, has Diebold backed any protections for a woman's right to choose?"

"Hell no!" cried someone in the back.

"What has Diebold done for you?" Patty asked.

"Nothing!" someone replied.

Patty cupped her hand to her ear. "I can't hear you."

"Nothing!" the crowd thundered.

Patty raised her fist above her head. "That's right, he's done nothing! You all know I smashed through the glass ceiling to become the first woman governor of California. I used my office to work tirelessly for equal rights for working women. Why can't our president do the same? Where can we find a president who will fight for us, fight for the oppressed, fight for the victims of male privilege? Who will fight to unite the women of the world?"

Here she paused and waited. And waited. Would just one person in the crowd—anyone—shout the words she so longed to hear?

"You will! Patty Pitypander will! Pitypander for president!" a woman in front yelled.

Patty shot a big grin at the woman and held her arms out wide in a Christ-like embrace.

"Yes, you're the one! Pitypander for president!" cried a second woman.

A third woman repeated the incantation, and a fourth, and within seconds the frenzied cry of "Pitypander for president" was resounding back and forth across the convention hall. Hundreds of pink hats began jumping out of their seats, raising their fists and cheering.

A thrill shot through Patty's body. After so many years in the wilderness, she still had her old magic. Even now, she, Patty Pitypander, daughter of Luigi the mayor, Diva of the Dispossessed, could still make the multitude roar. She had lit the fire of destiny, and from here it would engulf the continent.

True to her word, she kept her speech short and stepped down quietly from the podium. A gaggle of admirers gathered offstage to meet her, pressing forward through the crowd with pen and paper to get her autograph.

Two older women approached from the VIP table. Patty immediately recognized both celebrities. Margot Lewiston was an elegant blonde actress who had starred in dozens of hit movies and earned two Oscars. Sally Snack was the chunky, irrepressible comedy host of the late night show "Midnight Snack." Lewiston asked if Patty and Nigel would join the two of them for lunch.

Of course they would.

PATTY POINTED TO a table in the corner of the restaurant, hidden behind a column, where the four of them would not be noticed.

Margot Lewiston and Sally Snack put the question to her at once: Would Patty consider jumping into the race?

Patty opened the bidding with a faint chuckle and a nonchalant grin. This was no place to declare her intentions. These women were practically strangers.

They were rich enough, no doubt. Both celebrities had to be worth at least a hundred million dollars apiece. Margot must be pulling down twenty million per picture, and Sally had to be making that much a year from Midnight Snack.

"So will you?" Margot asked urgently.

"Run? Me?" Patty looked down the menu. "Do you think I would have a shot? What about Clement?"

Margot leaned forward. "Are you kidding? Clement is toast. He'll never get over the blackface thing. I heard this morning Brown has almost tied him in the polls, can you believe it?" She stuck her tongue out like she was going to be sick. "Ugh! Brown? Never."

Patty made a mental note of Margot's attitude: yet more proof of Brown's low likability rating. "What about Krieger and Sartini?"

This time it was Sally who stuck her tongue out. "Not a chance. Krieger is a dork. Santini won't even take Indiana."

"Ohio," Nigel corrected her. "And it's Sartini."

"What?"

"His name is Sartini, not Santini," Nigel declared. "Tony Sartini. He's a first-term congressman from the third district of Ohio, on the east side of Columbus. But I agree his prospects are dim."

"You can take that to the bank." Patty pointed her thumb at her former aide. "Nigel here keeps the stats on every voting district in the country stored away in his head. He's a walking electoral encyclopedia."

Sally shrugged. "Have it your way. Sartini, Santini, whatever. With that schnoz, not even Houdini could take Ohio. Wherever he's from he won't take that place either."

Patty stifled her urge to defend Sartini's schnoz. Nothing was wrong with the brash young congressman's substantial Italian nose. It gave him character and reminded Patty of Uncle Salvatore, who used to sneak candy to her when she was little. She offered her disagreement in the guise of a mild grin.

"So, with all these men running, we felt we had to talk to you, Patty," Margot said. "We can't believe what a steaming pile of poo the Democratic candidates are. Where are all the good women this year?"

"The pickings are pretty slim," Patty acknowledged. "Some people thought Betty Hickham might run."

"What stopped her?" Sally asked.

"Family issues," Nigel replied. "Her husband had a second heart attack."

Margot smiled cynically. "Uh-huh, and I'll bet he had it just to keep her from running."

"I'll have a heart attack too if the Democrats don't come up with a better candidate," Sally threatened. "What if we lose to Diebold again? I can't survive another four years of him. Somebody's gotta do something fast."

Patty buttered her bread rolls. "Well, I'm flattered you two were thinking of me. Of course, I haven't given it much thought."

"Well, you have to. You're the only one with the right stuff," Margot said. "You heard those women in there. They were screaming for you, all ten thousand of them. Pitypander for president!"

Patty responded with a coy smile. "They weren't serious. Just kind of worked up."

Margot reached across the table and seized her by the wrist. "No, it's you they want, Patty. You would win the women's vote hands down against Diebold."

Nigel seconded the motion. "Exactly what I've been telling her. America wants Pitypander for president, now more than ever."

"Well, that's nice of you all." Patty stirred her tea slowly, allowing their approbation to linger in the air. "Not saying I would do it, of course, but just for the sake of argument, suppose I did want to throw my hat in the ring. Would you two be interested in donating? I mean, to get things off the ground?"

Margot's face went blank. "I don't understand. Why would you need us? With your money you could buy and sell us both a hundred times over."

If they only knew. Should Patty reveal her secret? They might mistake her confiding in them as begging. So be it. Even the worthiest politician must stoop to conquer. She could grovel with no loss of dignity.

Patty rubbed her chin. "Just between you and me... No, I'm afraid to tell you... No, no, I shouldn't tell you."

Sally leaned forward, her eyes wide open. "We won't say a word."

"All right, I'll tell you. I'm not as rich as you think." Patty looked down at her napkin in shame. "You see, I don't have any serious money of my own. I've spent my whole working life in government, in education and politics. I can't come up with even a million dollars."

Margot's reflexive laugh quickly gave way to confusion. "You're pulling our leg. What about the Pitypander casinos? You must be rolling in dough."

Patty put on a brave smile and confessed. "The casinos, the hotels, the restaurants, the golf courses, all of them belong to my husband, one hundred percent. And Benny doesn't want me to run."

"But why?" Margot asked. "He backed you for governor, didn't he?"

"Yes, and it's because of that experience he's against my politicking anymore."

"Why?"

Patty stared blankly at the tablecloth. The question begged for an answer. "Benny found it's not easy being the spouse of a well-known politician, especially if you have a global business empire to run. It's inconvenient. It also, well, it overshadows him."

Sally slapped the table with the palm of her hand. "Oh, so it's his ego that's holding you back. I should have known a man would be standing in the way."

"Inconvenient! That's no excuse!" Margot bristled with outrage. "You can't let him get away with that! Let one man stop us from putting a woman in the White House? Hand him power over half the country? For what, to save his stupid ego? No way, sister!"

"Yes, that's the way it is, I'm afraid." Patty shrugged helplessly. "One awfully greedy man is standing in the way of a hundred and sixty-five million deserving women. It's a crying shame, but without Benny's money what can I do?"

Sally's face filled with defiance. "Like you told us in your speech, you can fight, that's what you can do! Fight, fight, fight, isn't that what you told everyone up there?" She banged her fist on the table.

"Forget your husband. How much would it cost to get you into the race?" Margot asked.

Nigel looked up at the ceiling, as if calculating the figure in his head, carrying the ones and zeros. "Ten million dollars. We shall need to set up a few SuperPACs with vague-sounding names to get around the individual contribution limits, but that's a minor detail. With some creative accounting, big donations can be turned into lots of little ones. Not that it would ever occur to anyone to question whether Patty Pitypander had ten million of her own money."

Margot was stuck on the amount. "Ten million? That's a big donation."

"That's only for setting up a starter organization, you understand," Nigel said. "It would go toward office space, campaign materials, hiring a little staff and such. For the primaries we'll need much more. Iowa will cost ten million, New Hampshire fifteen, and South Carolina eight. But ten million would light the fundraising fire—if only we had it."

Patty looked forlornly at her ham sandwich as America's fate hung in the balance.

Margot's face broke into a smile. "I can spare two million, Sally. How about you?"

Sally pressed her lips together. "I'll match it. Where can we get the rest?"

"We'll pass the hat in Hollywood," said Margot. "Plenty of showbiz people are dying to kick that jackass Diebold out of the White House. We'll spread the word and scare up another six million in pledges."

Nigel rubbed his hands together. "How long will it take you? We haven't much time."

"A few days," Margot replied. "I'll start making calls today."

Sally picked up her wineglass. "A toast! Patty Pitypander for president! Down with the patriarchy! Up with the infestation! Bug, bug, bug, bug, bug!"

The four clinked their glasses together.

Sally turned to Patty in triumph. "Now there's nothing holding you back. You can tell that crazy husband of yours to go pound sand."

Patty smiled faintly. The Casino King would not be so easily dismissed.

CHAPTER 5

The Rookie Reporter

THE RED ENGINE light came on as soon as Jack pulled out of his parents' driveway. He shifted into first gear, maneuvered the ancient Honda Civic back under the carport, and popped the hood.

Oh no, not today.

An amber ooze was dripping down the side of the intake manifold like melted butter off a dinner roll. But it wasn't butter, it was oil. Something was making it curdle into goo—maybe a blown head gasket.

Jack looked at his watch. He had thirty minutes to get to *The Burbank Bee* and his first real job ever.

Fumbling for his wallet, Jack found eighteen dollars, not even enough for a one-way taxi ride. As if he had time to wait for a taxi this morning, of all mornings.

If the problem wasn't the gasket, maybe he could make it. Besides, what was the alternative? Jack jumped back into his car and took off, rattling down the road toward the interstate.

Four lanes of cars crawled in front of him as wisps of blue smoke spiraled up from under the Civic's rusted hood. The needle on the temperature gauge was climbing steadily toward the "H." Jack pulled off the freeway, parked, and switched off the ignition to let the engine cool. Minutes later, he drove back onto the superhighway, where traffic continued to inch forward.

Fifty yards ahead a big orange detour sign pointed right, diverting traffic onto a jammed two-lane road where stoplights waited for him every fifty yards.

Jack pounded his fist on the steering wheel. "Doggone it."

The Civic continued to smoke.

An hour later, Jack and his Civic fumed into the parking lot of the *Bee*. He kicked the car door shut.

"Need some help?" a female voice said.

Jack looked around. Over in the corner a petite young woman with curly blonde hair was studying him.

"Hi, I'm Fanny Flowers."

"Jack Snap. Nice to meet you." He looked at his watch again.

"Are you late?" she asked.

"Yes, how did you know?"

"Gus told us he was starting a new reporter today. I thought you might be him."

"You work for Gus?" As soon as the words left his lips, Jack wondered why he'd asked such a dumb question. How else would she have known about him?

"Yep, on the Metro desk." Her eyes fell on the Civic as blue smoke billowed up from under the hood.

Jack shrank with embarrassment. "It's really my father's car. I'm hoping to get a new one soon."

She looked at the smoking ruin. "Awesome. Looks like you'll need one soon."

They entered the building and headed for the elevator. Jack reached for the "2" button. "Second floor?"

She nodded, smiling sweetly.

"Cool. Same floor as me. So, like, how long have you been here at the *Bee*?"

"Six months, full time," she said. "But I interned here part-time before I graduated from Pepperdine."

"Cool, I just graduated too."

"Awesome." She put her finger to her chin. "UCLA's J-school, right?"

"I guess Gus told you that too?"

Her smile turned playful. "No, I'm psychic."

Jack stopped to check in with the receptionist. Fanny showed her employee pass, waved back at him, and disappeared into a thicket of cubicles around the corner.

After an hour of signing forms at human resources, Jack was escorted to an open area of desks surrounded by glass-lined offices. Someone had already laid his nameplate on his desk. He scanned the floor for Fanny. A sign above the cubicles on the far side of the building read "Metro."

Minutes later he looked up and saw a pear-shaped man waddling toward him. It was Gus Masterson, summoning Jack to his office.

Jack knew Gus's bio by heart. The old editor had worked almost everywhere during his forty-five years in the newspaper business: *The New York Times*, *The Washington Post*, and a host of lesser papers in mid-size cities. A graduate of the Columbia School of Journalism, he'd been a reporter, a columnist, and an editor of various descriptions.

Despite Gus's long experience, the sagging fortunes of the newspaper industry had turned him into a refugee, driving him from one shrinking newspaper staff to another. Not long ago he had landed in the top slot of the humble but respectable *Burbank Bee*, where he probably figured he would finish up his illustrious career, if the *Bee* could stay afloat a few more years. Gus was the newspaper's undisputed captain. No one else there had anything like his experience, as most of the editorial staff was well under thirty.

Gus's big mahogany desk was a mess, covered with stacks of paper threatening to topple over. His floor-to-ceiling oak bookcases groaned with volumes on history and politics. Dozens of inscribed plaques and journalism awards hung on the back wall, forming a circle around the Pulitzer prize he had won twenty years ago for investigative reporting. The smell of stale coffee pervaded the room.

Gus shut the heavy oak door behind his new reporter. "Jack, about your interview with Pitypander—great job getting in there. You're about the only reporter she's been willing to talk to since she lost her re-election. She's cut off practically all communication with the press. But you got in to see her. Very resourceful of you."

"Thank you, sir."

"The problem is, you didn't come out with anything."

"Sir?"

Gus folded his hands together. "Jack, your story was about Pitypander's warm and happy feelings about her glorious term as the first female governor of California. You brought me a big wagonload of fluff. There was no news in it. It wasn't worth editing."

Stunned, Jack felt a lump in his throat. He tried not to flinch.

"This isn't a college newspaper," said the veteran journalist. "We do real news here. We can't print a puff piece just because you like Pitypander. Even if any of her BS was true, which I doubt, it's old news by now. You had a golden opportunity for a hard-hitting scoop, something with meat in it. For example, you could have found out where Pitypander's going next with her political career. I'm sorry to say it, but you blew it."

But Jack *had* asked about her political plans. And if he had blown it, why had Gus hired him? Jack's shoulders tensed up. "I tried to get her to talk about that, sir, but she wouldn't tell me anything."

Gus lay back in his armchair and grinned. "Son, they never do, not willingly. Politicians are the slipperiest damn liars in the whole damn world. To get them to tell you the truth, you have to know more than they know about themselves, so they can't wriggle away from you. You have to trap them."

"How?"

The old man's eyes gleamed. "You chase 'em, corner 'em, run 'em to ground. It's a sport. Sort of like they're the fox in a foxhunt and you're the master of hounds. Tally-ho, Jack!"

"Tally-ho, sir?"

"Forget it. I was making an analogy. Listen, son, I know it was your first big interview. You weren't ready for it. You're a rookie. You went into that interview unarmed. But you'll get the story next time."

Unarmed? How could Jack trap a powerful woman like Patty Pitypander, his mother's college chum?

He held his tongue.

Gus leaned across the desk. "The important thing now is that you got in to see Pitypander. You penetrated her defenses. Mort couldn't have done that. Hell, the woman hates doing interviews. She can't stand reporters. But for some reason she liked you, Jack. She even sent me a nice little note recommending you for this job."

"Great."

So that was why he'd been hired. It wasn't his sheaf of clips from the student newspaper, or his brilliantly written story on Pitypander. He had simply gotten in to see her—thanks only to his mother.

"Son, sometimes half the battle for a reporter is getting access to powerful people, and you proved you're enterprising enough to do that. After the speech Pitypander gave to the Ladybugs, I'm more convinced than ever she's going to run for president. And when she does, the *Bee* will have a secret weapon, better than anything they've got at *The New York Times* or *The Washington Post*. That's you."

"Me?"

Gus pointed at him. "You've got something. I don't know what it is, son, but you've got it. I guess Pitypander saw it too. People like you, Jack, or at least women do. Women are the gatekeepers of this world, and if you can charm women, that'll get you in like Flynn nine times out of ten. That's why I hired you. You're a charmer. You're gonna make me proud."

Jack drew himself up in his chair. "I'll try, sir."

"Meanwhile, you're gonna need retraining before you cover the campaign. First, I want you to forget the bullshit they taught you in journalism school. Rookies have to learn the ropes of a real newspaper. We'll teach you what you need to know, right here at the *Bee*. I'm loaning you out to another department for a few weeks until the presidential campaign heats up and the fun begins."

"Which department, sir?"

"Metro." He motioned toward a group of cubicles across the floor. "Over there."

"Really?"

"Now don't be disappointed. I know you were expecting Mort's old political beat, so you might find Metro to be small potatoes—car accidents, house fires, zoning regulations, that sort of thing. But you'll learn. Hell, even Woodward and Bernstein did a stint on the *Post's* Metro desk. And they were several years older than you are. So be patient."

"Who do I ask for at the Metro desk?"

"Fanny Flowers. While you were in HR, she came to me and asked for you. I understand you two have already met." Gus winked at him. "See, you are a charmer."

Jack got up and walked to the door.

"And don't be late again," Gus yelled after him.

Jack the Charmer headed for the Metro desk with a pat on his back and a smile on his face, sure his luck must be changing for the better.

CHAPTER 6

Diebold's Outrage

THE PORTLY MAN with the florid face raised his palm to his brow to block the lights, squinting at the hundreds of black baseball caps bearing his name.

One might have mistaken him for an ordinary man. In a parallel universe he could have been a car salesman, a stockbroker, perhaps a neighborhood plumber. In this universe, by dogged ambition and ill chance he had wound up as P. Trayson Diebold, president of the United States.

He swaggered across the stage with a smile as big as Texas. The auditorium, packed with his most devoted admirers, exploded in applause.

It was great to be home, away from the White House and the Washington swamp. Diebold soaked up the adulation for a few seconds, thrust out his arms, and clapped for himself, along with the crowd.

"Hellooooo, Dallas!" He bowed, faced one side of the stage, and spun around to the other. "Are y'all feeling safe with Diebold?"

A thunderous roar went up.

"Mighty fine, mighty fine." Diebold pumped his fist.

They felt safe with Diebold, safe as a bank vault. The vault joke still worked as well as ever. It wasn't merely a play on his name. His re-election depended on it.

In his first presidential campaign, Percival Trayson Diebold, former wildcatter from Waco, had stumbled upon a crucial insight: His supporters didn't care a whit that he was not related to the family that made the ubiquitous Diebold cash machines and bank vaults. All his voters wanted was to believe something in their world was safe from change, and nothing said safety like a safe. That was why a bank vault with glittering gold bars inside had been stitched onto the black baseball caps. Single-handedly holding back the tide of revolution, Diebold kept his people safe.

A bank vault needed a banker, one who looked the part. Every morning Percival lost his effeminate first name, divided his hair in the middle, waxed his handlebar mustache, donned a three-piece suit, and placed a gold watch in his vest, morphing into P. Trayson Diebold, nineteenth-century banker. He and his safe would protect his voters, their dreams for the future, and their money from the meddling hands of their government—which, he reminded them at every rally, did not work for their benefit.

He began his act as he always did: with his gold watch. Diebold dug his fingers into his vest and pulled it out.

"What time is it?" he called out.

"Diebold time!" the crowd answered on cue.

"Ah, yes, so it is." He grinned. His supporters not only knew his shtick by heart, they looked forward to every line. The repetition of his comic routine made it fun. "Time to crack the safe! Let's do it!"

"Be bold, Diebold!" someone hollered back.

He pivoted toward Glenda Gomez, the small Hispanic woman at the center of the stage. The interview would be easy, his advisers had told him. The local news anchor was a Diebold contributor, lured with the promise of a major policy announcement. He followed her to two chairs at the front of the stage.

Gomez cast her eyes at her script. "Mr. President, could you summarize your goals for your second term? What do you hope to accomplish?"

Diebold turned to the audience. "Glenda, the federal government is like an overgrown shrub. The dang thing grows so fast we can't keep up. Instead of pruning it back like we've been doing, I mean to get serious. To hell with pruning it, I want to chop the sucker down to the ground and start over. Chop chop!" He stood up, raised his right arm, and slashed the air. "Chop chop!"

Applause broke out across the auditorium.

"To the ground, Mr. President?" Gomez asked. "Chop chop? What do you mean?"

Diebold glimpsed a white-haired man in the first row, chopping back at him. He pointed at the man. "See him? He gets it!"

The president pulled a piece of paper out of his coat and cleared his throat. "Glenda, I have my new plan for America right here. I call it my Clean Slate program. We're gonna wipe the slate clean by reducing the government to the few departments we had when the United States was new: State, Treasury, Justice, and War. If those four departments were enough for George Washington, they should be enough for us. We gotta get back to basics. It's our only way out of this mess."

"But what will you do with the other departments, Mr. President?"

Diebold swept his hand through the air, as if across a chalkboard. "Wipe 'em out, Glenda! Clean the slate."

She stiffened up. "What? All of them?"

"Yes, ma'am, all other federal departments added since the 1790s, and all the burdensome laws and regulations they impose on the American people."

Gomez looked puzzled. "But, Mr. President, isn't that most of the government?"

"Why, sure it is, Glenda. That's the point." Diebold held up both hands and counted off the ten doomed departments on his fingers. "Education, Interior, Agriculture, Commerce, Labor, Health and Human Services, Housing and Urban Development, Energy, Veterans Affairs, and Homeland Security. They gotta go. Chop chop!"

"But what about the federal employees in those departments?"

"Gone!" Diebold abolished their jobs with a flick of his wrist. "They'll be released to work in the private sector. Let 'em learn what it's like to do a real job for once."

"What will you do with the Post Office?"

"Sell it to the highest bidder, Glenda. We're gonna sell off all the federal assets we can—buildings, national parks, national forests, you name it. Do you have any idea how much land the federal government owns?"

"No, sir."

"Six hundred and forty million acres, Glenda. Twenty-eight percent of the whole country. Why do we have to own it? We could sell it for trillions. When I think of the acreage we could free up to boost the economy, why, I get goose bumps up and down my back. Think of the growth we could unleash."

Diebold explained how his program would reap trillions of dollars in savings from massive budget cuts. Trillions more, raised from asset sales, would be used to pay down the federal debt and abolish income taxes. Henceforth the government would be funded from tariffs and excise taxes.

"Is that really enough for all the revenue the government needs?" Gomez asked.

"Didn't it work in the 1800s, Glenda? Why, this country boomed back then! And we're gonna do it again. We'll slap a big federal excise tax on luxury items. We can start with overpriced coffee drinks, brie, Pilates classes, designer jeans, electric cars—the crap nobody needs."

"Those things are mostly used by progressives, Mr. President. Is that your intention?"

"Absolutely, Glenda. If those wine-and-cheese progressives want a huge federal government, I say let them pay for it. Why should the rest of us suffer? This sucker's been growing out of control for two hundred years. We're gonna cut it back to the ground, as soon as we get my Clean Slate bill passed. Chop chop!"

A hundred arms in the audience swung up and down, chopping along with Diebold. A thrill rippled through his body. This was democracy in action, the way it was always supposed to be. Serving the people—the real people, the ones who lived in what the coastal elites called flyover country—this was why he had gone to Washington in the first place.

An ear-splitting shriek erupted from the audience. Diebold saw a Secret Service agent to his right drop into a crouch.

"Down with Diebold!" someone cried out.

The president peered into the crowd. A woman with a pink hat had stood up in the middle of the auditorium and was yelling her head off.

She pointed at him. "Misogynist!"

Three security guards dashed toward her. They wrestled her down and carried her away, her fists swinging wildly.

Diebold turned to his left. In a back row another woman in a pink hat had popped up. She hollered, "Down with the patriarchy! Up with the Ladybugs! Bug, bug, bug, bug, bug! Pitypander for president!"

Two security guards clambered over some empty seats to subdue her. She let her body go limp so they would have to carry her out.

Diebold sat back with an uncomprehending stare, scanning the audience for more pink hats. "Pitypander? Is she kidding?"

Gomez wrinkled her nose at her script and put it aside. "There's an interesting question. Let's explore that, Mr. President. What about Pitypander? Ever since the Clement scandal broke, there's been talk that the Democrats should run the ex-governor against you."

Diebold's face tightened. "Crazy talk, Glenda. Nothing but crazy talk."

"So you don't think Pitypander will run?"

Diebold paused. "I'm not sure if she will, but I do think she's nutty enough to try." He smirked. "Hell, I'd love it if she did, Glenda."

"Why?"

What a stupid question, Diebold thought, puffing up his chest. "Because Patty Pitypander would be a pushover. That woman couldn't run a PTA meeting on her best day. She damn near drove California into bankruptcy with her crazy spending. What the dickens would a woman do to the whole country?"

Had he just said *what the dickens would a woman do*? Noting the surprise on Gomez's face, Diebold rushed to rephrase his question. "I didn't mean *any* woman, you understand. I meant Patty Pitypander. Just her."

Gomez's demeanor changed. Clearly irritated, she went on the offensive. "Are you opposed to a woman being president, sir? Are you afraid of what a woman might do?"

Diebold turned to the television cameras, quaking as he imagined the millions of female voters hanging on his next words. He glowered at his bald-headed press secretary, cringing in the front row. The idiot! Where in tarnation did he find this interviewer? Gomez should have been helping him climb out of this hole, not entrapping him in a major gaffe.

How best to wriggle away? Come down foursquare for women in general but dead set against the only one who stood a chance against him.

Diebold took a deep breath and let his answer fly. "No, I wouldn't mind a woman president. Hell, I'd welcome one. And I'm sure we'll have one someday. But Patty Pitypander? For president of the United States? C'mon, Glenda, don't be ridiculous."

CHAPTER 7

The Decision

PATTY WAVED FROM her veranda at the raucous crowd gathering on the beach. Ladybugs swarmed over the sand in their pink hats, shouting up at her through megaphones and holding up homemade placards marked "Run Patty Run! See Patty Run!" One woman beat a drum. Another sounded a trumpet.

The telephone rang for the eighteenth time. As Patty was ending the call, Nigel walked in.

She laid the phone on her side table. "That was the National Organization of Women. Their website has been overwhelmed. Their members can't believe what that idiot Diebold said about me. The phone won't stop ringing. I can't even drink my coffee."

The phone rang again.

"Let your secretary take a message," Nigel said as she reached for it. "We need to talk."

Patty collapsed into her chair. The Englishman stood over her, grinning down at her with that superior look of his.

"Hmm, I think America wants Pitypander, don't you?"

She looked up and laughed. "I should never have doubted you."

He stabbed the air with his forefinger. "More importantly, you shouldn't have doubted yourself. Are you out of your funk now?"

She rubbed her chin. "I think I've just traded one funk for another, and it's your fault."

"My fault?"

"Well, just look at them down there," she said, peering out the window. "They're expecting me to do something. Wipe that awful smirk off your face, Nigel, and tell me what we're going to do now."

"We'll give them Pitypander, of course. All the Pitypander they can stand."

"I mean, what's our next step?"

Nigel sat down and folded his hands. "Getting money, so we can start hiring your staff. Hopefully, Margot and Sally will come through for us soon."

Why had she gone to Hollywood for funding? All she needed was ten million dollars. She could have sold one of her Picassos for that without Benny ever noticing. Pawning her household decorations hadn't occurred to her. Instead, she had unwisely entrusted her destiny to Tinseltown, home of the flightiest people on earth.

She threw her head back, looked up at the gilded ceiling, and sighed. "Oh, if only I had Benny's blessing, none of this begging would be necessary."

"You don't need a blessing, least of all his." Nigel poured himself a cup of coffee. "What you need for a presidential campaign is money. With enough hard cash you can buy a blessing from the bloody Pope."

Still, it didn't feel right, and it wouldn't look right. Benny had stood alongside Patty in her other races. Benny should be on board. They should be a team, smiling, arm in arm, waving into the cameras together, beholden to no one.

The phone rang again. This time Patty picked it up. It was Mama.

Olympia sounded hopping mad. "Patty, I'm just calling to let you know how upset I am about what our awful president said about you yesterday. The nerve! Of course you're qualified to run. Don't listen to that man. You do what you think is best, baby."

"Thanks, I'll do that. Mama, can I get back to you? All hell is breaking loose here right now and I've gotta go."

"Sure, honey. Talk to you later."

Patty's secretary walked in and handed her a slip of paper. A message from Margot Lewiston was scrawled on it.

Patty fell back against her chair. "Incredible! Margot and Sally did it!"

Nigel pumped his fist. "Aha! There you are."

"It says here we have twenty million dollars in commitments. Money is pouring in. Diebold's little insult to women opened the floodgates!"

Nigel sprang to his feet. "It's a go!" He stopped suddenly and looked down at her. "Or is it a go? You have made your decision, haven't you? You can't waffle now. Please say yes."

Patty stepped to the window. Down below at the rim of the indoor pool, Mylo was on his knees replacing a light bulb. She closed her eyes. There would be great sacrifices ahead. Mylo would be only the first. No more ogling the pool boy. It was a jarring thought.

The stack of paperback novels beside the recliner caught her eye, striking her with dread. The pile seemed to reach for the sky. Jenessa Fuller would never stop having affairs, not with Marjorie Mickle pumping out four potboilers a year. If Patty didn't change her ways, she might become the first woman in history to drown in pulp fiction.

Her weakness for pool boys? Her addiction to romance novels? What did they signify? Surely some improvement in her habits was called for. Should she run for president of the United States?

"Patty, when will you ever get this chance again? Please do make up your mind," Nigel pleaded. "The entire world is waiting on your word."

A voice boomed from the hallway. "No, it isn't."

Patty swung around. "Benny!"

BENNY DARKENED THE doorway, his owlish brown eyes hurling daggers at Nigel. "The world doesn't want Patty Pitypander for president."

Nigel turned to face him, as if standing at attention. "And why not, my good man?"

"'Cause she's not qualified, my good jackass."

Nigel leaned his head back. "Oh, I see. Is that how it is? I suppose you consider yourself somehow qualified to tell her she's not qualified? And how would you know?"

Benny pointed his forefinger at the Englishman. "Look, pal, I know what you're up to. She doesn't need a scam artist like you rolling in here and putting wacko ideas in her head so you can—"

The blast of a Ladybug's trumpet rattled the windows. Benny jumped back. "What the hell was that?"

Nigel pointed at the pink hats on the beach. "You see that crowd down there? There are hundreds of women outside your home. They believe, as I do, that Patty should run and that this is entirely her decision."

Benny's stubby arms hung from his shoulders like pendulums, his fists clenched. "No, bozo, it's our decision! Hers and mine. She's my wife! Who do you think you are, filling her head with this crap?"

Nigel stiffened up. "You may have missed the memo. It's the twenty-first century. She doesn't require your permission. Are you going to tell your wife what she may or may not do?"

"You bet I am." Benny drew closer. "She married an Italian, the old-fashioned kind, bub. It comes with the territory."

Nigel threw up his hands. "Ah, you're Italian. Somehow I don't think that's the problem here." He shook his head. "I'm afraid you two will have to work this thing out. I've done what I can. Patty, let me know what you want to do." He spun around on his heels and walked away.

"Good riddance!" Benny turned to Patty. "So what are you gonna do?"

The stack of novels caught her eye. The one on top was *Seize the Night*, with the dark-haired stranger on its cover. Patty wondered what heroine Jenessa Fuller would do in the face of such patriarchal oppression.

It became clear in an instant. Jenessa wouldn't stand for such treatment, not for a minute. Jenessa Fuller—the proud, high-spirited temptress who knew a thousand ways to master the hearts of men—would be her own woman.

Patty walked up to Benny and stood inches from him, fists on her hips, her face defiant. "*Carpe diem.* Seize the day!"

"What?"

"I'm going to run for president, Benny."

He folded his arms. "Not with my money, you're not."

"That's right. Not with your money. You aren't going to control me anymore, Benny. I've got my own money now. Twenty million bucks. How do you like that?"

He stopped smirking.

She glared at him. "You said we were partners, but you wouldn't back me. So I went out and raised my own money. Did you think you could stop me, Benny? Have you ever been able to stop me?"

Benny plodded across the floor and back, his hand against his temple. "Look, sweetie, we've got a good thing going here. Don't you see this could wreck everything for us?"

"Why would it?"

He turned around. "Because everything about you will be investigated, doll, including me. As long as you're in the spotlight, the press will dig and dig until they find something. They'll never stop digging."

"I'm not afraid of the press."

"Oh, yeah? Then you're a damn fool! Tell me, what happens when reporters start investigating my casinos? Our deals with the regulators? What about our foundation? How about my tax records? You don't think they'll come after me to get to you?"

Patty wondered if she would ever live down Benny's pay-to-play schemes. Giving a fat contribution to the Pitypander Foundation, doing a hotel deal with Benny, or granting him a casino license made people expect things of her when she was governor—like relaxing some state regulation or leaning on a department head to get a no-bid contract approved. Benny had gone behind her back, compromising her right and left with his illicit deals. She had never been able to stop him, not once.

That was in the past now. She wouldn't let him betray her interests again.

"Someone has to rescue the country from Diebold, Benny. He's power-mad. He'll wreck everything Democrats have fought for in the last century. It's going to take a woman to beat him. It's up to me."

"Power-mad?" Benny laughed. "Patty, you love power more than anyone. You want to control everybody else, but you can't control yourself."

She waved him off.

"You'll lose, doll. Then you'll go menopausal all over again. You'll turn back into a big puddle of tears, boo-hooing day and night like five years ago. Having fantasies again. All the shrinks in California won't be able to bring you back this time."

She stuck out her finger and poked him in the forehead. "No, this is where the real self-control problem is, Benny. It's right in here—your ego. You're not afraid I'll lose. You're afraid I'll win!"

He took a step back. "That's not true. I'm just worried about you, doll."

She jabbed him again, and once more he retreated. "You can't stand the thought of not being in control of me. You won't be able to do business like before. Your life won't be the same if I win."

"It's worse than that. Nothing will be the same if you even run. Ever." He turned and walked out.

So nothing would be the same. Thank God. America wanted Patty Pitypander, and dammit, it was going to get her. All the Pitypander it could stand.

Patty walked across the house and up the stairs to her bedroom. In the back of her closet, on a high shelf, lay her little pink hat, where she had left it years ago. She set it squarely on her head and looked in the mirror. It still fit.

She walked down to the beach, raised her fist, and called out to the other pink hats, "Pitypander for president!"

A cheer went up from the astonished Ladybugs.

CHAPTER 8

Early Stumbles

STEPPING DOWN FROM the Gulfstream, Patty tightened the belt of her overcoat, bracing herself against the cold Iowa wind. Bright sunshine reflected off the new campaign bus awaiting her arrival across the tarmac. She walked up to it, put her hands on her hips, and admired the red letters painted on its side: *Empathy Express*.

"Magnificent."

Eighty feet long, the articulated land-based vehicle was more battleship than bus, outfitted with sofa beds, a bathroom, a kitchen, television screens, and enough telecommunications equipment to command an invasion force. Below its name were emblazoned the words "Pitypander for President" in red, white, and blue.

Her new staff, two dozen in all, spilled out of the vehicle to greet her, led by Nigel.

Patty raised her fist. "On to victory!"

They returned her salute. "Victory!"

Patty entered the vehicle and conducted an inspection of its interior. She smiled at the Jenessa Fuller novels thoughtfully placed in her cabin. Her butler must have suggested bringing them.

Her followers were so young, even her top lieutenants. After Nigel, who had hired them, the oldest was Colleen Cook, a forty-something television reporter who had signed on as communications director, and thirty-ish campaign pollster Chassidy Navarro, from Patty's gubernatorial campaigns. The others were a motley collection—local activists, volunteers hailing from around the country, and Ladybugs—all united in one mission: drive the hated Diebold from office.

The Empathy Express turned onto the highway, while Navarro briefed Patty on the status of the campaign. "The race has tightened. Clement is polling at twenty-seven percent, Brown at twenty-four, Krieger at eighteen, and Sartini at eight. You're at twenty-three already."

Third place after only three weeks in the race! Women, Chassidy told her with a confident grin, were flocking to her side, but further progress would be harder to achieve. As cornfields rolled by, the subject turned to strategy and how best for the Pitypander campaign to make up lost time. The other primary candidates had been stumping around the state for months. To win Iowa, Patty must land big punches fast.

"We have to hit the farmers hard," Nigel said. "Everything depends on your making a good first impression. What do you know about cows?"

"Nothing."

"A pity. Our first stop is a dairy farm. Today you're a cowgirl. You're crazy for cows."

"Me?" Patty laughed. She had never come within ten feet of a cow.

"Relax, you're not here to kiss cows," her campaign manager assured her. "The voters want to see you, that's the main thing. Today you'll score points with farmers and environmentalists in one go."

The photo-op would showcase Patty's bold new ideas for tackling global warming while allaying farmers' concerns about government interference. She would win over the environmentalists by favoring technology to reduce greenhouse gases.

Patty nodded. "Right, I'm an environmentalist." That was one of the top five items Nigel had sketched out in a long list of core values—the

Pitypander Principles—explained in detail on the campaign website. She could read more about her principles later, when there was time. Today her mission was to attack Diebold's dismissive attitude toward climate change.

She wasn't in deep-blue California anymore, where she could hit a few key regions like Silicon Valley, Hollywood, and the Central Valley, and play to a crowd of like-minded people. She must broaden her appeal to encompass all of America.

"Campaigning has changed since you were governor," Nigel said. "The pace has quickened. We have to be more responsive, flexible, and open-minded. Be ready for anything. Even cows."

The big bus pulled off the highway onto a macadam road. A sign posted along the fence pointed to Dapper Dairy Farm, where a crowd of reporters and television crews was waiting next to a fenced stockyard.

The stench of cow manure blasted Patty's nostrils with such force she jerked her head back. "My God, I can hardly breathe. How can anyone live out here?"

An elderly man in overalls, Elijah Johnson, greeted them. He was accompanied by a bespectacled man in a white lab coat who introduced himself as Dr. Hardy, founder and CEO of Bovine Modification Systems.

The farmer led Patty and her team into the stockyard, where Dr. Hardy held forth on the manifold dangers of cow flatulence.

"Most people have no idea how deleterious bovine methane can be for earth's atmosphere," the scientist said. "Methane accounts for a tenth of this country's greenhouse gas emissions, and enteric fermentation from the digestive process of ruminant bovines is a major component of our total methane load."

"Our methane load?"

"Cow farts, that's what he means," farmer Johnson whispered to Patty. "I'd always thought they just smelled bad. Then I come to learn from the good doctor here that cow farts is worse than cigarettes. He says our Holsteins is melting the polar ice caps."

"That bad, eh?" Patty noticed piles of manure dotting the stock-yard like a minefield. She stepped gingerly around them as Johnson and Dr. Hardy led her past one ruminant bovine after another, the reporters traipsing after them.

Johnson leaned his arm against a fence. "Why, Governor, when the wind is still, the farts can get so thick around here they knock you down. Don't know how we survived out here so many years. Damn good thing we caught it in time."

"Oh, but it's more than the flatulence, Elijah," Hardy pointed out. "These animals emit even more methane through eructation."

"Eructation—burps, he means." Johnson walked farther on, trans-lating for the scientist as he went. "The doctor says a cow's mouth is even deadlier than her ass."

Patty heard a moo so deafening it almost knocked her down. "Oh!" She jumped a step backward and grabbed onto a fence post. The cow responsible was eyeing her.

"She won't hurt you." Johnson patted the cow's head. "She's just curious. She ain't never seen a politician before. I'd say she's just a mite suspicious. There, there, Bessie. The governor ain't gonna hurt you none."

Patty turned to a Holstein munching contentedly in a feed trough, taking no notice of her. It seemed to have no regard for the destruction it was wreaking on the planet's climate. "How much does a cow eat, Mr. Johnson?"

"Oh, about a hundred pounds of feed corn a day. It's like eating beans. Imagine how gassy you'd be if you ate a hundred cans of beans. You'd be fit to explode, I reckon."

Patty's stomach rumbled. "So what can be done to fix them?"

"Gotta catch the methane," Johnson said, "before it gets away and kills the ice caps."

"Who catches the methane?"

"Dr. Hardy and his boys."

"And exactly how do you do that, Doctor?"

"With this." Dr. Hardy walked over to a gray metal box about three feet high resembling an air-conditioning compressor. It was hooked up by copper tubing to other boxes placed every fifty feet around the stockyard. It made a whooshing sound.

The scientist opened the top of the box, revealing the fan and copper coils inside. "This is our firm's methane extraction unit. It continually ingests the ambient air, extracts the methane molecules from it, and disaggregates them into carbon and hydrogen. The carbon is piped to that big storage unit over there and removed for burial. The hydrogen can be mixed with oxygen in the air to make water fit for drinking."

"You can drink fart water? It's actually safe?"

"Yes, quite safe."

"Very impressive technology." Patty wished she understood it so she could ask him an intelligent-sounding question.

She surveyed the faces of the reporters. They were paying more attention to the scientist than her. Was there anything extraordinary about Iowa's cows she could say, somehow linking these splendid animals to Dr. Hardy's amazing breakthrough?

Flatulence, she gathered, was an Iowa cow's outstanding feature. "I assume you started your tests here because Iowa's cows are extra gassy. Is that right?"

"As a matter of fact, Governor, you're exactly right. They are phe-nomenally gassy." The scientist bent down and scooped up a handful of dirt. "You see this rich black topsoil? This is some of the most fertile soil in the world, deposited when the glaciers retreated during the last ice age. It gives Iowa corn an extremely high carbon content. That's what turns these innocent-looking Holsteins into super-emitting planet killers."

Johnson grasped the shoulder straps of his overalls. "Depend on it, ma'am. An Iowa bessie can outfart any cow in the world with her eyes closed. Why, on a bad day here—"

"Thanks, I think I get it." Patty turned to the reporters, eager to distill the complexity of the methane menace into a sound bite even they could understand. "It's not so complicated," she said knowledgeably. "Iowa's black dirt makes super-gassy corn, which makes super-gassy cows."

"Exactly," Dr. Hardy said. "But of course all bovines generate profuse amounts of gas. Iowa's are just the worst offenders, which is why we picked this state to test our technology."

"Doctor, how many of these machines would it take to stop Iowa's cows from defoliating the earth?" Patty asked.

Dr. Hardy was ready with the answer: Total bovine methane abatement would require deploying two million of his patented gas-absorbing units statewide, at a cost of twenty billion dollars for the first ten years, not including regular maintenance and replacement, which only his fledgling firm was qualified to do.

Twenty billion sounded like a lot of money. "Just for Iowa, for only ten years?"

Dr. Hardy looked at her glumly. "Yes, and that's the problem. Farmers can't afford my gas-absorbers. To pay for them, milk prices would have to rise to twenty dollars a gallon. Farmers will need federal help. That's why we called your campaign. We're hoping you'll help us raise awareness of this issue."

Patty turned to the cameras. "I'll do a lot better than that, Dr. Hardy. On my very first day in office, I'll direct the Department of Agriculture to offer federal subsidies for your machines. We'll tax milk to pay for them."

Minutes later communications chief Colleen Cook came running to her in distress. A campaign staffer in Durango Beach had relayed an alert about some breaking news.

Patty pulled the story up on her phone and read the banner headline on her screen:

HOLY COW! PITYPANDER PINNING BLAME FOR CLIMATE CHANGE ON IOWA, PROPOSES TWENTY-DOLLAR MILK

How much was a gallon of milk? Patty had no idea; she hadn't set foot inside a grocery store in years.

She modified her plan on the spot. Consumers who couldn't afford twenty-dollar milk would receive food stamps. Her milk tax would pay for everything.

Too late. The media people were heading to their vans.

"Wait, come back!" Patty yelled, waving her arms frantically. "Let me explain my position!"

As soon as she said this, her right leg changed its position, sliding forward on something slippery underfoot.

"Whoa!" she cried, flinging out her right arm and grabbing a fence rail just in time. She looked down in disgust at the excrement clinging to her shoes.

Steadying herself, Patty scraped the mess off on some grass and frowned at a nearby Holstein. "Okay, Bessie, you got me. So what is the price of milk?"

"Moo!" the cow replied, sending her scurrying back to the bus.

THE SNOW, ALREADY six inches deep in the airport parking lot, pelted against the windows of the Empathy Express, driven by a howling wind. Patty watched the snowflakes swirl with rising alarm. Would she be stuck in New Hampshire overnight? Even the weather had turned hostile to her.

Nigel leaned across the aisle and carped some more about her weak performance in Iowa. "One can't very well go prancing about the countryside bashing Iowa's farmers for their gassy corn and cows, proposing a fivefold increase in milk prices, and expect to win the Iowa caucus, can one?"

He was almost as insufferable as the reporters. Patty threw her head back in indignation. "I didn't insult Iowa, the media did. What's wrong with those people? They twist everything I say like a pretzel."

"They don't care much for you either. You're not connecting with the press. That's your biggest problem."

Brown had taken Iowa with twenty-seven percent, followed by Krieger with twenty-five and Patty with twenty-three. Clement, at eighteen, had continued to spiral downward. Sartini, disappointed by his seven percent share and unable to raise enough money to go on, had dropped out, but hardly anybody except Patty noticed. Now that the handsome young congressman with the fine Italian nose had been eliminated, she wondered whether he would like to be her vice president.

Nigel's brow was knotted in thought. "We must turn things around here. The first order of business is to repair your relationship with the media. Let's concentrate on that."

"It's hopeless. They all hate me," Patty said, sulking. "They did in California, and they're even worse here."

Nigel turned to the woman sitting in the row behind them. "It can't be hopeless. What do you suggest, Colleen?"

The ex-reporter leaned forward, offering an overly eager grin, like she'd been dying to be asked for her opinion. "We need to take direct action. If you want to win the press over, you have to wage a charm offensive."

No, reporters were out to get her. There was no charming them.

Colleen swept the long black hair out of her eyes. "Stop thinking of the media as your enemy. Reporters are regular people with a job to do. Respect them as professionals and they'll return the favor. Show them you're human. They think you're aloof."

Aloof. What a ridiculous accusation. Patty had been raised in the middle class. Luigi Ingratelli was no Boston Brahmin. He ate pasta, attended Red Sox games, and sent his kids to modest Catholic schools. Patty was every inch her father's daughter.

"I have to agree with Colleen," Nigel said quietly.

The two of them had discussed her aloofness problem behind her back. This was an intervention, planned and rehearsed. Her top lieutenants were plotting a coup.

Nigel would not drop the subject. "Right or wrong, you have the image of being elite and standoffish. I've heard it said many times before."

"That's silly. I may be reserved but I'm not elite."

Nigel's eyes opened wide. "Rubbish! You're a billionaire's wife. You own five homes, one of them a castle, and eat like a gourmand. You do weekend shopping trips to Paris for lingerie, jetting away on your Gulfstream 650 the way normal people drive their SUV to the mall."

"You know perfectly well it's all Benny's money. So I like nice things. So what?"

"You must close the gulf separating you from the press," Nigel said. "Come down from your castle and be a people person. Humble yourself, Patty. Connect with them."

His glibness was so grating. It was easier to connect with some people than others. Patty recalled how she once solicited votes in a Los Angeles barrio by working in a soup kitchen for a couple of hours, doling out potato salad to gang members. She could relate to gang members. Their needs were much like hers, revolving around money, power, and protecting their turf. The media, in contrast, was antagonistic by nature. It was their job to be nasty. "How do I connect with the press?"

"Pretend you're hosting a cocktail party for them. Be warm and giving. Get to know them personally. Isn't that what you have in mind, Colleen?"

"Yes, that's it exactly. Connections win elections," the communications director said in a firm voice.

"There you go," Nigel said. "Remember that. Tattoo it to your left wrist: Connections win elections."

How trite. Very well, she would humor them. She eyed the press bus stalled in the snow on the other side of the parking lot. If she wasn't going anywhere, the vipers on that bus weren't either.

Take direct action. Be warm and giving. They're ganging up on me. I'll show them.

Patty walked to the drink machine. She poured hot chocolate into eight plastic cups, put lids on them, and laid them on a tray.

"Where the devil are you going?" Nigel asked as she carried the tray to the front of the bus.

Patty stuck her nose in the air. "To the people, to be a people person."

She stepped down from the Empathy Express and trudged across the parking lot to the vipers' bus, carrying the steaming beverages. The startled bus driver opened the door.

Patty entered and saw the shocked faces of thirty reporters looking up at her.

"Would any of you like some hot chocolate? Joe? Mary?" She handed out the cups on her tray. "Come on over to my bus, folks. There's plenty more where this came from."

The reporters, their faces full of curiosity, filed out of the press bus and shuffled through the snow to the Empathy Express.

"That's it, all the drinks you like." Patty directed traffic as they made their way to the kitchen. "There's sherry, gin, and vermouth back there too. Help yourselves."

Her eyes zeroed in on a young blond man, his head covered in a hooded parka, waiting at the end of the queue.

"Hello, Governor." Jack Snap pulled back his hood and smiled.

Patty blinked, took a step forward, and touched him on the shoulder as if to make certain he was real. What was Jack doing here, among the vipers?

"Jack! It is you. How marvelous to see you again." Her face began to tingle. "So you did get the job at the *Bee*?"

His blue eyes beamed down at her. "Yes, and Gus assigned me to follow your campaign. How cool is that?"

Jack Snap was assigned to her? That was very cool. "My campaign? How lucky for us!" The tingle, intensifying, ran down Patty's leg. The sensation was too agreeable to be a recurrence of her sciatica. It must have emanated from Jack.

"It's Gus's idea. I'm covering all the candidates, but he thinks you're gonna go the distance."

Going the distance, with you, Jack? Be still, my heart. Patty leaned against the side of the bus, her eyes locked on the boy with the wonderful blond hair.

CHAPTER 9

The Road to Super Tuesday

P. TRAYSON DIEBOLD chucked *The New York Times* across his desk in disgust. "'Pitypander bursts upon the political scene with a welcome breath of fresh air,' my ass. How can they make this stuff up with a straight face?" He picked an official White House pencil off the Resolute desk and snapped it in two.

It wasn't just the *Times*. Across the media landscape, resentment of the ex-governor's wealth and aloofness had mutated into gushing admiration.

"'Riding to the rescue,' my ass. Are they nuts? That woman is plumb dangerous," Diebold grumbled to the man with the long face. "She'd never have made it to governor if it weren't for her husband's money. She's got no qualifications. She'll be the death of this nation if she gets to sit in this chair. I'm the one riding to the rescue. Can't those idiots see that?"

Pitypander had transformed her image. She needed to, her handlers knew it, and the liberal press obliged. Perceptions of the candidates were being tested and redefined by their campaigns weekly to suit the fickle public mood. Four years earlier Diebold had remade his own image, tapping into a rich lode of voter sentiment with his comforting slogan "Be Safe With Diebold." Pitypander, abetted by the complicit media, had stumbled upon a vein of her own.

Her metamorphosis began with her second-place showing in the New Hampshire primary, where she finished on Brown's heels by playing up her New England roots and rallying the Ladybugs to her side. Her supporters' fervor awed the pundits. That alone made the cuckoo ex-governor a serious contender. A lightweight only yesterday, she had gravitas today.

That was the most galling part: that Pitypander could suddenly have substance. How could anyone believe this tripe? But believe it they did.

The *Times* was the first to change its tune. Anxious to atone for its earlier backing of Clement, the newspaper published a feature on the former governor, pontificating that "though inexperienced, Pitypander brings diversity and femininity to an otherwise bland group of boring male also-rans. Committed and energized, she is riding headlong to the Democrats' rescue."

The Washington Post scrambled to catch up, chiming in with an impassioned front-page piece about how valiantly the ex-governor had battled for California's immigrants. *People* magazine splashed Patty across its cover wearing a pink Ladybug hat, under the headline "Champion of Women's Rights." Nightly news anchors reporting on her rallies burbled with hopeful anticipation.

The cheerleading for Pitypander had begun in earnest. Her second-place finish in New Hampshire was generating a tidal wave of media fawning.

Diebold wasn't entirely surprised. "Politics is horseshit from top to bottom," he said. "It's make-believe. That's all it ever is."

Attorney General Tosh Cooper plucked the newspaper off the president's desk. "They got one thing right in there. She sure is tearing up the campaign trail. At five rallies a day, she'll outwork the others if nothing else. Anyway, we know Clement is a goner."

According to the *Times*, the beleaguered senator was circling the bowl, shamed and shunned by donors in the wake of his blackface scandal. Only five people had shown up at his rally in Columbia, South Carolina. They wandered down the street from a homeless shelter for the free drinks.

"Did the FBI ever find out where that old photograph of Clement came from?" Diebold asked.

"No, sir. We haven't been able to trace it to anybody. We're not even sure it's real."

Diebold leaned back. "I've been wondering about that, Coop. Maybe it wasn't real. The timing was awful suspicious. Do you suppose Pitypander could have been behind it?"

"She had the most to gain, no doubt about it," Cooper replied, dutifully following the president's logic. "It sure cleared the way for her."

"My thoughts exactly."

"Yes, sir."

Diebold spun around in his chair and looked out the window at the Washington Monument. He could handle the bloviating, posturing, and fraudulence demanded by this job just fine, but not the character assassination. Pretending to be what he wasn't came naturally. Calumny didn't. The vicious, take-no-prisoners kind of scandal-mongering they did in Washington turned Diebold's stomach. Sometimes it even made him homesick for Texas, something which normally only the smell of pork barbeque could do.

For what little he knew of Pitypander, having met her only once, she might actually be a fine woman, despite her do-gooder pretense, even if her ideas were bat-crap crazy. Casting aspersions about a woman wasn't how Texas men behaved. John and Muriel Diebold, good Baptists both, had raised their son Percival to respect women, most of the time.

Respect be damned, Diebold thought, Washington's swamp creatures weren't leaving him any choice. The Democrat smear merchants and their media allies had been setting traps for him since his first presidential campaign. They were even sabotaging Harry Clement. If they would frame a faithful old soldier in their own party, what would they do to a hated arch-conservative like himself?

Would anyone in his right mind go into battle unarmed against such lowdown scum-suckers as these? No way. Not this boy. That would be political suicide.

He turned back to Cooper. "Suppose they pull a trick like that on me. Have we got anything to fight back with? What do we have on Pitypander?"

"Plenty," said the attorney general. "Her husband owns the Pitypander Palaces. There's a lot of dirt in the casino business."

The problem was the ex-governor had no role in her husband's far-flung empire. "That's close, but not close enough. I mean Patty Pitypander herself. What have we got on her personally? I mean real personally."

Cooper scratched his chin. "If you want, sir, we can look into it."

"Do that. Look into it. We'll be facing her in November. I'm sure of it now."

PATTY STARED UP at the big television screen in the hotel ballroom and bit her lip. "How're we doin', y'all?"

"There's no further need for your y'alling now," said Nigel. "We're going north tomorrow. You can give it a rest."

The last y'all had just slipped out. For the past three days she had been y'alling across the South like a beagle chasing rabbits. She had y'alled to voters outside a polling place in Birmingham this morning, y'alled to the workers at a Greensboro toy factory this afternoon, and y'alled to her supporters at a Pitypander rally here in Richmond. As Patty's voice withered to a husky croak, for the life of her she couldn't stop y'alling.

Were there any more hands in the entire South to shake? Patty's right hand ached, the skin on her palm rubbed rawer than her nerves.

But *bless her little heart*—a Southern phrase she had come to despise even more than she hated casually dropping her g's—she had made it to Super Tuesday, and it was time "to let the voters do the talkin'." With twelve primaries at stake in a single night, the vote totals poured in.

"Massachusetts, Vermont, Minnesota, and California are in the bag." Nigel crossed those states off his scorecard, writing a "P" next to each. "Clement will take Texas and Oklahoma. Brown has Utah. Krieger is leading in Arkansas. It's neck and neck in Alabama, North Carolina, Tennessee, and Virginia."

Ah, Virginia. If Patty could beat Clement in the heavily populated counties between Washington and Fredericksburg, the Old Dominion—a perennial bellwether—would fall into her calloused hand like a ripe plum.

As Nigel predicted, Loudoun, Arlington, Fairfax, and Prince William Counties began to tip her way.

"It's nine o'clock," the news anchor announced. "Pitypander has run the table in Northern Virginia, thanks to her strong showing among suburban women. Seventy-five percent of Virginia women under forty have thrown in their lot for the erstwhile California governor."

Fist-pumping women in pink hats marched across the screen chanting "Bug, bug, bug, bug, bug!"

North Carolina and Tennessee soon followed Virginia into the Pitypander column. Shouts burst out across the ballroom.

"I'll be damned! It's a rout!" Nigel jumped up and down on his toes. "We're running the table tonight."

Minutes later a white-haired old man standing in another ballroom far away appeared on the screen with a hangdog look in his eyes.

Patty squeezed Nigel's shoulder. "My God, it's Harry Clement. He looks like he's been run over by an eighteen-wheeler."

"Harry, Harry, Harry!" the senator's supporters cried out, thrusting their campaign signs up and down like pistons.

Clement waved back at them, his fleshy jowls trembling as he struggled to maintain his smile. He let his people go on cheering for half a minute before finally raising both hands, signaling he wished to speak.

The cheering died down to a murmur.

"Despite extremely unfair press coverage," the senator called out in a somber tone, "we've run a clean race, one we can be proud of. Whoever framed me with that blackface photo should be ashamed. I repeat, I have absolutely no memory of having worn blackface in kindergarten. But, dear friends, that's behind us now. It's time to face the truth."

"No! Don't do it, Harry!" yelled someone in the crowd. "Harry, we love you! Stay in the fight! We need you, Harry!"

Clement flashed a thumbs-up sign at the supporter, but continued. "Seeing no path to victory, I am hereby suspending my campaign. We need to get behind the Democrat with the best shot at sending our miserable excuse for a president back to Texas. Tonight the voters have told us who that is: Patty Pitypander." Clement raised his fist in salute. "Patty Pitypander for president!"

Patty slapped her forehead in disbelief.

"Clement's endorsed us!" Nigel thrust his arms in the air. "Nothing can stop us now! We're going all the way!" The ballroom erupted in cheers.

The words "BREAKING NEWS" appeared on the screen.

"Long before any observers thought possible," the news anchor said, his voice tinged with the high drama of the moment, "the Pitypander campaign has steamrolled its way to victory. With the addition of Clement's delegates, Pitypander has cobbled together enough votes to take the Democratic nomination. The Brown and Krieger campaigns are expected to concede shortly."

The commentator next to him looked flabbergasted. "What an incredible comeback, Marvin. Who would have believed it? The ex-governor of California, four years after suffering a humiliating re-election defeat widely thought to have ended her political career, has risen like Lazarus from the dead to clinch the Democratic presidential primaries, thanks to the implosion of Clement's scandal-plagued candidacy and a massive turnout among her feminist base. It's a most improbable upset for a newcomer to the national scene. A woman who many, notably President Diebold, derided as unqualified to run."

Nigel raised his fist. "Unqualified to run! Ha! The buggers! What do they know? I told you we could do it! Didn't I tell you?"

The ballroom became a sensory overload of jubilation, popping champagne corks, and unbridled joy.

Amid the din of the celebration, Patty's phone rang.

It was Benny. "You did it, doll! I don't know how, but you did it!"

"Thanks, Benny."

"I take back what I said, babe. You do have a chance. I checked with the bookies downstairs. They're laying forty-seven percent odds on you beating Diebold."

Patty turned up the volume on her phone to make sure she'd heard him right. "Forty-seven percent, you say? Is that good?"

"Good? Of course it is. You just started, doll, and already you're within shooting distance of Diebold. Forget what I said before. I'm behind you all the way, babe."

If a troglodyte like Benny could be converted, anyone could. His phone call had made her victory complete. All things were possible now.

Patty's doubters, with the exception of herself, were in full retreat. The primary battles had been expected to last well into the spring. This triumph had come so fast, so easily. Was it real, or a dream?

Patty pinched herself. It felt real. Hadn't she reached out to the press and tamed them? Yes, she had shown them even a billionaire's wife could be a genuine people person. The reporters lined up behind her now, talking up her campaign on the nightly news shows. The country was learning to appreciate her hopeful message. She had discovered her authenticity.

Patty turned to her exultant campaign staff and raised her fist alongside Nigel's. "We did it, y'all!"

CHAPTER 10

The Arrangement

EVEN BY THE standards of the Las Vegas Strip, where the Eiffel Tower and canals of Venice are neighbors, the visitor in the baggy brown suit looked phony. Benny knew a counterfeit when he saw one.

The first thing he noticed when Gorok Krok entered his office was the man's hair. Much too light for his skin, it lay precariously on his head, and could only be a wig. The second clue was his heavy accent, some kind of Eastern European mishmash Benny had never heard before. The third oddity was Krok's business card, which lacked a street number and a postal code. "Pudding Lane, London" was the entire address.

Too vague to be real, Gorok Krok was from everywhere and yet nowhere, a mosaic of geographic fraudulence as blatant as Las Vegas itself. Some people might have been repelled by the man's brazenness, but not Benny. In Vegas the bigger a fake was, the more respect it commanded. The most audacious, like the sumptuous Pitypander Palace itself, were sixty stories tall and drew huge crowds.

Krok's brown eyes twinkled below his bushy eyebrows. "I grow up in Budapest," he said, declaring himself a Hungarian. "I leave many years ago when communists let us go. I have lived in many places: Europe, Africa, Middle East, America, Asia. You name it, I have been there. I have many contacts everywhere."

So Krok was selling international contacts. He must be some kind of consultant. With whom, and for what? Benny lay back with his hands behind his head. "Exactly what does Krok Business Services do, Gorok?"

Krok dug into his briefcase, pulled out his firm's glossy brochure, and handed it to Benny. It was full of pictures of foreign places where Krok had performed his supposed services, alongside hazy descriptions of what those services were.

"We find deals for making good business, yes?" Krok said. "We find investments as you like them, okay?"

Talking to Krok was like playing charades, but the Casino King liked games. "So you're a search firm, is that it? You look for customized investment opportunities around the world?"

"Yes, that is it."

Thumbing through the brochure, Benny stopped on a page showing the skyline of Hong Kong. Krok had supposedly arranged the sale of a large hotel there to an unnamed buyer. "Ah, I see you work in China. Do you have good Chinese contacts?"

"Only the best," Krok assured him. "I find you anybody in China."

"Anybody?" Benny considered that an impressive boast, but a little over the top. The population of China was almost a billion and a half.

"Anybody in Communist Party," said Krok, scaling down his claim to ninety million.

"We're already in China—big time."

"Ah." Krok lifted an eyebrow. "Where?"

"Macau," Benny replied with a satisfied smile. "Anybody who is anybody in this business is in Macau."

The gambling industry in Macau already dwarfed that of Las Vegas, and it was still growing apace. The Pitypander Palace in the former Portuguese colony was the jewel in Benny's crown and his most profitable venture, justifying the years of bureaucratic hassles he had endured to get it built.

"You like Macau?" Krok asked. "I go to Macau for you. No problem."

"No, Macau is overbuilt," Benny replied. "There are too many casinos there already. We are looking to expand in Asia, though. Maybe you could look around for us someplace else."

"We go there. We go to someplace else."

Benny rubbed his chin, wondering whether Krok had access to the right people someplace else. The last thing the Casino King wanted was to run another interminable bureaucratic gauntlet like the one he'd faced in Macau. If only someone could slash through the red tape and expedite the permitting process for his next big project, Benny would hire him in a heartbeat. "Do you know many government officials in Asia?"

"Yes, of course," Krok replied with an air of supreme confidence. "To be arranging investments inside their countries, we must always have their okay. We work with them."

So far so good. Working closely with local officials was crucial to getting big projects built. "Do you find that officials do not give their okay easily?" Benny asked.

"No, it is never *easily*. In *easily* there is no profit for officials."

Benny knew that only too well. Official palms required greasing. "It's the same here. Believe me, our government doesn't give its okay easily either."

"It is big place, the American government. The bigger is the government, the harder to get okay, yes?"

"True," Benny said. "And that could get much worse after the election. My wife, you know, plans to double the size of the government, maybe even triple it. If she's elected, you won't believe how hard it's gonna be to get things done in this country."

The corners of Krok's mouth curled upward. "Maybe soon you will have something better than money to trade. You can trade getting things done easily."

For now money would have to do. Benny smiled back at Krok and handed him his own business card. "Do you work on retainer or commission, Gorok?"

RECLINING ON HIS gilded settee, the round-faced dictator Kim Il Bong grasped his Havana cigar and took a hit. He held his breath for two seconds and exhaled. A perfectly formed O-ring of smoke floated up, up, and away.

He paused to admire its exquisite roundness, as it was in fact the most circular smoke ring he had ever made, and probably the most circular one ever produced anywhere at any time in human history. Even so, it failed to reach the thirty-foot ceiling of his palace intact.

Perhaps he could hit the ceiling with the next one. He sucked in a deep breath and puffed out a second impeccable smoke ring, and up it flew, farther even than the first. But, to his dismay, it also broke up, at about twenty feet in the air. He launched another smoke ring, and another, to no avail. Each one vanished before reaching its target.

His nuclear-tipped missiles were having the same problem. The prototypes for the YZ-5 missile had been dropping out of the sky at a range of only five thousand kilometers, not nearly far enough to reach Washington. His last five defense ministers could not explain why. Executing them with anti-aircraft guns had not improved his missiles' range or accuracy.

The Supreme Leader looked out the palace window at his yacht in Wonsan harbor. A dozen workmen were crawling over every inch of the two-hundred-foot vessel with buckets, mops, and sponges, busily preparing for his afternoon pleasure cruise along the coast. His favorite dancing girls would be there, including the plump one with the naughty smile, Poo Koo-Wong. Kim had had his eye on Poo for a long time.

He began to work the buttons on the television remote, his eyes scanning the list of classic American movies. He stopped on the one labeled *High Noon*. The credits rolled down the screen.

Kim had seen that one. He had seen all of Gary Cooper's movies, and Grace Kelly's too.

"They don't make 'em like that no more, pardner," he said aloud, practicing his American English.

He pushed some more buttons and worked his way down the list of Star Wars movies until he reached *The Empire Strikes Back*. His favorite character, Yoda, appeared on the screen.

"Do, or do not," Kim said, quoting the revered Jedi Master. "There is no try."

A five-star general in a green uniform, standing about four feet tall if one included his enormous officer's cap, appeared in the doorway and saluted. "A thousand pardons, Dear Leader. The new Russian ambassador has landed. He should arrive momentarily. Would you like to receive him here or in your office?"

"Here."

"Very good, Great Leader of the People."

Within five minutes a man with bushy eyebrows and oily hair, wearing a baggy brown suit, was escorted into the room by a pair of armed guards who came up to his elbows. A female Korean translator stood at his side.

"Ambassador Boris Bubkov, at service of Great Chairman Kim," said the emissary through the translator. "President Bludinov conveys warmest salutations to you and valiant people of your happy country."

"And I return them to him." Kim Il Bong put down his cigar. "What the hell does Bludinov want?"

Bubkov reached into his coat pocket for a piece of paper and handed it to the translator. "It is with greatest courtesy and respect President Bludinov has sent me here," the translator said, "to solicit favor of Great Chairman's cooperation in his latest American project."

"The Americans? I thought Bludinov was the expert in dealing with them. He seems to think so. What does he need me for?"

Kim watched as Bubkov conferred for a moment with the translator.

"It is because our two countries share great struggle against the Americans that President Bludinov appeals for your assistance, Great Leader," the translator said. "It is opportunity to benefit through mutual unity of purpose, our common will to prosper in world oppressed by American dominance, and—"

Kim could almost hear Poo's mellifluous voice calling him. *Il Bong! Il Bong!*

He must hurry this meeting up. "Enough! You will make me late for my cruise. Get to the point! Why are you here, Ambassador? What is Bludinov's crazy scheme this time?"

Bubkov whispered something to the translator.

"Scheme, O Great One, Master of All He Attempts?" The translator bowed deeply, her lip quivering.

Kim leaned toward Bubkov. "Yes, his scheme, you idiot! You insult my intelligence. Are we not talking about Viktor Bludinov? When does the president of Russia not have some scheme?"

"It is about the American election for president, Great Leader," said the translator. "We have penetrated the inner circle of one of the candidates and—"

"You mean the photograph of the little boy?" Kim thought back to the news report about Clement quitting the U.S. presidential race. "How can a photograph of a child decide who will lead such a big country? The Americans have lost their minds."

"There is woman candidate to replace him—Patty Pitypander. It is her I have come about, Great Chairman."

Pitypander? Kim searched his memory. That was the governor of California he had shaken hands with in Davos, Switzerland, years ago. She was a foolish-looking woman, he remembered. She had a smile so fake it seemed glued to her face. "I have met her."

"Her rich husband wants to meet important people in Asia, to make big deals. He is very greedy. If his wife becomes president of America next year, there will be many opportunities through him."

"For whom?" Kim asked. "What do you want from me?"

"We want that you will meet Pitypander's rich husband, about making a deal."

So that was it. Bludinov, incorrigible as ever, was up to his old tricks, creating political scandals in other countries to sow chaos and weaken his foreign enemies. Only this time, operating behind the scenes to avoid blame, he wanted an ally to do his dirty work for him.

"What's in it for me?" Kim asked.

"We are willing to pay, Great Leader."

Kim settled back in his chair and displayed a sardonic smile. "Oh, you will pay, Ambassador. You will pay."

"President Bludinov has trusted me to bargain for him," the ambassador said. "I make bargain. Name price."

Kim took a puff of his cigar and blew a smoke ring into Bubkov's face. The Russians already knew about the YZ-5. "Very well. As I'm sure your satellites have detected, my new missile keeps falling into the ocean. I am tired of shooting defense ministers and hoping for the best. I'm sure some Russian technology could fix my problem."

Bubkov understood. "I try to arrange this technology."

"Try?" Kim laid his head back and launched a smoke ring at the ceiling. "No, Ambassador. Do, or do not. There is no try."

CHAPTER 11

The First Debate

THE WHITE HOUSE had worked its magic on P. Trayson Diebold. The man had grown in stature. Patty recalled when he was only a pompous Texas congressman known for his wacky ideas about turning the clock back two centuries. The trappings of power—and the fact sober people now had to take him seriously—rendered him fierce and dangerous. He had an unmistakable aura.

Tonight, girded for combat in his three-piece banker's suit, he looked like a rattlesnake ready to spring. His angry blue eyes were set on high beam. He twiddled his mustache with his finger, presumably plotting how he would strike her down with a single blow.

Patty squinted at the klieg lights above the stage as their heat poured down on her face. Sweating at a televised debate had cost Richard Nixon the 1960 election. She must not sweat. If her life depended on sweating, she would not do it. She had caked her face with powder three times to make sure.

The new agenda developed by Nigel for the Pitypander-Sartini ticket would be the key to Patty's victory tonight. She had rehearsed every day since the Democratic convention with the campaign team, preparing to present her grand plan to the nation.

"Relax, focus on the supporters you have out there," she heard Nigel saying behind her, like a trainer rubbing down his prizefighter at ringside. She surveyed the thousands of eyes looking back at her from the audience.

Nigel was right. Her people—the women of America—were in that crowd, in every living room in the land. Tonight she would incite her legions to rise up.

"Ladies and gentlemen, the candidates," the debate moderator said.

Now for the handshake. Nigel had reminded her how it could set the tone for the whole night. She must control her body language and not let Diebold tower over her with his heavy six-foot frame in a show of physical dominance.

Patty walked to center stage. While Diebold was still four feet away, she thrust out her hand like a spear. At a distance of two feet he clasped it firmly in his and tried to move in close, but she stiff-armed him.

Patty presented her iciest smile. "Best of luck, Percival." She awaited his reaction. *Percival. That'll get him.*

A dark rage smoldered in Diebold's reptilian eyes. Mocking his awkward first name had rattled him as planned.

The moderator reviewed the rules. After the candidates introduced their platforms, reporters selected by lottery number would ask follow-up questions. Patty would go first.

She cleared her throat, turned to the cameras, and delivered her opening lines as she had rehearsed them with Nigel and Colleen. "My fellow Americans, the president proposes taking us back to what he imagines was a simpler time, to the founding of our country. Back then, limited government was well-suited to our agrarian nation, but times have changed. A post-industrial urban society cannot function as if it existed in a bygone era. We must have a government tailored to the needs of our own century.

"Since the president keeps trying to take us back to our past, let's look at our history. In 1776 America was founded on the revolutionary idea that everyone has a right to the pursuit of happiness. But did the founders go far enough? Don't we have a right to happiness itself? Is life nothing but a cruel game of fruitlessly pursuing happiness? Do you really want your government to turn a blind eye to your real day-to-day needs and leave you to fend for yourself on your own? Of course not.

"It's not 1776 anymore. Most of us live in cities, not on farms. To serve our needs today, government's role must be expanded, not rolled back. We must ensure not only that our citizens can pursue happiness, but that they actually catch it.

"To that end, the Pitypander administration will propose the creation of a special department—a Department of Happiness. Its mission will be to bring happiness to everyone, not just the super-rich. It will be empowered to intervene in any situation causing you unhappiness you might call or email about. We'll have an eight hundred number and—"

The buzzer sounded. It was Diebold's turn.

The president grabbed his microphone and chortled. "There it is, my fellow Americans, now you've heard it from Governor Pitypander herself. She has just presented her nutty scheme for the federal government to take over every last aspect of your lives. A Department of Happiness, she calls it! Darn it, I have a better idea: Let's go two centuries the other way, toward self-reliance, and create our own happiness. Let's get government off our backs. My Clean Slate program will free American business to create trillions of dollars of new wealth. It'll enrich all Americans and return our country to the liberties our ancestors enjoyed.

"Now, unfortunately for the people of California, Mrs. Pitypander's Department of Happiness is not her first crazy idea. As governor of that fine state, she was the West Coast distributor of crazy. For example, she pushed through a ban on plastic straws and appointed a state bureaucrat to oversee her straw abatement program—at a cost of five million dollars per year. But did her unelected Straw Nazi stop at straws? Of course not! Bureaucrats always grab for more and more authority. He started regulating everything from Styrofoam cups to plastic spoons, and soon he was spending fifty million dollars a year telling Californians how to eat.

"Governor Pitypander is why California is broke. Oh, yes, she's just full of concern for your welfare. That much is true. She's got a well-intentioned program to solve every little problem you have. And you'll pay for it too. If you let this foolhardy woman loose in the Oval Office and let her bribe you with your own money, she'll smother you with her regulations and spending."

"That's a lie!" Patty shot back. "My straw initiative didn't cost fifty million dollars, and we kept forty tons of plastic out of the environment."

Diebold waved his hand. "My time's not up. I didn't interrupt you, Governor!"

"I didn't call you crazy!" Patty replied.

"Now you're getting hysterical too."

"Really, Percival? Come on, who are you trying to fool, Mr. Be-Safe-With-Diebold?"

"Okay, that's enough, Governor," the moderator warned. "Let's keep it civil, shall we? Let the president finish."

Diebold pivoted to explaining how selling off trillions of dollars in government assets would eliminate income taxes and the national debt, while restoring American freedom and ushering in a new golden age.

After similar bitter exchanges, the opening segment ended, and it was time for the reporters' questions. The moderator called out the first winning lottery number: "Fifty-nine."

A man with a green tie stood up. "John Giddens, ABC News. Governor Pitypander, exactly how would your new department work? Let's say I was unhappy about something. How would your Happiness Department help me?"

Patty kept her smile going full blast. "Well, John, we'd have an eight hundred number you could call, or you could go to the department's website and fill out a complaint form. Then they'd get back to you and solve your problem."

Giddens wrinkled his brow at her. "Would it be that easy? Could you be more specific? Say I have a flat tire, or a bad date, or maybe I think my pay is too low. How would they fix my problem?"

Patty had seen Giddens in action many times on television. He was a pit bull, famous for his snide interviewing style. The puzzled look on his face was part of his act, which he used to unnerve and humiliate his victim. She stood her ground. "John, the department would be empowered to intervene to enforce your right to be happy. They'd call up the tire maker, or the girl you had the date with, or your chintzy boss, and give them a nasty warning. If that didn't work, the government could sue the guilty party on your behalf."

Giddens pursued his line of questioning further. "But what if the government's solution to my unhappiness made the tire maker, or the girl, or the boss unhappy? What about their rights?"

Patty gritted her teeth. "We'd look into that too. We'd set up some kind of resolution court to handle conflicting claims of unhappiness."

Giddens looked even more perplexed. "This country has three hundred thirty million people, and they have a lot of conflicting claims. How many employees will it take to staff your Happiness Department?"

The moderator cut him off. "Sorry, Mr. Giddens, that's all the questions you get. Next question. Number twenty-four."

A thin woman with short brown hair took the microphone.

"Alice MacIntosh, *Chicago Sentinel*. President Diebold, what is your response to the charge that the Diebold administration is not taking sexual harassment seriously enough?"

Diebold laughed. "Why, it's poppycock of course. The charge was invented to whip up the female vote for the Democrats. Sexual harassment isn't a federal issue. Washington needs to get out of the business of trying to police relationships between men and women. That's for state and local governments to handle."

MacIntosh directed the same question to the governor.

"Alice, hair-sniffing gropers like our president are the problem," Patty said. "We need to make toxic masculinity a federal crime. The Pitypander administration will propose jail time for men who prey on women. And while we're on the subject, I support a man tax—a fifteen percent surcharge on the income of men earning above two hundred thousand dollars. That will reduce unequal pay."

Diebold slapped his forehead. "A fifteen percent man tax! What in tarnation? This woman is plumb crazy. A tax on men is unconstitutional."

"Oh, really? Since when did the Constitution stop men from discriminating against women?" Patty replied. "We don't even have an Equal Rights Amendment."

"Governor, please," the moderator said. "Next question. Number sixty-seven."

The microphone was passed to a tall female reporter with red hair. "Wilma Jenkins, Fox News. Governor, what is your position on the recent election of Prime Minister Valmo and the unrest in Riga? Are you concerned?"

Patty froze, puzzling over the name Valmo. Was Valmo a he or a she? Where was Riga, who was rioting there, and why?

Forcing a smile, Patty pinched the microphone between her thumb and forefinger. The heat radiating from the lights grew more intense. "Thank you so much for that question, Wilma. It's a troubling situation they're having in Riga, isn't it? Yes, the election of the prime minister is very concerning. I'm following the situation over there closely and I favor keeping our military options open."

Jenkins dropped her jaw. "Military options? Are you serious, Governor? You would consider invading Latvia to put down its striking miners?"

Patty paused. A miners' strike in Riga, Latvia—so that's what this was about. She gathered from Diebold's smirk and the reporter's incredulous stare that the idea of invading Latvia to quash a miners' strike would be ludicrous, especially coming from a pro-labor progressive like herself.

But first she must settle the more basic question of where Latvia was. Patty dimly recalled it was somewhere in Europe, but not near her favorite cities for shopping, Paris and Milan. Was Latvia somewhere around Prague? She hadn't noticed it during her sojourns in Central Europe. No, it was probably part of Scandinavia, up around Moscow. Sending U.S. troops into Scandinavia to end a miners' strike did sound absurd, unless of course it was absolutely necessary, in which case Patty must back it to the hilt so as not to appear vacillating and weak like everyone was expecting a woman to be.

The klieg lights grew hotter. But she must not sweat.

Patty swung at the question like a blindfolded child flailing at a piñata. "Invade Latvia? No, of course not, that wouldn't be prudent, not unless there's a unanimous consensus among our NATO allies to do so. Military action must always be our last resort."

Jenkins rolled her eyes. "But Latvia is a NATO ally, Governor, so it seems very unlikely they would give you consent to invade them. I just wanted to know if you're worried about the right-wing coalition taking power there and the possible political spillover effects on neighboring countries."

Neighboring countries? The reporter was setting another trap for her. Which countries bordered Latvia? Norway? Finland? Romania?

Groping for an escape, Patty seized on the first bromide that entered her head. "I fully support the will of the people of Latvia. We won't let anything spill over onto anybody, not in Riga or Latvia, or anywhere else."

The moderator looked down his list. "Time for the next question. Let's see, that would be reporter ninety-three." The microphone was passed to a startled young man in the back.

"Good evening, Governor," he said in a voice she instantly recognized.

Shading her eyes with her hand, Patty looked through the lights to make sure. Her heart fluttered with excitement. Yes, it was him. It was Jack Snap!

Jack fumbled with his notepad, riffling through it to find his question. "Uh, Governor, building on your awesome record of success as governor of California, what do you hope to be your most awesome accomplishments as president?"

In his panic, Jack had forgotten to introduce himself. Patty would do it for him.

"Jack Snap of *The Burbank Bee*, isn't that right?" she said with a wink. He smiled back. "Yes."

"Well, Jack, following up on what I achieved for California, I would hope my most awesome accomplishment for the country to be that I used the power of our federal government to save those left behind in this grand experiment we call America: the poor, the homeless, the unemployed, the disadvantaged, the unfortunate of every race and creed, no matter how modest or miserable their circumstances. If I can help those people, well, to me that would be just so...so awesome."

She bared her teeth in a broad smile. Jack sat down with no further questions, seemingly satisfied by her answer.

Allowing herself to exhale, Patty made a mental note to thank the young reporter. He had not only rescued her from Latvia but returned her safely home to California, where she was awesome.

CHAPTER 12

The Rumor

JACK PUSHED THE elevator button with modesty on his mind, determined not to strut into the morning staff meeting. He would pretend as if last night's debate had never happened, as if he hadn't been on television raising the *Bee* to national prominence, questioning Governor Pitypander before tens of millions of viewers. He would wear his celebrity as lightly as humanly possible for one so famous.

Despite his valiant attempt at nonchalance, Jack could feel everyone's eyes following him around the table as he walked across the conference room. Oddly, he heard no applause. No one uttered a word.

As he sat down, someone to his right snickered. He turned and saw John Hobart, the *Bee's* sports reporter, grinning like a dog.

Hobart held up his fist like it was a microphone and pointed it at Gus Masterson, sitting at the head of the table. "Governor, building on your awesome record of success as governor of California, what will be your most awesome accomplishments as president?"

The room erupted in laughter.

Jack turned to Gus in bewilderment. "What was wrong with my question?"

"Your most awesome accomplishments?" Gus labored to conceal his amusement. "That was the toughest question you had?"

Hobart howled. "We have a new pitcher for the *Bee's* softball team!"

Jack searched the room for some sign of support, but everyone was laughing at him. "Seriously, what was wrong with it?"

"Son, you set her up," Gus said gently. "You could have had a real zinger ready. Like going after her record in California. Or questioning her proposals. Instead, you threw her a softball right through the heart of the strike zone. You looked like a cheerleader for her campaign, like she'd planted you there. She even winked at you. You aren't working for her, are you?"

"Working for Governor Pitypander? No, of course not."

Cheerleader. Like she'd planted me there. Jack's face went flat, the words resounding in his head. He didn't hear much after that. When the meeting ended he wandered back to his desk, his shoulders sagging under the weight of his humiliation.

Fanny Flowers followed him. "Jack, don't take it so hard. It wasn't such a bad question."

He waved her off. "No, they're right. It was the stupidest question ever asked in the whole history of journalism. I'm the world's suckiest reporter. I blew it, and this time I did it on national television. When will I ever get a chance like that again?"

"Probably never," Fanny conceded, standing in front of his desk. "Okay, I'll admit your question was kind of sucky, but it's not the end of the world. You just have to be a lot tougher on Pitypander next time."

"They think I should have gone for the jugular," Jack said with a whimper. "I couldn't do that to the governor, could I?"

"You have to." Fanny lectured him on his obligations as a reporter. "She's a politician. That makes her fair game. You're not in J-school anymore, Jack. Gus is a real journalist. If you tell him you can't go after Pitypander because you like her, you'll be signing your own pink slip. And anyway, she's not as nice as you think."

"What do you mean by that?"

"There's a rumor about Pitypander, from back when she was governor."

"Rumor? What kind of rumor?"

Fanny looked around to see if anyone in the newsroom was listening. "A sex scandal."

Jack fell back into his chair. He examined her face carefully. Was she teasing him again? If so, her timing was terrible, as he was in no mood for jokes. "You're putting me on."

Fanny was serious. "My brother told me about it. He went to Burbank High, in the same class as a boy named Rod Collier. He's about our age. Did you know him?"

"No, I went to Clark High."

"According to my brother, this Collier kid was supposedly bragging to the other boys about having an affair with Pitypander. How creepy is that?"

It sounded to Jack like standard high school locker room talk. "No. That's impossible. Not the governor. I know the governor."

Fanny snorted with laughter. "Jack, you're such a Boy Scout."

How did she guess? His eyes narrowed. "An Eagle Scout, and don't you forget it."

They could ridicule Jack's reporting skills, but not his six exemplary years in the Boy Scouts of America. Troop 524 was Burbank's finest. The olive-green sash still hung proudly above his bed, covered with dozens of merit badges his mother had lovingly sewn on. The one for competitive rowing, the first of his many triumphs in the sport, had led to his earning a coveted spot on the UCLA crew team.

"An Eagle Scout, excuse me. I didn't mean to demote you," Fanny said with a restrained grin. "Anyway, I never liked Pitypander after I heard about her and Rod Collier."

"I don't believe it," Jack replied. "That's totally impossible."

Fanny sat down on a corner of his desk. "It doesn't matter whether you believe it or not. Imagine what would happen if the rumor got out now—in the middle of a presidential campaign."

"It's not true. It can't be. I know Governor Pitypander. My mom knew her in college. People you know don't do sick stuff like that."

"Oh, yeah? Well, that rumor about her was all over Burbank High. It might get out now that Pitypander's running for president. With all the reporters following her around now, it's only a matter of time before one of them hears about it."

Jack snapped his fingers. "You know, I think you're right. I should warn her. She'll be grateful for the heads-up."

Fanny stared at him like he was a visitor from another planet. "You think Pitypander doesn't already know about the rumor? My God, you are naïve."

"I am not." Jack crossed his arms. "I'm trusting. I give people the benefit of the doubt. I don't believe in smearing them—especially friends."

Fanny shook her head. "We can't be trusting in this business. You have to have a killer instinct, like a shark going after blood in the water. You want to impress Gus? Investigate the Pitypander rumor before the national media gets wind of it. Bring Gus a big story and he won't call you a Pitypander cheerleader anymore."

Fanny's idea wasn't half bad. He could disprove this ridiculous rumor, clear the governor's name, and impress everyone—all at the same time. There was just one thing: Why him?

"If this is such a great story, why haven't you gone after it?"

"Politics isn't my beat. It would have been Mort's story, but he's gone." Fanny patted him on the shoulder. "Lucky for you. Now it's yours."

GUS CLOSED HIS office door and let Jack make his pitch for the Collier story.

The old editor's chair creaked under the strain of his two hundred and eighty pounds. "You need some solid facts. You don't have a story yet. What you've got is an unsupported rumor put out by some high school boy—locker room talk. Without facts to back it up, that's less than worthless. It's dangerous—to you and the *Bee*."

Jack felt a blast of cool air from a vent overhead. Gus always kept his thermostat turned down too low. "Yes, sir, I know. That's why I want your okay to check it out to see if there's anything to it."

Gus folded his arms and took a hard look at his rookie reporter. "You've met Pitypander. Do you really think she'd have sex with a high school boy? With all she has to lose?"

"No, sir, I don't believe she would."

"Then why are you interested in the story?"

"Because the rumor is out there. It's a story by itself, even if it isn't true," Jack said. "If we don't get the scoop, someone else will and we'll be kicking ourselves. If it's about a Burbank student, shouldn't we be covering it anyway? It's local news."

"Good point. So what else do you know other than what Fanny told you?"

"Nothing. But if there's anything to it, sir, think what a story it would make!" Jack turned his gaze to Gus's wall of journalism awards: his Henderson prize for best investigative journalism, his Maury Cleveland award for best political coverage, and of course, his Pulitzer for exposing corruption in Chicago.

Gus followed Jack's eyes. "I have to admit, it would be a helluva story. Yep, one helluva story."

"Then you'll let me do it?"

Gus rubbed his jaw. "Are you gonna hit it hard this time? I mean real hard, no more fluff? You promise you won't pull any punches with Pitypander?"

"Yes, sir!"

"If this didn't involve a presidential campaign, I'd say the story's not worth the trouble. But politics is so nasty these days, hell, even a high school boy's locker room talk could turn into a big deal. I'm going to let you go for it."

"Thank you, sir."

The old editor leaned across his desk. "But you better watch out," he said with an admonishing wag of his finger. "Get the facts—and make damn sure you can prove 'em. You'll be digging into the private business of a powerful woman. Patty Pitypander is not only a presidential candidate. She's a billionaire's wife. And she's always seemed a bit off to me."

"Off?" Jack replied.

"Pitypander strikes me as a Jekyll and Hyde type. It's that vacant stare she gets on her face sometimes, like her mind has gone wandering off. Other times she looks like a female tiger who'd claw a man to pieces if he got in her way."

A tiger. Jack hadn't noticed anything abnormal about the governor, but Gus had observed her a lot longer than he had. "You think she's nuts?"

"A little," Gus said. "Politicians are all a little nuts. They're not dealing in truth like us. They're constantly twisting facts to fit their views. That makes them lose their grip on reality. They're paranoid about being exposed as frauds. Also, in Pitypander's case, well, there's the female thing. Moodiness, hormones, it's like pouring gasoline on a raging bonfire of insecurity, you know what I mean?"

Jack didn't really know what Gus meant, but nodded anyway. *A moody, paranoid tiger.* Pitypander might tear him to pieces. And to think she was his mother's college chum and had been normal once.

Jack promised not to set off any hormones or bonfires. All he wanted was a scoop.

"I don't think she's as crazy as Diebold claims," Gus said as Jack stood up to leave, "but get on the wrong side of Patty Pitypander, son, and you might see a tiger."

PATTY AWOKE FROM a brief nap as the Empathy Express steered into a parking lot outside yet another auditorium, her fifth stop of the day.

"Are we still in Massachusetts?" she asked Nigel, fighting off her grogginess.

"No, Portland, Maine." Her campaign manager, holding a clipboard, read his notes from the day's itinerary. "National Organization of Women rally. Red Meat Speech Number Two is best suited for this audience. Four electoral votes. Say something nice about lobsters."

She walked across the stage. Where was she? Oh, yes, Maine, land of lobsters.

"Women of Maine!" She throttled her microphone by its neck and raised her fist. "Yes, I am a feminist. Like you, I have a vagina. Therefore, I do not have equality in this country.

"As my first act as president, I will demand tough new laws against sexual harassers, including mandatory jail time. Because when one of us is harassed, all of us are harassed.

"Our bodies are our battleground, and we intend to win the battle. I ask you, what part of 'no' don't men like P. Trayson Diebold understand? Why do we put up with a catcalling, hair-sniffing, girl-grabbing Republican like him in our White House?"

She bashed Diebold's regressive Clean Slate program for its calamitous effects on the poor. She reminded the women how unrelentingly earlier generations had fought for their right to vote, smashed barriers to employment, and championed laws guaranteeing them equal pay for equal work.

Her eyelids drooping, she caught sight of Nigel making a pincer-like movement with his hand. *Lobsters, oh yes, I forgot!* If she wrapped up her speech with lobsters, she could go back to the Empathy Express and get some sleep.

"You women of Massachusetts—I mean Maine, excuse me—have a long, proud history. For centuries you fought for your rights, ever since the Revolution when this state first stood up against England's unjust tax on lobsters, throwing them into the harbor, winning for you and your posterity the right to tax your lobsters however you like."

Patty departed the auditorium, the pink hats parading behind her to the Empathy Express. Only steps from being able to lie down, she saw a young man standing in the parking lot. It was Jack Snap.

He came running up to her, pen and paper in hand. "Governor! Got a minute?"

"Not now, Jack," she said, rushing past him. "Can it wait?"

He dashed after her. "I have a question. Just one question."

"I'd love to, but this isn't a good time. I'm absolutely bushed."

"Do you know anyone named Rod Collier?"

Patty stopped in her tracks. She turned around and put her hand to her chin. "Rod Collier? Uh, yes, I did know a Rod Collier. What about him?"

"Could I get an interview when you have some time? Just a few minutes is all I need."

"About what?"

"Rod Collier."

"Oh, yes. Rod Collier. I hardly know anything about him. Not worth your time." She turned toward the bus door.

"It won't take long, I promise."

For anyone else her answer would have been a flat no. But there was an infectious earnestness in Jack that couldn't be denied. As she looked again into his wonderful sky-blue eyes, her resistance melted away. "I'll have someone set up an interview."

She boarded the bus, staggered to the pull-out bed in the rear, and collapsed. As she drifted off, Jack's pleasant face reappeared in her thoughts.

Some time passed.

"Patty," a voice said. "We have to talk."

Patty lifted an eyelid. Someone was in the bus window. Was it her own reflection? No, it was a voluptuous young woman with flowing brown hair. She was smiling mischievously and beckoning with her finger, as if Patty should come outside. The hair, the face—they were familiar somehow.

Patty sat up with a start, blinked several times, and rubbed her eyes. The image slowly faded away to nothingness. It must have been a dream. There was no one in the window, and no reason to worry at all.

CHAPTER 13

The Interview

PATTY LAY IN a lounge chair dabbing SPF-8 tanning lotion on her face, hoping it was strong enough to protect her from the intense sunlight pouring down through the pool roof. She took a deep breath and exhaled. At last, a well-deserved break from the hectic campaign trail.

Her corgies, Cain and Abel, curled at her feet, jumped up and growled at the clickety-clack of footsteps on the stairs. It was the butler escorting Jack down from the house. Patty sat up, ran her hand through her hair, and tugged the top of her bathing suit upward.

The reporter stopped fifty feet away and checked his watch. "Oh, sorry, Governor. I must have gotten the time for our interview wrong."

Patty smiled. "Not at all, Jack. I hope you'll forgive me, but this is the first chance I've had in weeks to get any sun, and as you can see, I'm pasty white. Come on over. We can do the interview here while I catch some rays. We'll multitask."

He stood at the pool's edge, gazing at his feet.

Patty turned her head. "What are you doing over there? Come, pull up a chair next to me."

He dragged a chair over to her and obediently sat down.

"That's better. Now you wanted to ask me something about Rod Collier, was that it?"

Jack kept looking away from her, at the pool. He fumbled for his pen. "Yes, uh, you said you knew him?"

She paused a moment before answering. "That's right. There's not much to tell you. In the governor's office we hired high school interns every summer. Rod Collier was one of them."

"Why high school interns?"

Patty eased her head back on the lounge chair and closed her eyes. "For most of the kids, it was their first job. Some were poor and wouldn't have been able to get another job. It was also a great chance for them to see how their state government worked. It gave them an educational experience."

"So how did you know Rod Collier?"

"He was a nice young man who worked with the mail."

Jack pulled out his notepad and jotted something down. "Just the mail?"

Patty opened an eyelid. "What's this about?"

The young reporter was reading his notes, avoiding her stare. "Rod Collier might be involved in a story I'm working on."

"Oh, what's the story about? Is he in some kind of trouble?"

"I don't know. He might have been."

"Dear, dear, I hope he's all right."

Jack was looking at a ship out on the ocean, still averting his eyes. Was her bathing suit too revealing? *Good thing I didn't wear my bikini.*

Cain jumped up on Jack's right leg and sniffed him.

Patty sat up. "Stop that! Get down! Bad dog!"

Jack bent down and stroked Cain's back. The dog licked Jack's face, promptly rolled over, and begged for a belly rub. Cain was a shameless flirt.

If only I could get away with that. If only I were a dog.

She grabbed her bottle of sunscreen off the table. "Would you be a dear and rub some of this on the back of my neck? I'd hate to burn. I won't look good on camera with a red neck."

"Uh, okay." Jack took the bottle, squirted some lotion into his hand, and spread it across Patty's neck.

A thrill rippled down her back as she felt the warmth of his hand on her skin. "That's a good boy. A little lower. That's it. Yes, there. Right there. My, my, you do have the touch, don't you, Jack?"

She shouldn't have said that. He stopped at once.

"So, Governor, what else did Rod Collier do in your office?"

She turned onto her side and closed her eyes again. "Hmm, I don't exactly remember. The interns reported to my aides. They were gophers."

"What did they do?"

"They did odd tasks," Patty replied. "You know, typical gopher things."

"Like what?"

"Oh, like filing, sorting through mail from constituents, fetching things, taking mail to other government offices, running to get pizza or coffee, doing little projects no one else had time for. A new bunch came and went every summer. I would see them running down the corridors. I only got to know a few of them. Of course, as the governor I was very busy."

"But you do remember Rod Collier?"

"Yes, you couldn't miss him. He had a purple spiky mohawk—electric purple. You could see him from a hundred yards away. He brought me my mail every morning. He was the kid with the funny hair and the big smile. He should be just about finished with college by now, about your age. What's happened to him?"

Jack was scribbling something on his notepad. She leaned over and saw the words "purple spiky mohawk, big smile, brought her the mail."

Jack slipped his pen back in his pocket and got up to leave. "I don't know. I've been looking all over creation for him. He's disappeared."

SOON AFTER JACK left, Patty decided she'd had enough sun. It was time to indulge herself in one of her favorite guilty pleasures. She pushed a button to close the pool's roof and opened her latest Jenessa Fuller novel, *His Winsome Ways*.

Patty pulled out the bookmark and resumed reading. The heroine, it seemed, had met her match this time. Ever since chapter four it had been clear Jenessa would have her hands full trying to bed the recalcitrant but charmingly naïve Dirk Swails, who was from a different world, a different time:

> And if he hadn't yet responded to her flirting, perhaps it was nobody's fault. Dirk was a man of mysterious origins whom she'd met quite by accident that evening on the pier. Most obviously, he didn't belong to her social set, and that was precisely what she found most alluring. His eyes, those sparkling eyes, spoke in a language only eyes can understand, something intimate and piercing her mind could only guess the meaning of. Jenessa knew him. Dirk, with his winsome ways, did belong to her somehow. Deep inside, she had sensed the gravitational pull of his heart even if she couldn't understand where it came from. As the invisible, unknowable force emanating from him drew her ever closer, she hungered to learn more about it.

Patty laid the book down and looked at its cover. Shirtless and brawny, Dirk was locked with Jenessa in a permanent sweaty embrace. *His eyes, those sparkling eyes.* Were Dirk's eyes enough by themselves to draw Jenessa to him, even if he was from a different world? It seemed improbable eyes could have such power.

Something about Dirk made her think of Jack, or was it vice versa? In any case, they were much alike. The reporter was winsome and from a different world. Jack's eyes sparkled, generated an unknowable force, and appealed to her like no others had before.

Patty heard a noise. She looked down to see the two corgies dozing at her feet.

"Patty," whispered someone behind her. "Over here."

Patty turned her head and sat bolt upright.

It was the beautiful young woman with the lustrous brown hair she had seen in the bus window in Maine. This time the woman wasn't a reflection or a dream. She was wearing a short white skirt and a blue blouse. She was talking.

"Patty," the woman repeated.

Patty drew back in terror. "Who are you? How did you get here?"

"I'm Jenessa Fuller. Pleased to meet you."

"*The* Jenessa Fuller?" Patty looked at the cover of her novel.

"Yes, that one. I'm your imaginary friend."

Patty stared her up and down. The woman didn't exactly match the book cover, but there was a striking resemblance. This woman was brunette and about Jenessa's age of twenty-five. Still, the idea was absurd.

"That's impossible," Patty said. "I don't have any imaginary friends."

Jenessa grinned. "You're a politician, Patty. All your friends are imaginary."

Patty tossed her head back. "Nonsense. I've never met you. I don't know how you would know anything about me."

"Ah, but you have met me," Jenessa replied. "You've followed me for thousands of pages. And I know all about you. I've come to talk to you."

"About what?"

"About Jack."

"Jack Snap?"

Jenessa giggled. "Don't be coy with me, darling. There's no other Jack in your life. Sad to say, there's no other man in your life, other than that worthless billionaire husband of yours. Which is why I've come."

"What's Jack to you?"

Jenessa took a cigarette out of her purse and lit it. "I think he's awfully handsome. I can understand your fascination. What do you think of him? Do you think you have a chance?"

"I'm not sure," Patty replied. "I don't really know much about him."

Jenessa smiled. "No, I'm certain you don't. That's why I'm here—to help you figure out what makes Jack tick. You want him, don't you? You know you do."

"I'm trying to give up young men, Jenessa. I'm much too old for them. I wish you would—"

"Give them up? Ha! We never give them up, not women like us."

"Like who?"

"Women with serious romantic needs. Unfulfilled needs. We never get old enough to outgrow those secret yearnings. Honestly, I don't know why you would want to, when you can have any man you want. Correction—*we* can have any men *we* want."

"We? Who is we? If you're imaginary, you can't have Jack," Patty said.

Jenessa's shoulders drooped. "And that's so unfair, isn't it, when you've had my men, in my world, one after another. Let's see. Randall, Simon, Everett, Peter, Darrell, Willard, Tom, Harold, Norman, Aaron, Frederick, and now I see you're working on Dirk. Must I name them all? I've allowed you to fantasize about my men to your heart's content. You didn't ask if I minded you monitoring my most intimate encounters with them. Or did you think vicarious pleasure was a one-way street?"

"If you mean, did I think a character in a romance novel would mind her own business and stay between the covers of her book where she belongs, yes, I did," Patty said with some annoyance. "Evidently I was wrong."

"Don't be so selfish, darling." Jenessa took a drag from her cigarette. "You've been in my head through a hundred novels. Now I'm in yours, sharing your young man with you, and there's nothing you can do about it. It's payback time."

What impudence was this, Patty thought. Novels should come with warning labels if characters were going to pop out of them and harass their readers without provocation. She would set this Jenessa character straight. "Listen, whoever you are, I've given up young men. I have much more important things going on in my life now. I'm running for president of the United States."

Jenessa burst out laughing. "President? Hmm, I'm sure that's terribly important, running the country, fighting for watered-down legislation, proposing budgets that will never pass, pressing the flesh with horrid world leaders, making war on the wrong people. Oh, what a crushing bore! I know you crave power, but the world doesn't run on power, it runs on love."

Patty scrutinized the cover of *His Winsome Ways* again. "The world runs on love? I don't see that anywhere in here. What does that even mean?"

She looked up, intending to express her opinions about what the world actually ran on, but Jenessa Fuller was gone.

A YELLOW BUTTERFLY alighted on a poppy flower, prompting Cain and Abel to stop and bark. They started to take off after it, but Patty yanked on their leash, pulling them back onto the footpath to the beach.

The fact that her dogs pursued the butterfly proved it was real. Dogs weren't smart enough to have visions. They only chased after real things.

Sitting atop a rock in the cove, Patty reviewed her options. She could go back to Dr. Snopes, if she dared. No, that was impossible. If word got out she was seeing a psychiatrist, her bid for the presidency would be over in a day.

If she did visit the doctor again, how would she explain what had happened? Her previous visions weren't like the one she had just witnessed. They were daydreams, vague sexual fantasies about real young men. Frequent and mostly innocent. No fictional character had ever appeared before her in the flesh, speaking in full sentences with the impertinence to advise her about her love life.

Dr. Snopes had chalked up Patty's recurring daydreams to repressed anxieties, arrested sexual development during puberty, or some such Freudian malarkey. All Patty knew was that young men who looked hot when she was seventeen still stirred her blood at fifty-five, and they weren't supposed to.

What should Patty make of Jenessa?

The product of Marjorie Mickle's prolific brain, Jenessa Fuller was the gorgeous young protagonist of an unending series of steamy novels in which the heroine, using her matchless feminine wiles to overcome impossible odds, always bedded her man. Males were her hapless victims, sex objects she bent to her will as readily as Circe turned Odysseus's hapless sailors into swine. No man, however obstinate at first, stood a chance against her. That was Marjorie Mickle's implicit promise to her lonely readers. For fifteen dollars and the time it took to read a few hundred pages, they could conquer hearts too.

And now, Jenessa, moonlighting as romantic consultant par excellence, had set up shop inside Patty's busy head to help her get Jack, a fantasy so palpable, yet so potentially destructive to her other fantasy—winning the presidency—that no one must ever know it.

No one.

CHAPTER 14

A Person of Interest

THE 1980S POP music pounding through the walls of Perogi's restaurant hit Jack and Fanny before they even got out of his Civic.

"Ah, 'Material Girl,'" Fanny said with an accommodating smile. "I love Madonna."

That was a good thing, Jack thought. They would get their fill of Madonna at Perogi's.

The popular Burbank eatery was famous for two things: low prices and the car flying through its wall. The owners had mounted the back end of a turquoise 1957 Chevy convertible, tail fins and all, into the wall above the booths, so it looked like it had come crashing through from the street.

From what Jack could tell, Fanny seemed to like Perogi's as much as he did. Even better, she was light on his wallet. When the waiter came for their drink orders, all Fanny wanted was a beer. She didn't mind talking shop, and relished listening to his problems.

"So, any progress on the Collier story?" Fanny asked in a solicitous tone, as if sensing things weren't going well.

Jack's frustrations had been building for weeks. At last he could pour them out. "No, and I don't get how somebody could just disappear so easily. It's weird. Nobody has a clue where the guy is. I found the two classmates your brother mentioned, but they hardly knew Collier. He didn't graduate with them, according to the yearbook. I guess he dropped out of school."

"What did Pitypander tell you?"

"That Rod Collier had a funny haircut and delivered her mail with a big smile."

"That's all you got out of her?"

Jack raised his beer to his lips. "Yeah. I can't find his haircut or his smile either."

He had tried contacting Collier's parents, but they were gone too. No one in his old neighborhood knew where they were. The post office had no forwarding address.

Fanny sipped her beer. "Whenever I can't find leads for a Metro story, I post notices on social media sites in the neighborhood where my story is, asking for information."

"Yeah, I thought of doing that," Jack said. "The thing is, posting notices is so passive. It's like waiting for somebody else to do my job for me. I want to find the leads myself. I need the glory."

"It is passive, but sometimes I get lucky and people show up out of nowhere. I don't care how I get a story, as long as I get it."

Fine, Jack would plaster every website in the area with a notice about Collier. Why not? The old shoe-leather method wasn't working.

He watched as a young man walked up to a video game near their booth and dropped in a coin. The screen displayed a stone citadel full of space aliens blasting away with ray guns.

Fanny, drumming her fingers to the tune "Lucky Star," smiled up at the 1984 video of Madonna writhing suggestively on the floor, her hands caressing her belly button. "So what do you think of Pitypander now? Isn't she strange?"

"I feel sorry for the governor," Jack said, biting into a pretzel. "It's sad how she lives in that great big mansion by herself. The way she looks at me is a little weird, but I can handle her. I just hope I can handle Gus."

"You can. He's tough but fair. Get the story and he's happy."

"Yeah, I hope so."

"So tell me about your life before you came to the *Bee*," Fanny said. "How did you get so much into the Boy Scouts?"

Jack had been expecting this question. They all asked it sooner or later. He took a swig of beer. "It was one of the few activities my mother allowed me to do."

Fanny raised an eyebrow and gave him a knowing look. "Hmm, sounds like your mother was a little over-protective."

Jack laughed. "You could say that. The Amish are pretty strict with their children."

Fanny gasped. "Holy crap, I was just thinking you had helicopter parents. You mean you're Amish?"

"No, but she was."

"Tell me about her."

Jack described his mother as a headstrong girl who rebelled against the rules of her Amish community. "She didn't want to ride in a buggy, wear a bonnet, and have seven kids, so she quit the church and went off to college. That's where she met Dad. She's still pretty old-fashioned, though. She pushed me into the Boy Scouts to keep me clean, brave, honest, and reverent. It was her penance for defecting to the modern world."

Fanny smirked. "I'd say her little plan worked."

"Well, I don't know about that, but it did keep me busy. I was a super Boy Scout."

Their first date was going so well. Fanny hadn't completely freaked out about his mother. She seemed to understand him—until the waiter came back to take their dinner orders.

"You didn't tell me you eat meat." Fanny's eyes turned sullen. She withdrew her hand from his.

Jack studied the menu again. He had ordered the sirloin steak. What was her problem?

"I'm a vegan," she announced. "I've taken the Vegan Vow."

"The what?"

"The Vow is our oath of abstinence from consuming anything derived from animals," Fanny said with an air of fervent religiosity. "Meat tops our list of forbidden foods."

Jack looked up at the waiter. "Give us a few more minutes." The waiter nodded and stepped away.

A vegan. Uh-oh. That was way more serious even than a vegetarian.

"So you were telling me about your parents. What do they do for a living?" Fanny asked.

"Uh, well, they work for the government," Jack replied, still focusing on the menu. "They're in charge of, uh…safety. By the way, what's wrong with meat?"

The indignation welling up in Fanny's eyes told Jack his question was thoughtless, even provocative. It was a question that had no right to be asked.

Fanny's face flushed. "What's wrong? A poor animal suffered and died for your dinner, that's what's wrong! You think slaughtering a cow is okay? You think it's natural and moral?"

It was natural for Jack. That eating could be a question of morality had rarely occurred to him. His stomach had its own rules, clear and unmistakable, and Jack obeyed them. When he got hungry, he ate. Simple as that.

"It's immoral to eat animals because you're hungry," Fanny declared.

"It is?" Jack was mystified. Fanny's convictions were at serious odds with his stomach's.

Fanny pulled back in her chair. "It is if you know better."

"So you've never eaten meat?"

"Sure, I used to," Fanny admitted. "I was a meathead once. I never thought twice about eating animals before I evolved and joined the vegans. Now I can't stand the sight of meat anywhere. Ugh!"

Anywhere included his plate, Jack surmised. "Sorry, I didn't know it was such a big deal with you. Or anybody for that matter, unless you were a Hindu or a fundamentalist Jew or something."

"My last boyfriend was a meathead. My feelings weren't important enough to him. We broke up over a Big Mac."

Jack took that as a shot across his bow. She was setting forth her prerequisites for a relationship. He gallantly offered to change his order to macaroni and cheese.

Fanny smiled half-heartedly, acknowledging the magnanimity of his gesture but informing him that his dinner order was still morally repugnant. "Cheese is an animal product. We vegans don't eat any kind of animal product."

"Cheese? It's just cheese," Jack said.

"No, cheese isn't just cheese! Think of the cruelty that went into making it."

Jack had never realized cheese was cruel. The cow didn't die for it. She squirted some milk out of her tits and the cheese people made cheese out of it, as cheese people had been doing since the dawn of time.

Jack had it all wrong.

The very mention of cheese sent Fanny into a whirl of deep distress. "How would you like to be penned up your whole life, fed corn laced with antibiotics, and hooked up to a milking machine? What a horrible existence!"

Jack tried to stand his ground. "It's only a cow."

"No, it's an animal with feelings, like us," she replied. "Can't you see that?"

"I never thought of it that way. But then I'm not a cow. I don't know what they're feeling. Not much, I expect. They're pretty stupid."

"Well, feel like one! Empathize!" Fanny's eyes were ablaze. "Some poor cow who never did you any harm was jailed for life and stuffed with chemicals to make your stupid cheese. You should be overcome with guilt."

Seeing cheese in a new light, Jack called the waiter back. "Okay, make mine a macaroni and a side order of, let's see, asparagus. That's okay, isn't it?"

"Yes, that's more like it. Now, about your shoes. Are they made of leather?"

"Yes," Jack admitted.

"What's the difference between a cow dying for your stomach or dying for your feet?"

"I like my stomach and my feet, so I appreciate the cow dying for either one."

"No, I mean there's no moral difference as far as the poor cow is concerned. Meat or shoes, you're complicit in the cow's destruction."

"But I need shoes," Jack said.

"Yes, but not leather ones. What your shoes are made of is a moral choice." Fanny lifted her foot. "See my shoes? My shoes are plant-based."

"I guess you'll want me to get rid of my leather belt, too?"

"Should a cow die to keep your pants up, Jack?"

He smiled playfully. "You want them falling down? On our first date? Hey, I'm beginning to like this vegan thing."

The stony look on Fanny's face told Jack this was no laughing matter. "They make belts of nylon and vinyl, you know. Nobody needs a leather belt anymore."

Meat, cheese, and now shoes. So many things came from animals, and it looked as if Jack's budding relationship with Fanny would cost him all of them. Besides chicken, turkey, beef, fish, eggs, and honey, there were silk ties, wool sweaters, down pillows, and probably hundreds of other items he didn't even know about yet, each a single step in a marathon of self-denial required to get Fanny's moral approval.

Was the little blonde from Pasadena worth it? Jack hoped so. So Fanny had a little quirk—no big deal, so did he. She seemed to understand him like few girls he'd ever known. They shared work, journalism, and so many other things, so why not this? He looked into her big green eyes and swore the Vegan Vow.

AT MIDNIGHT JACK stepped out the door of Fanny's apartment and saw someone moving in the shadows. At least he thought it was someone. It might have been his imagination.

He walked a few paces toward his car, glanced over his shoulder, and stopped at the sound of something rustling. He turned toward the large shrub behind him, stood for a moment, and waited for the bush to move, but it was still.

Jack pretended not to notice anything. He walked further, swung around, and this time saw the silhouette of what looked to be a man, short and stout, standing in the moonlight, twenty yards behind him. The figure studied him momentarily, then turned and ran. Jack sprinted after him across an empty lot.

Within seconds Jack was on him, tackling him by the shoulders of his dark blue jacket. He pinned the man to the ground with his powerful arms. "Who the heck are you?"

The stranger, middle-aged with wire-rim glasses and a big nose, panted but said nothing.

"Why are you following me?" Jack demanded.

"None of your business," the man replied in a gravelly voice.

"Yeah? Well, maybe the cops won't think so." Jack whipped out his phone.

"No, stop, don't call the cops! You don't want to do that!" said the man.

"Okay, then who are you? If you don't tell me, I'm gonna call 'em."

The stalker reached into his pocket and pulled out his badge. "Agent Seven, FBI."

Jack lifted his knee off the man's chest and saw a handgun sticking out under his coat. "How was I to know you're with the FBI? You were following me."

"Well, you didn't have to attack me." Agent Seven stood up and dusted himself off. Bending over, he touched his right knee. "Aw, now look what you've done. My pants are torn. That there's gonna cost me sixty bucks, dammit."

"Sorry."

"You know, I could've shot you," Agent Seven said. "I still could, you know."

"Shoot me? Why would you shoot me?"

"I'm sure I could find some reason. I might consider not shooting you if you paid for these." The agent held his hand out.

Jack looked at him with astonishment, wondering what kind of FBI agent he had caught. "I'm not paying for your darn pants, mister. You were chasing me, remember?"

The G-man took out a handkerchief and wiped a smudge off his glasses. "The bureau won't pay for them either. This is the thanks I get for protecting the public. I think I should at least get hazard pay for this. You know, I have kids almost your age to put through college."

Agent Seven seemed very whiny for an FBI agent. Next he'd be complaining about his retirement plan. "Why were you following me?" Jack asked.

"I'm on official business," the agent replied.

"Involving me?"

"You're Jack Snap, aren't you?"

"Yeah. How did you know?"

"Never mind that. I need to know something, Mr. Snap. Where is Rod Collier?"

Where did that come from, Jack wondered. How did this guy know about Collier? Wherever Collier was, it was none of the FBI's business. Jack reached for his phone again. "To heck with this. I'm not telling you anything. I have rights. I'm calling the police."

"No, you won't. You assaulted me, remember?" Agent Seven pulled out his badge again. "Which of us do you think the cops would haul off to jail, the FBI agent or the young punk? It'll be your word against mine. I could charge you with assault."

Jack shoved his phone back into his pocket. "I'm not a punk. I'm a newspaper reporter, and I don't have to put up with this. FBI or no FBI, I've got rights. You were tailing me."

Agent Seven laughed. "Oh, you're more than a reporter now, Mr. Snap. You're a person of interest."

"Why?"

"The bureau never says why. Never has to." Agent Seven slowly disappeared into the shadows. "A little advice for you, kid. First, be careful with Pitypander. There's a lot you don't know about her. Second, you never met me. This never happened."

THE GULFSTREAM PICKED up speed and lifted off the runway. The few days' rest at home had given Patty time to clear her head.

She decided her vision of Jenessa Fuller must have been caused by the extreme stress of the campaign. Running around the country at a furious pace, traveling at all hours, giving speech after speech, strategizing with advisers in meeting after meeting, not to mention the tense interviews with reporters—it was enough to make anyone see things. Nothing about Jenessa could have been real. She should forget about the incident. Tanned and re-energized, Patty was off to conquer the Midwest.

Nigel, spreading his materials on the table between the seats, reviewed Red Meat Speech Number Eight, which had been written to appeal to urban voters. Patty must hammer away at the devastation Diebold's Clean Slate program would wreak on the poor in Chicago's south side. Benefits were at stake—welfare, food stamps, healthcare, and school programs. A big turnout was critical. Illinois must not be taken for granted.

Nigel turned next to administrative matters. "I had our man investigate Jack Snap, as you asked."

Patty's ears pricked up. "Oh? And what did he find?"

Nigel flipped a page in his notes. "Jack Snap is a solid Pitypander supporter, works at *The Burbank Bee* covering politics, and lives at his parents' three-bedroom home in Burbank. He's six foot two, one hundred eighty pounds, blond hair, a recent journalism grad from UCLA. Captain of the crew team, led it to the state rowing championship. Mother is Mimi, father is Bob. Both parents work for the Department of Agriculture. The family moved to Burbank from Omaha, Nebraska, a few years ago when their farm went bankrupt during a drought. Jack was a teenager at the time."

The pieces of the Jack puzzle were fitting together. A corn-fed Nebraska boy with a streak of Midwestern honesty and forthrightness, the son of the shy, unpretentious Amish girl Patty had befriended in college. Yes, that was Jack. Captain of a championship rowing team? That explained his fabulous muscles, earned no doubt by years of dedicated training.

"And he's on our side," Patty said. "Maybe he can be persuaded to leave the Collier thing alone."

"One more thing," Nigel replied. "Snap got into a scuffle last night."

"Oh, dear." Patty sat up straight. "Was he hurt?"

"No, the other fellow got the worst of it. Probably a mugger. Snap easily overpowered him. He was walking back to his car around midnight from his girlfriend's apartment."

Patty's face fell. "What? Jack has a girlfriend? You didn't mention that."

"Yes. They started dating recently."

Only recently? Maybe it hadn't gotten serious yet. Patty wrenched her lips into an indifferent smile and paused a few seconds. "What's her name?"

"Fanny Flowers, another young reporter at the *Bee*."

"And what do you know about her?"

"Hmm, somehow I thought you might ask." Nigel turned a page in his notes. "A reporter for the Metro section. Twenty-two, blonde, five foot five, recent journalism grad from Pepperdine. Militant vegan. Chairperson of the California Animal Activists Association. Demonstrates at animal rights rallies almost every weekend. Arrested twice in college, once for chaining herself to a chicken coop, another time for leading a sit-in in front of a steakhouse. In both cases the charges were dropped."

What had Jack gotten himself into? His new girlfriend sounded like a wild woman. What had attracted Jack to her? Did Jack have a thing for wild women? Nigel, as thorough as he was, wouldn't have the answers to such questions.

"What does Jack know about Rod Collier?" she asked.

"He doesn't seem to know much of anything yet."

First Rod Collier, and now a rival girlfriend. Patty's concerns about Jack were piling up fast. Something must be done.

"I'll have our man stay on him," Nigel promised.

"Go ahead. Meanwhile, I think I'll do some investigating of my own," Patty said with a roguish smile.

Nigel laid down his notes and gave her a hard stare. "Isn't the campaign keeping you busy enough? Don't you have quite enough to do without inviting more distractions?"

Patty patted him on the hand. "Relax. There's only so much your man can learn about Jack skulking behind a bush. I'm just going to invite Jack to our little party at Aspen."

Nigel sat up. "The fundraiser? Why in heaven would you invite Snap? He doesn't have any money. He'll be completely out of his element among those people. It's too dangerous."

"The party will be just the place to learn more about him," Patty said. "We'll get to know him in a more sociable setting. He'll have his guard down. Something we don't know about Jack is bound to pop out."

Nigel grimaced. "Or something about you."

CHAPTER 15

A Visit to Macau

THE CHARIOTS WERE still careening around the Roman arena when Kim Il Bong peeked out the window of the railcar to see his train pulling into the Zhuhai station near Macau. He paused the movie.

Inconveniently, the train had arrived at its destination in the middle of *Ben-Hur*'s chariot race, right before the best part when Messala would once again be trampled to a bloody pulp under the thundering hooves of Charlton Heston's horses.

"Let them wait," Kim said to his aide.

He clicked the remote again to continue his movie several more minutes, until Messala, groaning in agony, breathed his last. The dictator switched off the television and took one last satisfying puff from his cigar.

"Take that, Messala!" He shook his fist.

No sooner had the train stopped than the two hundred armed soldiers on it began jumping off. They quickly surrounded the station's perimeter as workmen hurried to unload the Supreme Leader's baggage onto the platform.

Kim stepped down to the red carpet unfurled before him, saluted the ranks of soldiers lined up at attention, and climbed into his armor-plated limousine. Twenty-five motorcycles formed a motorcade to escort the Dear Leader across the border of mainland China into Macau.

The entourage rolled into the casino district, past the MGM Casino and the Wynn Macau, and turned along the bay onto Avenue Sun Yat-sen, where Kim saw the golden glass windows of the sixty-story Pitypander Palace shimmering against the sky.

The soldiers lined up in front of the Palace, shoulder to shoulder in perfect parade formation starting from the limousine, past the fountain, through the front doors, and across the marble floors of the hotel lobby, each head turned upward and to the right at precisely the same angle. Kim exited his vehicle and went inside.

A five-star general, four feet tall, marched to the Palace's check-in desk, stood on his tiptoes, and glowered at the astonished hotel clerks. Waving a copy of an online reservation, he flung a bundle of U.S. thousand-dollar bills across the desk. A procession of soldiers lugged Kim's twenty suitcases into the elevators and up to the fiftieth floor VIP suite.

An hour later the Great Chairman entered the casino. The first thing he encountered was a shiny machine with a crank on its side. Having seen such devices only in movies, he stood before it for a moment, full of curiosity, protected by a circle of soldiers. His defense minister stood at the ready with large bags of coins and chips.

The strange contraption was ringing and dinging.

"A pleasure machine, Dear Leader, used for wagering," the defense minister explained. "It is operated by coins."

Kim pointed to it. The defense minister plucked a coin out of his bag and dropped it into the device. Kim reached up and pulled down the crank. Two lemons and a strawberry rolled down into the gizmo's window.

The defense minister regarded the pleasure machine with suspicion. He gave it a hard kick. Nothing happened. He pushed a second coin in for the Great Leader, who pulled down the handle once more. Two bars and a seven dropped into the window. A third try produced a seven, a bar, and a tomato.

The defense minister gave the machine a stern look and turned to Kim. "It is defective, Dear Leader."

The four-foot five-star general stepped forward, pulled his revolver out of its holster, and fired three shots into the tomato. The machine made a grinding noise before going dark and silent.

"Ha! Take that," said the Master of All He Attempts.

Kim took a swig of Jack Daniel's. A defective pleasure machine, what was the point of that? Perhaps another would perform correctly.

Bells began ringing nearby. Kim turned and saw a pleasure machine flashing "Jackpot" in bright red letters. Behind it stood a Chinese woman, jumping with joy, scrambling to scoop up the coins flooding into her tray.

The general motioned with his thumb. Three soldiers lifted the woman off her feet and carried her away screaming.

Kim walked over to the properly functioning machine and gestured with his finger to his defense minister, who dropped in a coin. Kim pulled the handle. A raspberry, a lemon, and a bar appeared. Another coin and another yank of the handle generated two tomatoes and a seven. A third coin and a third draw yielded a lemon, a seven, and a bar.

The second pleasure machine was summarily executed.

"Perhaps all such devices in this place are defective, Great Leader," the defense minister said.

"Enough!" Kim thundered, walking away from them in disgust. He took another swig of Jack Daniel's. "There are many other games here, are there not?"

"Oh, yes, Great Leader." The minister's eyes grew big. "We are informed that there are dozens of opportunities here for your pleasure."

A party of decadent round-eyed Westerners gathered around a roulette table nearby. The defense minister pointed to it. The soldiers shoved the patrons away.

The croupier, surrounded by gun barrels, froze with fear.

The defense minister pounded his fist on the roulette table. "Explain this game."

The croupier, his lips quivering, went over the rules of roulette. The Great Leader, hearing he could choose red or black, picked red.

The defense minister laid chips down for Kim's bet on red. The roulette ball rolled round and round the roulette wheel, and ended up on black twenty.

The defense minister leaned over to inspect the wheel. "Perhaps black is the proper choice, Dear Leader."

That was obvious. Kim would ensure success by laying his chips on the table with his own hands. "Black," he commanded.

The four-foot five-star general clutched his revolver as he stared down the croupier.

The ball fell on red thirty-four.

Four soldiers seized the croupier by his arms and prepared to dispose of him.

Kim waved them off. "No, let him go. I wish to play some more."

Betting on black, he won the next roll of the ball. This success restored his confidence and inspired him to continue. The Master of All He Attempts proceeded to lose twenty-five out of his next thirty rounds.

Kim fared no better at blackjack. Within hours two million dollars in sorely needed hard currency vanished from the defense minister's hoard. All that remained was a small bag of thousand-dollar bills with George Washington on the front and Abraham Lincoln on the back.

The casino cashier, holding a bill up to the light, refused to accept any of them. The general fired a warning shot through the cashier's window. The clerk dropped to his knees with his hands up, begging for his life to be spared.

"No, don't kill him. Bring me the owner," Kim said.

BENNY BIT HIS fingernails, terrified to leave his office and go downstairs. No Pitypander Palace had ever been invaded by foreign troops before.

He debated his options. Calling the local Macau police would be useless, as they were no match for the North Koreans. The Chinese army could handle the intruders, but it was obvious China had sanctioned the raid. How else could North Korean troops have crossed China, if not with Beijing's permission? Who were these people?

The door to Benny's office suite flew open. A squad of six soldiers armed with AK-47s rushed in, followed by the four-foot five-star general, who discharged two shots from his pistol into the ceiling.

"Where are you taking me?" Benny asked as they seized him by his elbows and dragged him to the elevator.

As the elevator descended, the soldiers jabbered to each other in Korean. Dragging Benny to the casino, they hauled him before a rotund man with black hair sitting in a red leather chair and puffing on a cigar.

The soldiers plopped Benny into the chair across from him.

"Good evening, Mr. Pitypander." The visitor gazed at the Palace's soaring marble columns. "Nice place you have here. I've heard so much about your casino in Macau. I thought I should visit."

Benny, disheveled and dazed, pulled himself up in his chair. "You, you speak English? How do you know my name, Mister, uh—"

"Chairman Kim. I learned English in Switzerland. Also from your wonderful American movies." Kim extended his hand. "Put it there, pardner."

Kim Il Bong. Oh my God, it is him. "Ah, Chairman Kim." Benny shook Kim's hand with a tentative smile. "Welcome to Macau."

The Casino King found himself at a rare loss for words. His glittering resorts had entertained presidents, kings, princes, sheiks, dictators, poohbahs, and muckety-mucks of every description, but no potentate had ever brought his army with him.

Benny turned his head ever so slightly and noted that the muzzle of an AK-47 was a mere six inches from his ear. "Would you like a drink?" he asked his guest.

Kim dropped his cigar on the carpet and ground it in with his shoe. "Yes, a Jack Daniel's, neat."

Benny called over a waiter and ordered two. "What brings you to the Pitypander Palace in Macau, Chairman Kim?"

"We have a mutual friend, Mr. Pitypander."

Benny's face went blank.

"Mr. Krok," Kim said.

"Ah, yes, Mr. Krok, of course." Lifting an eyebrow, Benny suddenly remembered the shady consultant he had hired to scout for potential real estate partners in Asia. Gorok Krok had found him the murderous tyrant of North Korea. A heads-up would have been nice.

Benny searched his memory about Kim, recalling the dictator had once ordered a disloyal uncle to be shredded by anti-aircraft guns. Kim had another relative poisoned with radioactive isotopes, causing his agonizing death.

"Mr. Krok tells me you may be interested in doing a deal in Asia." The chairman pulled out a cigar and held it up expectantly as the defense minister rushed over with a match to light it. Kim puffed out a smoke ring that encircled Benny's head like a noose. "I too am interested in a deal."

"Um, a deal?" Benny wondered what kind of deal he could make with a starving country closed off from the outside world for seven decades. "I'm not sure I understand. I build resorts, Chairman Kim. Fancy ones."

Kim downed his bourbon. "I know. That's why I have come to you, Mr. Pitypander. I want you to build me a fancy resort."

"Why me?"

"Who better to do it than the famous Casino King? I want to play roulette and blackjack. They are delightful games of thievery."

"Where would this resort be?" Benny asked.

"On the sea, in Wonsan, where my yacht is docked. One of your pleasure palaces will make a lovely addition to mine."

Benny had never heard of Wonsan. "I'm sure it's a wonderful spot, Chairman Kim. Were you thinking of a hotel? A casino? A restaurant?"

"Yes, all of them. A fancy resort like this one."

Benny gulped. "But, Mr. Chairman, this hotel complex has seven thousand five-star rooms and two dozen restaurants. It cost me three billion dollars."

Kim sucked on his cigar. "You disappoint me, Mr. Pitypander. I was told you are an important businessman. Can you not raise a few billion dollars more?"

"Of course," Benny replied. "But a huge resort like this needs a steady flow of rich patrons to keep its occupancy rate at a profitable level. Where will the thousands of patrons to pay for it come from?"

Benny flinched as the cold steel muzzle of the AK-47 touched his earlobe. He had spoken too brashly to the Great Leader. He must show the proper deference. The dictator had only to wrinkle his nose and the thing would splatter the Casino King's brains across the room. Yet Benny sensed Kim needed him for some greater purpose than the transient thrill of committing a sadistic murder.

"The patrons will come from China, Japan, South Korea, and all over Asia," Kim said. "The casino must be built to the highest standards, to attract foreign tourists who will bring in hard currency. I offer you an exclusive concession, Mr. Pitypander. We will be venture partners in the Wonsan Pitypander Palace, the finest resort in Korea."

So that was it. Kim needed hard currency so badly he was proposing to open North Korea to capitalist investment. If Benny cooperated, he could get in on the ground floor of an exciting new gaming market with huge potential. But where would the workers come from to construct such an extravagant project?

"Could we use North Korean labor?" Benny asked.

The Great Leader smiled. "I can supply all the labor you need, Mr. Pitypander, for free."

Free labor? That would reduce Benny's construction and operating costs by eighty percent. The savings would make Wonsan the most profitable resort in the Pitypander empire, an even bigger gold mine than Macau.

Making this deal was a no-brainer. Not making it would also be a no-brainer, but of a much less pleasant kind.

"Put it there, pardner," said the Casino King, shaking the Great Leader's hand.

CHAPTER 16

The Spider's Web

WHEN JACK WALKED up to the Exclusive Excursions counter at the Aspen airport, the woman behind it looked surprised.

"Is this the place for the chartered helicopter to Mount Pitypander?" he asked.

"Yes. ID, please?"

Jack handed her his driver's license and ticket. She turned it over and held it up to the light. "You're Mr. Snap?"

"Yes."

She shrugged, crossed his name off her list, and gave him his ticket back with a bemused smile. "Welcome, Mr. Snap. Your flight to the castle is ready."

Jack expected to get that reaction a lot this weekend. At the fundraiser they would probably think he looked more like one of Pitypander's domestics than one of her fat cat donors.

Jack ducked as he entered the helicopter. *Wow, a helicopter. Awesome.* This would be his second new flying experience of the day. Until this morning, when the governor had sent her Gulfstream to take him from

Los Angeles to Aspen, he had never flown private. Jack marveled at the Sikorsky's plush leather seats, wet bar, television, and telephone. He had the cabin to himself.

A stewardess opened the cockpit door. "Would you like a drink?"

"A beer, thanks."

Jack took a Heineken from her and eased his seat back. His mind drifted to the Rod Collier mystery, and how weird it was that no one who had attended Burbank High remembered much about the guy. Collier's friends—the few he had—portrayed him as a loner. He didn't have a girlfriend and was more into video games than sports. No one believed his cockamamie story about having sex with Pitypander. Collier was just trying to show off.

So how was Jack going to track Collier down, now that he had exhausted his leads? He had pleaded on social media for anyone who knew Collier to contact him, but his calls for help had gone unanswered. Going to Pitypander's party was an unlikely way to find new clues, but Jack would at least get to know the governor better. She was half the story. Maybe he could shake some more information out of her.

The swooshing sound overhead grew louder as the helicopter blades picked up speed. Soon the aircraft was skimming over the tops of twelve-thousand-foot mountains carpeted with Douglas firs.

Minutes later the white walls and conical spires of the castle came into view. In the distance another helicopter was rising out of the dense forest, while a third hovered in the sky, awaiting its turn to land.

Jack's helicopter floated over the crest of another mountaintop and descended toward the trees. A red circle marked a helipad in the clearing below. The helicopter touched down, and its blades slowed to a stop. The pilot opened the door and Jack climbed out.

Above him soared the Pitypander Castle, seven stories of white stone walls built on a mountainside, punctuated by windows and balconies and ringed by crenelated towers, with a little fake moat and a wooden drawbridge for effect. Terraced gardens gushing with flowers spilled from the main courtyard. It was a fairy-tale castle on steroids, like the one in Disneyland, only bigger and gaudier. Sleeping Beauty would feel at home here.

Jack rolled his small suitcase across the drawbridge to the gate and entered the courtyard.

"Jack! Over here!"

It was the governor, standing to his left near the entrance. An assistant was sitting at a table, checking in guests.

"You're one of the first to arrive," Patty said. "You'll be in Room 502. Would you like a little tour of the place?"

"Sure."

Patty led him across the courtyard to the main entrance. "The land for miles around here belonged to John D. Rockefeller. He donated it to the national forest, except for this mountain, thinking he would build a retreat here, but he never did. Benny bought the mountain and built the castle when his plans for a resort were rejected."

"This place was supposed to be in Las Vegas?"

"No, Abu Dhabi. The sheiks didn't care for the turrets—too Crusader-ish. But Benny's not one to let perfectly good architectural plans go to waste, so he put the castle here. It took quite a feat of engineering to build it into a mountainside in such a remote spot. We're miles from the nearest road. The only way in or out is by helicopter. As you can see, it's very secluded."

The lush greenery in the courtyard struck Jack as unnatural. He touched a boxwood to see if it was fake. It wasn't. "I didn't know plants like this grew so high up. Aren't we at seven or eight thousand feet?"

"Ten thousand. And they don't." Patty snapped a chrysanthemum from its stalk and smelled it before tossing it back into the garden. "These will last a while, and then they'll be replaced."

"By helicopter?"

"Yes. They fly these in from Denver."

"How often do you come here?"

"Three or four times a year, usually when the weather is bad in Durango Beach. Benny meets me here sometimes. We throw parties every winter on our little ski run on the other side of the mountain. It's so private, and I love the fresh mountain air, don't you?"

They passed through a large entry room with a vaulted ceiling and curved marble staircases leading upstairs. Jack stopped to admire the two dozen medieval suits of armor mounted on the walls.

Patty noted his interest in them. "Oh, aren't they wonderful? Benny saw those hanging in a chateau in the South of France, and the only way he could get the armor was to buy the whole place. He sold the rest of it."

They proceeded to a grand ballroom. Jack looked up. Colored glass flowers—blue, yellow, red, green, and orange—covered the ceiling. Light streaming through the arched windows reflected the flowers onto the floor, creating a kaleidoscopic effect.

"These were hand-blown by the man who did the ceiling of the Bellagio in Las Vegas. We'll be having some festivities for the party in here, and some in the garden on the other side."

"How many people are coming?"

"Three hundred, but only half are staying the night."

Patty led him into a library walled by floor-to-ceiling oak book-cases. The room smelled of musty old books. "We bought these from an English earl who needed to sell his library to pay his taxes so he could hang on to his estate. We thought a fairy-tale castle ought to have old books in it."

Jack took a volume from a shelf. "Wow, *Don Quixote*. Translated in 1742. This is super old. Do you read novels?"

"Yes, modern novels."

Jack noticed a glass box in the corner. Resting on a metal stand, it was full of a gray, lacy material stretched between some wooden branches. On closer inspection, he realized the gray gauze wasn't lace, but a spider's web. "Are those—?"

"Spiders? Yes, as a matter of fact, they are." Patty chuckled. "It's an old arachnarium that came with the earl's library. The old boy was a little eccentric and dabbled in entomology. He had a vast collection of live bugs, which he kept in his library. Benny saved the earl's spiders, just for laughs."

"What kind of spiders are they?"

"Black widows," she said without a trace of concern.

"Those are dangerous, aren't they?"

"Only if they're not properly handled. Look closely down there and you'll see some crawling around. They're mostly females. Sad to say, black widows have a bad habit of devouring their mates. I suppose one would have to be awfully hungry to do that. Would you like to feed them?"

"Can't they feed themselves?"

"They need to eat twice a day, but they can't feed themselves when they're cooped up like this, so we have to help them." Patty stepped close to the arachnarium. "Here, I'll show you how the old earl did it."

Patty pointed to a separate glass enclosure. "He kept a little food supply for them over here." Using a big pair of tweezers, she plucked out a live caterpillar and dropped it into the arachnarium. The caterpillar started to wriggle, its legs quickly becoming ensnared in a web. Sensing the web's movement, a black widow crept toward her prey.

"There, she's trapped him," Patty observed as the spider closed in. "The poor widow's nearly blind, but the old girl can still tell when he's in her web. After she kills him, she'll tie him up with her silk, drag him back to her nest, and gobble him up."

Jack bent over the arachnarium and peered through the magnifying scope. The black widow injected her paralyzing venom into her helpless victim. As the nerve agent took effect, the caterpillar thrashed uncontrollably from side to side. It finally ceased moving. The spider bit off its head.

Patty handed Jack the tweezers. "Your turn."

There was something vaguely creepy about a woman feeding black widow spiders for sport. Most of the women Jack knew detested spiders.

He began to reach with the tweezers into the caterpillar enclosure, but stopped. "No, I'd rather not, thanks." He turned to give the tweezers back to Patty, but she was so close that his hand brushed against her breast. He jumped back. "Oh, sorry, Governor."

"Not at all." A strange grin appeared on her face. "You seem nervous. You're not squeamish, are you, Jack? A bug's gotta eat. It's just nature. We can't deny our nature, can we?"

Our nature? What does she mean by that? Jack laid the tweezers down and edged away from her. "Thanks, I think I'll pass."

COCKTAILS IN HAND, the donors wandered like cats from the ballroom to the great hall, through the study, and out to the garden. Waiters stood among the potted boxwoods armed with caviar, crème fraiche tartlets, shrimp, and refills of the best French wine.

Patty flitted back and forth between the garden terraces, attempting to meet her three hundred guests. She thanked everyone for coming and promised to fulfill her campaign promises to serve the oppressed.

She found Jack behind some shrubbery, looking as shiny as a new penny in his rented tuxedo. He was admiring the mountain valleys below the castle's stone walls.

He raised his beer in salute. "I can see forever from here. Is that Aspen?"

"Yes, and if you look hard, you'll see Denver out on the horizon." Patty pointed to it.

Jack put his hand to his brow to block the setting sun as he gazed down at the Mile-High City. A waiter holding a tray of shrimp appeared at his elbow.

"Would you like some hors d'oeuvres?" Patty asked.

He began to pick a shrimp off the tray, but quickly put it back. "I can't. I promised my girlfriend never to eat any animal product again as long as I live."

"What?"

Jack solemnly explained he had taken the Vegan Vow.

"Veganism? Oh, dear, I hope it's not catching. We have piles and piles of food here that would go to waste."

Jack looked at the shrimp longingly. "If she was here, Fanny would say how much those poor shrimp suffered when they were caught, and how selfish I am to want to eat one."

"Hmm, that does sound serious," Patty said. "Well, suit yourself. I'll have one for both of us." She grabbed a shrimp off the tray and bit into it. "Oh, that's wonderful. You don't know what you're missing. That waiter over there has some Camembert and caviar, if you like."

"Camembert?" His eyes brightened, but only for a second. "Oh, wait, that's cheese, isn't it?"

Patty laughed. "Yes, Jack, Camembert is cheese."

"Darn it, cheese is off-limits too. So is caviar. Fanny's orders."

Patty was impressed. Fanny must be quite a catch to warrant such sacrifice. "Sorry, we would have had some vegetables ready for you if we'd known, but it's not long until dinner. Let me introduce you to some people before you pass out from starvation."

Patty turned to a man standing nearby, next to a stone fountain. "Howard is the CEO of Mammoth Technology. You know, the people who make the phones."

Mammoth didn't just make phones. It made half the phones in the world, including Jack's. Howard Steinfeld, Mammoth's founder, had pioneered the design of smartphones. He was a cult hero in Silicon Valley and one of the ten richest men on the planet.

Jack shook the CEO's hand. "Wow, pleased to meet you, Mr. Steinfeld."

Patty led Jack into a small courtyard, introducing him to an assortment of other titans of industry, government, and academia: the German ambassador to the United Nations, the founder of Hasty Broadcasting, the CEO of TRP Motion Pictures, the president of Harvard University, and the prime minister of Australia.

"Gosh, Harvard." Jack looked back over his shoulder as they walked farther.

The next courtyard was framed by a portcullis leading to another part of the castle. There they ran into Benny, recently back from Macau, making a scene with the chairman of the Democratic Party, a tall, thin fellow with a gray beard.

Benny's voice boomed loud enough to be heard twenty feet away. "Yeah? Well, you still haven't told me what's in it for me."

The chairman leaned his shoulder against the portcullis and regarded the tycoon with disdain. "How about the good of mankind? Or does that not interest you?"

Benny scoffed. "No, it sounds pretty lame, actually. What does that mean, anyway? The good of mankind is crap, just another excuse for you guys to grab my hard-earned money." He turned to Prince Alawari of Saudi Arabia, a swarthy man in a flowing white robe and traditional Arab headdress. "What do you think, Prince? Do you people in Saudi Arabia pick leaders who rob you of everything you've sweated for all your lives?"

The prince stroked his beard and smiled. "Sweated? I'm sorry, I don't understand."

"Never mind. How do you pick your leaders over there, Prince?"

"Ah, we do not choose our leaders," said the prince. "The Kingdom of Saudi Arabia is passed by inheritance from the king to the prince he considers most suitable for the throne."

Benny sucked an ice cube out of his martini and crunched it between his molars. "Well, your system may be old-fashioned, but I'd say it's working pretty well for you. At least there's some logic in it. Our system doesn't get us good people anymore. Maybe we should put this democracy thing on hold and get us a king temporarily, until we can straighten things out. I don't guess you'd be available for the job, would you? It would be a promotion."

The prince glanced at Patty and hung his head in tactful silence.

"Excuse us." Patty hustled Jack out of earshot. "So what do you think of these people?"

"I think there's enough firepower here to wage a world war," Jack replied with a laugh. "Enough to start one anyway."

He left to get another beer. Seconds later Hollywood donors Margot Lewiston and Sally Snack descended on Patty, accompanied by a bottle-blonde actress in a low-cut sleeveless dress, Bridgette Allsworthy.

Margot pointed at Jack. "He looks like fun. Who's he?"

Patty sensed it was best to be tight-lipped. "A reporter."

"What's he doing here?" Sally asked.

"Someone's boy toy, I'll bet," Bridgette suggested with indifference, as if she would be unsurprised.

Patty lowered her brow, recalling some gossip about Bridgette. The actress was reputed to be a notorious home-wrecker, responsible for three highly publicized Hollywood divorces, according to Nigel. Patty must be on guard with this woman. "Jack is the son of an old friend. His newspaper assigned him to follow my campaign."

Bridgette studied Jack as he stood at the bar. "How did he get here? Did his newspaper pay for his helicopter ride?"

"No, I paid for everyone's helicopter, including yours. Like I told you, he's a friend." Patty omitted that she'd also had Jack flown from Los Angeles on her jet.

"The poor boy looks out of place," Bridgette said.

"He probably feels strange among all these gray hairs," Margot speculated. "Too bad there's no one his age around."

Bridgette fluffed her hairdo. "Speak for yourself. I'm not so much older than he is, not even ten years. If Jack's a personal friend of our future president, someone should do their patriotic duty and keep him company. I hereby volunteer."

The actress wasted no time. When Jack returned, she sidled up to him and took a swallow of her chardonnay. "So, Jack, Patty tells me you're a reporter. Tell me about your newspaper job. Is it fun being a reporter?"

"Sure, totally," Jack replied with a friendly grin.

Patty, watching helplessly as Bridgette tried to work her spell, noted with frustration how Jack relaxed in the actress's presence, like she was one of his peers. The jezebel wanted to know if Jack liked his job? *The gall of this woman, preying on a boy of his age.*

Patty's eyes wandered to a corner of the garden, where she noticed a woman in a black evening dress lounging on a retaining wall. The woman turned around.

"Jenessa? What are you doing here? You can't be here."

"Patty, my dear," Jenessa said, "we have to talk."

"About Bridgette?"

Jenessa nodded. "She's after our young man."

Patty bit her lip. "Yes, she certainly is."

Jenessa swept the flowing brown hair out of her eyes. "So what are you going to do about it?"

Patty shrugged. "What can I do about it, Jenessa? She's a glamorous movie star, she's ages younger than I am, and she has breasts."

Jenessa flicked her cigarette ashes into the flower bed behind her. "True, but they aren't very perky."

"Yes, but at least she has them. They are more than enough to do the job. Jack was noticing them. I saw him."

"They all notice them. You have a perfectly serviceable pair too."

Patty looked down at her chest. "Mine were like hers thirty years ago. Benny used to say they were plump. Now just look how they've shrunk. And then there are the wrinkles Botox can't seem to fix, my sagging jowls—not to mention my midriff bulge. Don't get me started."

"If only I could get you stopped," Jenessa said, raising her eyebrows in exasperation. "We go to war with the weapons we have. A weak body image is no excuse for inaction."

"I didn't know I needed an excuse from you," Patty snapped. "Say, why don't you mind your own business and leave me to wallow in my physical inadequacies? Go haunt someone else."

Sitting impassively on the wall, Jenessa made it clear she wasn't about to be run off so easily. She was on a mission, and came and went as she liked. "Being alone too long is what brought you to this pass. I'm not letting you suffer by yourself in a pit of self-loathing. Help has arrived."

Patty could see she had no choice but to listen. Jenessa would follow her anywhere, so she might as well hear the heroine out. "Okay, what do you recommend?"

"That's more like it. I like a cooperative attitude." Jenessa took a long drag from her cigarette and blew forth a plume of smoke. "Do you remember how I dealt with that awful Serena Munford character when she started moving in on my Rocky Starr in *How True Lovers Kiss*?"

How could Patty forget? The novel was one of Marjorie Mickle's finest efforts, its suspenseful plot featuring an epic battle between two temptresses seeking the same man. The wily Jenessa, initially caught off guard by Serena's mendacity, outwitted her rival by revealing her dishonorable intentions and scaring her off. She managed to snatch the unsuspecting Rocky from her grasp only seconds before the bomb Jenessa had planted under Serena's bed was due to explode.

Patty shook her head. "But I can't do what you did. I couldn't put a bomb under Bridgette's bed."

"Why not?"

"Even if I had a bomb, that would be much too risky for a woman in my position."

"Risky? Fiddlesticks!" Jenessa tossed her cigarette butt over the castle wall. "Life is risky, my dear. It can all be over in a few hundred pages. Always remember, nothing must ever hold us back from what we want. Go straight at him and take your shot, like you see that other woman doing. It's always the best policy when your man's up for grabs and being coy isn't cutting it. Take direct action—that's what I would do."

"Yes, I know it's what you would do, Jenessa," Patty replied. "But this isn't the right time or place. There are three hundred people here. Can't you see I'm running for president?"

"Not that again. I suppose you think the future of the world depends on your being elected. Get your priorities straight. If you're stopped by a few wrinkles now, just wait. In a few years there won't be enough Botox on the planet to save you. Jack is slipping away before your very eyes. You have two rivals for him already. Act now before it's too late."

"Before it's too late," Patty repeated.

"What's that, Patty?"

Nigel was standing beside her, holding a cocktail and looking concerned. Everyone in the garden was heading inside.

"I've been searching all over the castle for you. They're calling us to dinner." Nigel reached into his tuxedo and pulled out some printed pages. "It's time for your stump speech on inequality."

CHAPTER 17

The Naughty Negligee

THE LITTLE BLUE negligee, a fifth wedding anniversary gift
from Benny, still fit after all these years. Patty sucked in a deep
breath and wriggled her slumping body into it.

She examined the seams, relieved they had withstood the strain.
If the negligee had been skimpy at thirty, it was even more negligible
now. But didn't that make it all the more seductive?

As she walked about the room, Patty made a point of avoiding the
full-length mirror in the corner. The sight of the jellied folds of her
stomach and hips pressing out in all directions might undermine her
confidence.

Patty poured the last of her champagne bottle into her glass, gleaning
what courage she could from it. Now she must fortify herself with
inspiration. She opened *How True Lovers Kiss* to the critical passage
where Jenessa made her fateful move on Rocky:

> It was in the fading moonlight, in the sheer blackness
> of the night, that the courage at last came to Jenessa to
> go to him, with the stars as bright in her eyes as in the

heavens, and the drumbeat of her heart pounding within her breast. She must appeal to Rocky now, despite everyone and everything separating them, or forever lose her one last chance to learn how true lovers kiss.

Patty wrapped a bathrobe around her negligee and tiptoed down the castle's fire escape to Jack's room, carrying her glass of bubbly. Pressing her ear to the door, she heard the water from the shower running. She swiped an electronic key card against the door lock, nudged the door open a few inches, and poked her nose inside. Jack stood in the shower, the outline of his godlike form visible through the glass door.

Patty crept into the bedroom and reached for the light switch. She turned down the lights, casting a romantic shadow across the bed, and slipped behind the curtain.

Seconds later the water in the bathroom stopped running. The shower door clanged, falling back against its frame. A minute later Jack strolled into the bedroom in a bathrobe, his hair ruffled and wet.

The caterpillar had stepped upon her web.

"Jack." Patty crept out from behind the curtain.

He jumped back.

She held the champagne glass against her breast and took a deep breath. "It's me, Jack, it's Patty."

"Oh my God! Oh my God!" Jack pulled his bathrobe tightly around his body. "What, uh, uh, what are you doing in my room, Governor?"

She stepped closer. "Call me Patty, won't you? I've come for you, Jack." She pronounced the words "for you" slowly, slowly, slowly, with as much sultry fervor as Jenessa would. "I've come to make this a special night for you."

"What? Special? How?"

She took a deep breath. "To consummate our love, darling."

"Our what?" He jumped back again.

Patty untied her bathrobe and pulled it back, revealing her ancient blue negligee.

Jack began to tremble. So far, so good. She had captured his attention, perhaps even ignited his imagination, or even—if she dared to hope for it—his passion.

Patty sucked in a deep breath. "Do you like what you see, Jack? You know you want it. We both do. Let's stop pretending."

Jack lifted his hands to shield his eyes. "Oh my God! Oh my God!"

What was this? Jack was shy. Of course he was. Patty must overcome his reserve. She held out her champagne glass. "Would you like a drink? You seem a bit nervous."

"No, no! I don't want a drink."

Taking a sip, Patty pressed her fingertips gently against his bare chest. "Don't be nervous. I won't bite. I'm not a spider, I'm a woman. A lonely woman. Take me, Jack. Take me into your arms now. Please, please show me how true lovers kiss."

"What?" He thrust her hand away and backed up again, his face turning beet red. "No, please, Governor, I, I—"

"Oh, Jack." Patty stepped forward.

"No, Governor, please leave me alone!"

She took a step back. Leave him alone? He couldn't mean it. He simply stood there in terror, quaking before her, as if she were Medusa and the slightest glimpse would turn him to stone.

Yes, she realized, he could mean it. She could see it in his angelic face. Jack was a strangely inscrutable young man. It wasn't just his wonderful muscles, his perfect jawline, and his radiant eyes drawing her to him. He was complicated and mysterious and unattainable, and for all those reasons she found him incomparably desirable.

Yet Jack would not have her. He was pushing her away.

Patty struggled to comprehend his behavior. Was this merely some youthful bashfulness, reflecting his inexperience with women? This wasn't how things had gone in *How True Lovers Kiss*. Rocky Starr collapsed into Jenessa's waiting arms when she hurled herself at him this way. Rocky was a pushover compared with Jack.

Patty braced herself against the wall as Jack's plaintive cry "leave me alone" echoed in her head.

Leave me alone. What did those words really mean, the words that sounded so painful, so raw, even to the flinty ears of a politician? She wondered whether she must take them literally. Did the rules apply to her? Did "no" mean "no" when a man said it?

The answer was in Jack's fear-filled eyes. They shouted silently that "no" really did mean "no," contradicting Patty's deepest yearnings. What could she do now? She had no choice but to comply, to withdraw, to retreat somehow from the lost battlefield of love—to fight another day.

Patty took another swig of her champagne. She would grant his wish and leave him alone, for now. Staggering away from him, she dropped her glass on the carpet, ran to the door, and left in utter despair.

HER HEAD THROBBING, Patty looked out her window early the next morning and saw Jack rolling his luggage to the helipad. She flew downstairs and ran across the drawbridge. "Stop, don't leave!"

He spun around, his jaw clenched.

"Jack, you don't need to rush away like this. I forgive you. Please come back."

He lowered his brow. "You forgive me?"

Patty touched his forearm. "It's okay, Jack. You had a little too much to drink last night, that's all."

Jack shook her off. "What the heck are you talking about?"

"I know you didn't mean to come on to me like that. The beer got the better of you."

"Governor, you have it backwards. I wasn't drunk, you were. And you were in my room. You tried to jump my bones!"

Patty put her hand to her cheek. "Oh, no, that's not how it happened at all. I just got off on the wrong floor. My room is right above yours, and all the hallways look alike. I walked into your room by mistake."

"Really? Then how did your key card work my lock?"

"My card works all the locks. It's our castle, you know."

Jack's face filled with disgust. "I know what I saw. You're making up stories, turning things around. You're trying to cover it up and point the finger at me. It won't work."

"Make up stories? Why, I'm doing nothing of the kind. I forgive you. Let's leave it there and forget the whole thing."

Patty looked up. The helicopter was descending toward the helipad, its blades whipping the air.

Jack stepped back from the downdraft. "I was going to ask you some questions about Rod Collier while I was here, but you just answered my biggest one."

"What?"

"Whether you're creepy enough for the rumor about you to be true."

Patty's face reddened. She shouted over the noise of the helicopter, "Rumor? Is someone spreading lies about me? Is it that young man?"

Without answering, Jack grabbed the handle of his suitcase and turned away. The helicopter blades slowed to a stop, the door to the cabin opened, and he climbed aboard. The craft lifted off into the sky and disappeared over the crest of Mount Pitypander.

Patty plodded toward the castle, her shoulders slumped. She looked back at the mountaintop, hoping for another glimpse of the helicopter. Would she ever see Jack again? If she did, would he believe her?

"Oh, please, don't be so discouraged, darling."

It was Jenessa, sitting on a bench in the clearing with her legs crossed, holding open a paperback book.

Patty pointed at her. "You! Damn you, Jenessa Fuller, this is all your fault! Go straight at him, you told me. Why did I listen to you? Now look what's happened."

Jenessa laughed. "Don't worry. The boy's a tad upset, that's all. He'll get over it."

Patty stamped her foot. "You act like this is nothing. I've lost Jack's trust. He thinks I'm some kind of wacko. Now he's going to ruin me."

Jenessa flapped her hand and scoffed. "What an amateur. It's only a minor setback. I've survived a thousand scrapes worse than this. Don't you remember how I won Jude Remington back in *Two Lovers Lost?*" Jenessa held up the novel. "I have it here if you'd like to refresh your memory." She read some sentences to herself. "Goodness, these books about me are addicting, aren't they? They're like eating potato chips. I see why you can't put them down. How does Marjorie Mickle do it?"

Two Lovers Lost? Wasn't that the one where Jenessa drugged her rival? Patty folded her arms. "Don't be absurd. I'm not about to poison Jack's girlfriend. That would only make matters worse."

"I didn't poison the girlfriend," Jenessa said sharply. "Yes, I'll admit I considered it for about thirty thrilling pages, but in the end it wasn't necessary. If you remember, I made her overplay her hand until she self-destructed. It took a while to work everything out, but I succeeded. And so will you, sweetheart, if you do exactly as I tell you."

Patty rubbed her forehead as the throbbing from her hangover intensified. "Get Jack back! You think getting him back is my only problem now?"

Jenessa slipped the book back into her purse, took out a brush, and dragged it through her silky brown hair. "What other problem is there?"

Patty stood with her arms akimbo, her nostrils flaring. "Thanks to you, Jack no longer believes a word I say. He thinks I'm corrupt. He's out to blow up my campaign. Nothing will stop him now."

"So Jack has become a political problem for you as well as your love interest?"

"Yes!"

"I see." Jenessa set her brush down. "Sounds like an interesting plot complication. I'd love to help, but I don't do political problems. I'm a love doctor. Affairs of the heart are my bailiwick."

"Some love doctor," Patty replied with a grunt. "A good love doctor would be a general practitioner. You can't just suddenly specialize like that, on a whim, as if you were a chiropractor or podiatrist. Can't you see my personal and political problems are hopelessly intertwined?"

"That's only because you keep tangling them up, darling. Serves you right for running for office. You need to get your priorities straight. Do you truly believe a mere woman can win a young man's love and the presidency at the same time? I don't."

"A mere woman? Sexism! Not you too! Ahhhh!" Patty's hand flew to her forehead, her skull pounding like it was about to split open.

PATTY STARED AT the crown molding on her office ceiling, desperate for the weekly strategy meeting to end.

The drone of Nigel's voice halted abruptly. "Patty, are you listening?"

She wasn't. She hadn't heard a word her campaign manager had said since the part where they would barnstorm swing districts in the Southwest and lock up the Hispanic vote. "Sorry, Nigel, there's something on my mind. I have some bad news to tell you."

Patty said she'd had an accidental encounter with Jack at Pitypander Castle, caused by her innocently mistaking his room for hers. While there, she had inadvertently done something Jack had misconstrued as a flirtation, and he had left the castle in a big huff, determined to destroy her utterly.

Nigel was appalled. "No, not again! Why do you keep doing this sort of thing? Have you gone barmy?"

Fearing she may indeed have gone barmy, Patty declined to answer. Nigel, serious to his core, would interpret her visions of Jenessa as sheer madness and resign on the spot. And good campaign managers were hard to find.

Nigel prowled around the table, his hand clutching his forehead as he stared out the window at the traffic below. "Our problem isn't just Collier anymore. It's Snap himself. He's wise to you now."

That was the worst part. Patty had ruined her budding friendship with Jack. Disgusted him, alienated him, abused his trust. And what had she learned about the young reporter? That he had much more backbone than she had bargained for. Jack wasn't just a pretty face, not just a callow youth. Something of substance was emerging in him. Jack was becoming a man. Who could have seen that coming?

"Nothing happened," she swore.

"Oh, sure." Nigel shook his head. "A drunken flirtation in the middle of a neck-and-neck presidential race, with a reporter who barely shaves. My God, now you're at Snap's mercy!"

"But nothing happened, I tell you!"

Nigel wasn't buying it, and neither would a press corps ravenous for scandals. "We can't risk this story leaking out. Imagine the headline: 'Patty Pitypander, the Cougar Candidate.' They'll tag you with that and hang it around your neck forever."

"Oh, that would be so unfair."

"So was Clement's blackface scandal. Look where Clement is now."

Disgraced. Shunned. Cast into the outer darkness after a lifetime of public service, for a sixty-year-old crime he didn't remember committing. What would the party nabobs do to her for wrecking their chance to retake the White House? Her adult indiscretion was far more blameworthy than Clement's kindergarten blunder. If they banished him, they would crucify her.

Mitigating the damage was key, Nigel argued. "The first thing to do is to get control of Snap. We can't have him writing tabloid stories about the night Patty Pitypander tried to shag him at her castle in the clouds."

What better setting could she have picked for her crime, Patty wondered. The No-Tell Motel? The castle was her private residence.

Nigel snapped his fingers. "That's it. As angry as Snap may be, he still needs access to you for his campaign reporting. That will force him to come back to you. We could make him a friendly gesture, in the spirit of patching things up."

"A gesture? You mean a bribe?"

Nigel bristled at her vulgar suggestion of impropriety. "Nothing of the sort. I was thinking you could do Snap some small favor, to get him back on our side, without raising his suspicions. Maybe help fix something for him, something he depends on."

Something small that Jack depended on? "His phone," Patty answered without hesitation. "He can't survive five minutes without it."

"I have an idea. I'll put our tech people on it. Let Snap cool off for a few days. In the meantime, forget about him. Let's think about what you're going to say to Texas and Oklahoma."

CHAPTER 18

On the Road

NIGEL LEANED OVER the back of his seat and explained his strategy for the Lone Star State. "El Paso has the ideal demographic. If we can win here, we can take Texas."

El Paso certainly looked like part of the Pitypander Nation. The Empathy Express rolled past block after block of one-level stucco houses built on lots smaller than Patty's tennis court. How did these destitute people manage to raise such large families in such little places?

"Remember to be real. Authenticity is key," Nigel said. "It's the cornerstone of a candidate's credibility."

Being authentic was hard work, he reminded her, and she should forget any ludicrous idea she might have about how it ought to flow from her naturally. Authenticity was too complex to be natural. It was sociological, a function of ethnic identity. It differed markedly according to where she was in America. In Hispanic El Paso authenticity meant she must season her regular stump speech with some dollops of Spanish, without resorting to notes. The people here would notice and appreciate her effort.

Patty rifled through the dog-eared pages of her Berlitz Spanish phrase book. *"Te ayudaré"* still meant "I will help you" if one was speaking to a friend. But should she use the singular "you" or the plural "you" when addressing a crowd of strangers?

Patty wished she had more time to refresh her high school Spanish, largely forgotten after four decades of disuse. With a few more hours of study, the vocabulary, the grammar, the sound of the language, all these would come back to her from the dark corners of her memory. She'd lost so much of herself since high school; Spanish was the least of it.

"*Te ayudaré,*" she repeated. It would have to do.

The campaign bus squealed to a stop outside a high school gymnasium. Patty walked across the basketball court, waving at her cheering fans in the bleachers. A long banner strung across the back wall behind them was painted in red with the words "*Pitypander para presidente!*"

"*Te ayudaré!*" Patty raised her fist.

The bleachers responded with a loud round of applause. "*Si! Si! Ayúdanos!*"

At least they understood that. Patty smiled back at them. She could still do their lingo. *No problema.*

As she thought about what to say next, her throat constricted. Something to break the ice like "It's wonderful to be here, my good friends" might work, but what was the Spanish for that? After only two words, her tiny fuel tank of Spanish vocabulary was running on empty. The canned Berlitz phrases for ordering from a tapas menu, asking directions to the nearest bullfight, and buying pink lingerie in a Madrid department store melded into an irrelevant jumble in her head.

Patty fought off her anxiety, determined to push through. This speech was to be about heart, emotion, and her commitment to serve her supporters' needs. Pitypander people wouldn't mind her mangling their language a bit. Using the right tense or pronoun didn't matter. If she got the cadence right, they would understand her if she spoke Martian.

She must be specific about what she would do for them. If she spoke in vague platitudes, they would see her as another unprincipled pol bringing empty promises, there only for their votes. Being explicit would communicate sincerity, a language more difficult to speak than Spanish, with no phrase book at all.

What free things would she shower upon them? Everything. She pointed her finger in the air. *"Te daré palas y tortillas gratis hasta tus bucles de frutas."* ["I will give you free shovels and tortillas up to your fruit loops."]

She paused to take a sip of water and scan their faces. Her eyes fell upon a mustachioed man grinning hard in the front row. Her message of hope must have resonated with him.

With her next words she must proclaim herself a tireless ally in the Hispanics' long struggle for social and economic advancement. *"Sí, juntos podemos desenterrar los frijoles fritos en tu jardín."* ["Yes, together we can dig up the fried beans in your garden."]

Mr. Mustachio in the front row slapped his knee. Patty sensed she was on a roll.

Now, to drive home how committed she was to these people's welfare, she must back up her words with a solemn pledge that concrete action would be taken on their behalf. She would see to it that strong laws would be enacted to improve their lot. *"Me tiraré un pedo tan duro para ustedes que se escaparán para salvarse a sí mismos."* ["I will fart so hard for you that you will run away to save yourselves."]

Mr. Mustachio, visibly alarmed, pinched his nose in self-defense.

After issuing more promises, Patty wound up her pitch with a grand finale. Her supporters must go out and vote for her, or disaster would befall them. Diebold, with his cruel plans to eliminate their benefits, would destroy their hopes for a better life. She spread out her arms in a gesture of supplication, as if embracing them, and issued an impassioned plea: *"No olvides votar por mí en tus sueños húmedos!"* ["Don't forget to vote for me in your wet dreams!"]

This phrase set Mr. Mustachio to guffawing. Howls of laughter resounded across the gymnasium.

This could only be a friendly reaction. The crowd was laughing, so her speech must have worked. Her broken Spanish was good enough because she had communicated in the universal lingo of caring.

Truly, these were Pitypander people.

"Way to go, Patty. I think you got through to them," Nigel said, strolling back with her to the Empathy Express. "Voters can tell when you care. Compassion is what they're looking for."

THE EMPATHY EXPRESS headed west through the tumbleweeds, arriving at a bullet-riddled sign that read "Potowmack Indian Reservation." The big bus turned onto an unpaved road, as a caravan of reporters followed behind.

Windswept grassland stretched in every direction. For the next ten miles Patty didn't see so much as a cattle ranch.

"Potowmack? As in Potomac? Who are these people?" Patty asked.

Nigel shouted above the roar of the tires as the huge vehicle bounced over the rutted dirt road, churning up a cloud of dust. "They were the original inhabitants of what is now Washington, D.C. The Potowmacks have been stuck here near the Oklahoma-Kansas border for generations. An impoverished tribe, long forgotten, but proud despite centuries of hard luck."

"How did you find out about them?" Patty tried to remember whether she'd ever met a pureblood Indian before. The Native Americans she knew were more watered down than Elizabeth Warren.

"Colleen asked the Bureau of Indian Affairs which of all the tribes in America is the most destitute, and they told her that had to be the Potowmacks, without a doubt. Here we'll show the Diva of the Downtrodden bringing hope to indigenous peoples. It's the perfect photo-op for us."

"How did the Potowmacks become so downtrodden?"

Nigel pulled out his notes. "It's a long, tragic story. Before the advent of the white man they were a thriving branch of Maryland's Piscataway tribe, living at the confluence of the Potomac and Anacostia Rivers. Disease and wars with the whites took a fierce toll, and in 1790 the federal government wanted to build the new city of Washington on the small parcel of land they had left. The tribe, greatly reduced in size, was resettled across the Ohio River and in following decades driven farther and farther west by settlers.

"Eventually the dwindling band of survivors ended up in this desolate place. They were unable to adapt to their new home and learn to sustain themselves, so they became dependent on neighboring Oklahoma tribes, who resented having to feed them. The locals ridiculed the Potowmacks, dubbing them the *Nocawani petonka peepee kawa washin deesee.*"

"What does that mean?" Patty asked.

Nigel shuddered. "I'm ashamed to tell you. It's such an awful slur."

"Go ahead. I need to know."

"Fools from D.C. who pee into strong wind," he whispered in her ear.

Patty reacted with horror. "How insulting—especially coming from other native people. You'd think they'd be more sensitive to one of their own."

Nigel shrugged. "People will be people. It's only a small taste of how cruelly everyone has victimized the Potowmacks for centuries. Which is why you've come to save them. Here's the little script Colleen wrote for this skit."

Patty reviewed the first page. "Colleen wrote this? What does she know about scripts?"

"She once wrote and directed commercials for a New York ad agency. She gave us both a part, along with two of the Potowmacks. Oh, and I'll be giving you this prop toward the end."

It was a long brown pipe with feathers attached. Patty turned it over. The underside was marked "Made in China."

"I'll kill 'em with kindness," said Patty with determination, handing the pipe back to him.

"Yes, but please remember to stick to the teleprompters. Colleen was very careful in her script to be sensitive to cultural issues. We can't afford any gaffes."

The Empathy Express and media vans pulled up to the reservation headquarters, a two-story cinder block building with peeling yellow paint. After the camera crew set up, Colleen gave the signal to start taping.

On cue, an old man with long gray hair braided into ponytails wandered out. An elderly woman stumbled behind him with a cane, wincing with every step she took.

The old man's long red face was etched with age. Patty bowed low to him. "How," she said, raising her right hand in greeting.

"Howdy," the old man replied. "Good morning to ya. I am Chief Crazy Bird."

Patty stepped before the camera crews and pointed to herself with her thumb. "Me, Patty Pitypander, great former chief of California. Him, Nigel Windborne, medicine man."

Crazy Bird bit his lip and said woodenly, "Yes, we know. Wind talkers send message half-moon ago." He gestured at the old woman. "This is my squaw, Walks with a Limp."

"Walks with a Limp?" Patty squeezed the old woman's hand and looked at her leg. "Oh, dear, that's terrible, what's wrong?"

"I got plantar fasciitis." The old woman grimaced at the cameras and let out a dreadful groan.

"You poor thing," Patty said. "That must be tremendously painful."

Walks with a Limp lifted her heel off the ground. "Got that right, honey. It hurts like a sonofabitch."

Crazy Bird jabbed the old woman in the side with his elbow. "Squaw suffers much. She will speak no more."

"Great chief," said Nigel with a bow, "we are here to see your needle reclamation project. Would you be so kind as to show it to us?"

"Come with me." Tromping into the building, Crazy Bird led them down the hall to a back room filled with green storage bins, each brimming with plastic tubes. "Injectors," said the chief, pointing at the containers.

A uniformed agent from the Bureau of Indian Affairs stood by with a clipboard, busily taking inventory. The tubes, he explained, were syringe injectors. The Potowmacks were cooperating with the bureau in a needle recycling program, trading in their used heroin needles weekly for food, supplies, and drugs.

Patty peered into the bins. "My goodness, isn't that a lot of needles for only two hundred people?"

"Heap many." Crazy Bird raised both hands, his fingers outstretched. "More than the stars."

"The entire tribe is hooked on heroin?" Patty touched her hand to her cheek. "This is total degradation. How could the government have let this happen?" She looked mournfully at Nigel and asked why, instead of abandoning the Potowmacks to waste away on their barren reservation, the government couldn't simply return them to their ancestral homeland.

"Their true homeland is Capitol Hill," Nigel reminded her, his eyes tracking the teleprompter. "To make room, you'd have to relocate the lazy do-nothing Republicans, and then where would they go?"

Crazy Bird folded his arms. "We cannot return. The old ways are gone. Here we are fed and housed." He looked sternly at Patty. "So you gonna keep injector program?"

Patty slid her arm around the chief's shoulder, looked solemnly into the cameras, and swore she would. "Chief, I will not only keep the program, we will make reparations to the Potowmacks. Your people will have all the food, drugs, and needles they want."

"We not need to work for these things?"

"Oh, no, Chief," Patty assured him. "Everything your people need will be provided for free by the government. We're going to rescue you from this."

Nigel crossed in front of the teleprompter, inadvertently blocking Crazy Bird's view of it.

The chief began to stammer. "Since the days… Since the days… Since the days…"

Nigel jumped out of his way.

Crazy Bird forged on. "Since the days of my forefathers, the white man's words have been empty. First the white man says we may stay in our swamp in the east, then he tells us we must go to Indiana, but we may stay there forever. Then he moves us across the father of rivers to this place of tall grass and strong wind, but the buffalo are gone, killed by the white man for sport. Why should we believe your promises?"

"Because until now the chief and his people have been dealing with men," Patty replied. "Men will not help the Potowmacks. Men bad. Women good."

Crazy Bird chuckled, his dark brown eyes falling lasciviously on Walks with a Limp. "Squaw good sometimes, when the moon is full and the teepee is cold." He looked across the hall at the supply room, stacked high with provisions. "How long will we get free stuff?"

"As long as the wind blows and the river flows, Great Chief."

The chief seemed lost in thought, as if he'd heard it all before. While the cameras zoomed in on Crazy Bird's pensive face, Patty took the pipe from Nigel and cradled it in her hands. "We can smoke on it, if you like, Chief."

The chief turned his back on her. "I smoke no peace pipe with the whites," he said gruffly. "That was the big mistake of my forefathers. It is why we are in this awful place." A few seconds passed. Crazy Bird glanced at his squaw and roared, "I said, it is why we are in this awful place."

Jolted out of her daydream, Walks with a Limp hobbled up to the chief, wagging her finger at him. "This woman offers us kindness. So you will not have peace with her? Then I will." Turning to Patty, she lifted a necklace of beads from her own shoulders and placed it around the candidate's neck. "What the hell, honey, we gonna give you a chance."

"What?" Crazy Bird mounted a feeble protest, raising his fist stiffly. "I am the chief of the Potowmacks, woman, not you."

Walks with a Limp tossed her head scornfully. "I believe the white squaw's promises. She is fair and just, and she bends low in respect to us. You men cling to your wounded pride, which buys us nothing. It is high time for a squaw to be chief—here and in Washington."

"Never!" The chief threw his head back in contempt.

Undeterred, Walks with a Limp raised her right hand in salute. "Great Squaw, I give you the necklace of peace. From this day on we call you Peewaukamucka. It is a great honor among the Potowmacks."

Patty ran her fingertips over the plastic necklace's fine Chinese beadwork. "How wonderful! Thank you, Walks with a Limp. I will treasure this gift always. Peewaukamucka—what does that mean?"

"She who bows to her knees, Great Squaw."

Patty put on a cloying smile, holding her pose for a full three seconds until the words "THE END" rolled across the teleprompter.

"Cut!" said Colleen. "It's a wrap. Thanks, everyone. Great job."

CHAPTER 19

Small Favors

JACK THREW HIS keys on his dresser, kicked off his shoes, and flopped on his bed in exhaustion. His long hunt for Rod Collier had ended—in the worst way.

Collier was dead. And not newly dead either. He'd been dead for years.

A coroner's report had popped up on Jack's screen while he was searching the county database. "Rodney Hawkins Collier, male, seventeen years of age," the form said. In the Cause of Death box was a single word: pneumonia. The intern died only months after his alleged affair with Pitypander.

The tragedy had claimed two victims. Since Collier was dead, the tale of his affair with Pitypander was dead too. How could Jack verify a rumor started by someone he couldn't interview? Gus wouldn't dream of accepting the story without solid proof.

The reporter's eyes turned fondly to his trophy wall and the reassuring green sash covered with Boy Scout merit badges. He'd mastered dozens of skills—knots, hiking, trailblazing, first aid, and many others. Mounted nearby was his Ranger award for rock climbing, and below it the engraved wooden oars and gold medals he'd won as captain of UCLA's championship rowing team.

The laurels of Jack's excellent adolescence smiled back at him. Or did they? Maybe they were mocking him, daring him to take them down, box them up, and see how little was left of his pride in this cruel adult world where he had yet to prove himself. His wall of glory would turn into a wall of reproach unless he added a fresh victory to it.

Jack's head swirled with existential angst. If he failed in his first real job, would he ever earn enough to make a dent in his student loan, buy a car that wouldn't drip antifreeze on his parents' driveway, and escape his childhood bedroom? Had Jack peaked too soon? Was he cut out for journalism, or should he have majored in some field that paid, one that could put some economic distance between himself and a Starbucks barista? Maybe it wasn't too late to switch to something with a prosperous if stultifying future, like tax accounting or hospital administration. His storm of self-doubt was interrupted by the merciful buzzing of his phone.

An email had arrived in his inbox:

> TO: jsnap@mushmail.com
> FROM: vsylvester@mushmail.com
> SUBJECT: Collier
>
> Hi, I knew Rod Collier.
> Vinny

Jack didn't recognize the name. Had he missed Vinny Sylvester in the Burbank High yearbook? His heart racing, Jack hit reply.

Nothing happened. The reply form did not appear. The screen on his phone was frozen.

Jack tapped the back button twice to close the email app. Was his contacts app still working? He touched its icon.

Jack's contacts had disappeared. A second later his phone darkened.

In a panic he shook the device, tapped it, pressed its on/off button, but still nothing happened. He had charged his phone only an hour earlier, so it couldn't be dead.

A virus. It's infected.

Vinny Sylvester's message would be on his laptop computer too, so Jack rushed to his desk and turned it on. He sagged against the back of the chair and sighed with relief. There was Vinny Sylvester's email.

But listed underneath it was another email that had just arrived. Jack clicked it open.

> TO: jsnap@mushmail.com
> FROM: collections@greatscott.com
> SUBJECT: Second Notice
>
> Dear Mr. Snap:
>
> This is your second notification that we have not received last month's payment in the amount of $979.23. Per your student loan agreement, a 10% penalty charge of $97.92 will be applied to your next month's balance if we do not receive payment within the next thirty days. In that event, your total payment due for next month will be $2,056.38.
>
> Yours truly,
> Great Scott Student Loan Corporation

Come up with two thousand dollars by next month? Jack's heart sank. Sponging off his devoted parents to feed his student debt monster was getting old. It was shameful.

Seconds later, his laptop computer also went dark. Jack pounded on the keys. "What the heck?"

Jack looked up at the ceiling, wondering if life could get any harder. What was happening to his electronic devices? Would his Fitbit bite the dust next?

The phone in the kitchen rang. Jack went in and picked it up.

It was the governor.

"Ah, Jack, so glad to have caught up with you," she said. "I called to see if you got home from Aspen okay. Is everything all right?"

What did she think, that he'd gotten lost somewhere between Aspen and Los Angeles? That one of her Gulfstreams had crashed on the way without her hearing about it? How weird was this woman?

"I'm not really all right, but thanks."

"Oh, what's wrong?"

Should he bother telling her? Why not? Jack vented his frustrations, griping about his phone, his laptop, and his student loan. He let it all out, except for the tragic news about her intern's untimely demise.

"Your phone? Oh, dear. That sounds awful."

"Yeah, it was a good one too. Cost a thousand bucks." The words had barely passed his lips when Jack realized how trifling they must sound to a billionaire. Pitypander probably tipped her pedicurist more than a thousand dollars.

"Goodness! Are phones that much?" she asked. "Would you like a new one? I'd be happy to have it replaced."

"No, thanks."

"Oh, well then, how about the laptop?"

"That's okay. I'm guessing it's a computer virus. I'll take care of it. I have a geeky friend who fixes computers."

"Well, is there anything I can do about your student loan? Maybe I could help."

"No, thanks."

"Maybe we could get them to change it for you. Who's the lender? I'll have someone call them and have your interest rate lowered."

Lower my rate? Pitypander could make that happen? Of course she could—with the snap of her fingers. If the Democratic candidate for president asked, the stone-hearted Great Scott Student Loan Corporation would be falling all over itself to cut his rate.

But accepting her help would be wrong. Jack had principles. As he'd learned from his free trip to Aspen, there were no free favors, especially for an investigative reporter hunting big game.

"No, thanks, Governor," he said with an anguished sigh. "I'll figure it out." He thanked her for her concern and politely ended the call.

As Jack had hoped, his geeky friend was able to clear the virus off his phone and computer, and his lost emails magically reappeared. Greatly relieved, Jack rejoiced that his difficult day had ended with a breakthrough: a new source, someone who had known Rod Collier. Jack sent Vinny Sylvester a reply at once.

VINNY'S EMAIL SAID to be at the takeout window of Jumpin' Johnny's Pizza Parlor at three o'clock sharp.

Jack remembered the place from his high school days. A popular hangout for teenagers, the pizza joint was right on the Circle Beach boardwalk near the Muscle Beach outdoor gym and the skatepark, next to Ingrid's tattoo parlor and a Segway rental shop. Jumpin' Johnny's offered a hundred different toppings and pizza by the slice.

Arriving early, Jack took a seat on a nearby park bench. The street performers hadn't changed. The incredible English bulldog still zoomed down the sidewalk by himself with his four paws perched on a skateboard. The BMX dude still did one-handed wheelies on his bike, spinning like a gymnast. The fearless Glass Man still leapt barefoot onto slivers of broken glass and walked away unscathed every time.

Free spirits like them would always be here. Circle Beach was a kind of sanctuary for the professionally uncommitted, like a college campus but without the drudgery of classes and exams. Here nobody cared if you never grew up, never got a real job, never made it as a journalist. Life as a street performer had its advantages, like total freedom. As long as you could wow the crowd and fill your hat with tips.

At three Jack stood at the takeout window and asked to talk to Vinny. The cashier turned around and tapped someone in the kitchen on the shoulder. A door opened around the side of the building, and out came a young bearded man with brown hair.

"You're Vinny Sylvester?" Jack asked.

"Yeah, that's me."

"Jack Snap, reporter for *The Burbank Bee*. I'm the guy you emailed, the one who posted the online notice about Rod Collier."

Vinny blinked, looking down for a second. "Sure, what do you wanna know about him? We're kinda busy here, so we'll have to make it fast. I'm on my fifteen-minute break."

"How did you know him?"

"Let's go inside." Vinny led Jack to a table in the pizza parlor and handed him a menu. "We make the best sausage and cheese pizza in Southern California."

It was the best, Jack remembered, reviewing the menu. "Sorry, I can't eat it. Girlfriend's orders."

Vinny laughed. "The Vegan Vow, huh?"

Jack hung his head. "Yeah, it's killing me. How did you know?"

"Veganism's going around like a frickin' disease, man. It's an epidemic. I had a vegan girlfriend myself last year. Didn't last more than a couple months though."

"What happened?" Jack asked.

"Not worth the self-denial. A man's gotta eat. Food before females. It's a matter of priorities, dude. The hierarchy of needs."

Jack bought a slice of vegan pizza to go. Covered with red peppers and onions, it stank like rotting garbage. The reporter pushed it aside, pulled out his notepad and pen, and asked again how Vinny knew Rod.

Vinny looked around the restaurant. No one was sitting nearby. He turned back toward Jack. "Rod was a high school friend of mine," he said softly.

Jack leafed through some photocopied pages from the Burbank High yearbook. "Funny, I didn't see your name in here."

"Yeah, well, that's 'cause I went to Glendale High. Also, I didn't graduate, so I'm not in their yearbook either. Couldn't put up with school any longer. I never was into school anyway. Too much pressure."

What did Vinny know about the rumor? Jack thought about how to ask the question so as not to lead Vinny to any predetermined answer. "So, there's this, um, rumor about Rod back when he was in high school. Have you heard it?"

Vinny's face tightened. "Yeah, he told me about it. The idiot, he told all his friends about it. I didn't believe him. I don't think anybody believed him."

"Why not?" Jack asked.

"A fifty-year-old governor getting it on with a high school kid? Who would believe it? It's too weird."

Jack's heart quickened. So Vinny had heard the rumor. He was a qualified source. "I would believe it, if I had proof."

"Can't help you there." Vinny looked out the window at the boardwalk. "Anyway, what does it matter? Rod's dead. Yep, dead as a doornail."

"Tell me about it. What happened?"

"Car accident. His car went off a cliff, poor guy."

Jack put down his pen. "What?"

"Went too fast for the curve. Blew right through the guardrail and crashed into the ocean. Somewhere around Durango Beach. That's what I heard."

Jack leaned forward. "Wait a minute. The death certificate at the county records office says Rod Collier died of pneumonia."

Vinny scratched his beard. "Oh, well, maybe he died of pneumonia at the hospital. Maybe as a complication from a punctured lung or internal injuries or something like that."

Now Vinny was speculating. His dubious explanation wouldn't cut it with Gus. The old editor would demand hard facts and lots of them. The details of Collier's death had to be nailed down.

Jack would have to dig deeper. "Are you sure about this accident thing? Did you hear about it from Collier's family? Where are the Colliers? I can't find them either."

Vinny's eyes darted around the restaurant. "I learned about the accident from a friend, weeks after it happened, so I might have some details messed up. I heard his family moved back East, to Massachusetts, or maybe Connecticut. Or was it New York? I can't remember. Anyway, you won't find them around here anymore."

Vinny's information was hearsay, but it was better than nothing. "Who's the friend who told you about the accident?" Jack asked, pressing for more leads. "Do you know how I can contact him?"

Vinny shrugged. "No, I haven't seen him for a long time. But you could check with the police about the accident. They'd know." He looked up at the clock on the wall. "Hey, my break's over. I gotta go make some pies, dude." Vinny got up and disappeared through the swinging doors to the restaurant's kitchen.

Jack bit into his slice of vegan pizza and spit it out. Every bit as bad as expected.

"**DISPOSABLE DIAPERS AREN'T** resonating with the voters." Nigel paced the floor of the conference room. He seemed quite sure.

Patty lifted her eyes from the campaign status report. "Who says?"

"Chassidy. She had her pollsters ask a thousand seniors if getting free disposable diapers would make them more or less likely to vote for you. The answer was a resounding thumbs-down. Your likability numbers actually sank."

It was Mama's bright idea. Disposable diapers were a big expense for the ladies on the Horizons House pickleball team, and Mama thought giving the things away for free would be a surefire way to win over the senior set.

"Maybe Chassidy wrote the question wrong," Patty suggested. "Her wording may have had some anti-diaper bias in it. That's a thing, isn't it?"

Nigel clicked on the remote control for the television. "I don't think so. Look at this."

The video clip opened at an assisted living center at The Villages in Florida, with Patty speaking to a group of white-haired ladies in wheelchairs.

"And with this benefit added to your Medicare coverage you'll never have to worry about how to pay for your Depends again. You can Depend on me." Patty gave a cringe-inducing wink. The camera panned around the room for the elderly voters' reactions.

Nigel hit the pause button. The screen froze on a woman who was fast asleep, her mouth wide open.

"That doesn't mean anything," Patty said. "She's tired, the poor dear."

Nigel handed her Chassidy's report. "Our focus groups say the same thing. With all due respect to your saintly mother, free diapers don't poll well. At best they're a snore. To seniors they're a degrading subject. They think you're pandering to them."

"Pandering, me?" Patty skimmed through the report. "Maybe we're targeting our diapers at the wrong people. Young mothers will appreciate them, I'll bet."

"Possibly, but we have a bigger problem," Nigel said. "Diebold has launched another massive smear campaign against us." He clicked the remote again.

Black clouds rolled across the top of the television screen as the narrator described Pitypander's despotism in an ominous baritone: "Imposing her petty tyrannies on the people of California, the governor rammed a bill through the legislature appointing a fifty-million-dollar-a-year Straw Nazi to lord over consumers."

The head of the California Office of Restaurant Plastic Reduction, a bald man with a grim stare, appeared disapprovingly above a box of plastic straws.

"As this bureaucrat's power over the minutia of their daily lives expanded," the narrator continued, "Californians soon found themselves prohibited from using plastic cutlery."

The scene switched to the headquarters building of the Environmental Protection Agency in Washington. "Governor Pitypander wants to do to you what she did to California. Reject Pitypander's nanny state. Vote for freedom. In November, be bold—vote Diebold."

Patty scowled at the screen. "Oh, that's mean."

Nigel hit the pause button. "That's nothing. They're going after your fitness for office too. Look at this." Patty's interview with the host of *Meet the Media* appeared.

"Why do you think you have a shot at taking Texas from President Diebold, Governor Pitypander?" the interviewer asked.

"Because, Peter, Texans have been independent-minded throughout history," Patty replied, her voice brimming with confidence. "Ever since Daniel Boone beat the Indians at the Alamo, Texans have stood tall against oppression. That's why I believe they will stand tall with me in my efforts to bring economic justice to all Texans today."

The interviewer, biting his cheek, informed Patty that Daniel Boone opened up Kentucky, not Texas, and the Texans were wiped out at the Alamo—by Mexicans, not Indians.

Patty made an indignant face. "Oh, yes, I know that. I misspoke."

Two Fess Parker movies from the 1950s appeared on the screen, side by side. On the left, Parker was wearing a coonskin cap, playing Davey Crockett defending the Alamo in Texas. On the right, wearing the same hat, the actor was Daniel Boone fighting Indians in Kentucky.

"Remember the Alamo?" asked the announcer. "Patty Pitypander sure doesn't. Don't buy her Hollywood version of Texas. In November, vote for a real Texan, born and bred. Be bold—vote Diebold."

Nigel paused the video. "There goes Texas. Diebold's blitzing the whole state with this, portraying you as an ignorant fraud who doesn't know the first thing about Texas. Your poll numbers are tanking even in Austin. You can forget Kentucky too. Authenticity, Patty. We need authenticity!"

"So what do you propose?"

"We've got to hit back, good and hard. I asked our media people to develop some ads to counter Diebold's." Nigel clicked the remote again. "This one's only eight seconds, so we can afford to run it a zillion times. We'll burn it into the voters' frontal lobes until they're reciting it in their sleep."

Diebold stood on a stage with his hand resting on the shoulder of a young woman in front of him, seeming to nuzzle her hair from behind. The picture froze with Diebold's nose at the woman's ear, as a female voice-over followed: "Hair sniffing, groping, butt-slapping, misogyny. Had enough, ladies? Join the Patty Party and fight back. Vote Pitypander."

A dozen video clips followed, each an example of the catastrophic effects Diebold's Clean Slate program would have, especially on women: pregnant mothers banging on the doors of shuttered maternity wards, a woman with a fistful of food stamps rejected by supermarket cashiers, mothers with their tearful children standing at the padlocked doors of a school closed due to lack of government aid.

Patty's eyes perked up. "Ah, excellent. Diebold at his most heartless. Run them all."

"There's one other thing we need to discuss." Nigel turned off the television. "It's Jack Snap again. He's filed a freedom-of-information request to get the official police report on Collier."

Patty's face froze.

"He's stubborn, this one is. Your small favors didn't work. We'll have to try a bigger one."

CHAPTER 20

Benny's Deal

BENNY WAS A whirlwind of activity, running around the Palace and barking orders from the parking lot to the penthouse. Kim Il Bong's return to Macau must go off without a hitch.

This time Benny knew the dictator was coming. He could prepare.

The resort's employees scrambled to and fro. Between the marble columns they hung thirty-foot posters of the chairman saluting his people. In the hallways they mounted worshipful scenes of the Great Leader vanquishing greedy capitalists. Above the gaming tables they strung banners denouncing capitalist decadence.

They must make the chairman feel at home, Benny decreed. Any employee Kim was likely to encounter, from the front desk to the casino, must be fluent in Korean and smartly outfitted in the green military uniform of the Democratic People's Republic of Korea. A flask of Jack Daniel's and a mahogany box containing the finest Cuban cigars must grace every table in Kim's VIP suite.

At the appointed hour, Benny stood at the front desk with the jangled nerves of an expectant father, test-smoking a cigar for quality.

The doors of the hotel flung open. In marched the Great Leader's four-foot five-star general, trailing a squad of goose-stepping infantrymen brandishing machine guns. The front desk clerks raised their hands in surrender, dutifully handing over key cards to the rooms.

The soldiers unfurled a red carpet bearing a yellow hammer and sickle into the lobby. In strode the Great Leader himself.

"Chairman Kim." Benny bowed low to his guest. "Welcome back."

Kim acknowledged the hotelier's presence with a slight nod. "Mr. Pitypander." He proceeded to the elevator.

After an hour to refresh himself from his long train ride, Kim entered the casino, making a beeline for the roulette table. Benny, standing at the entrance with a tray in his hands, offered him a Jack Daniel's, neat.

"Thank you, Mr. Pitypander." Kim plucked it off the tray, gulped it down, and surveyed the roulette table. "Red twenty-five."

His defense minister, carrying a sack of chips, counted out a ten-thousand-dollar bet on red twenty-five. The roulette ball rolled around the roulette wheel several times and settled into a slot.

"The winner is…the winner is…forgive me, black seventeen," the croupier said in distress.

Kim emitted a low growl, his face forming a death stare. The four-foot five-star general jumped forward with his pistol. The croupier, his eyes bugging out, threw up his hands.

Benny rushed to the croupier's side, pointing to a table nearby. "We have prepared a special roulette wheel for you over here, Great Chairman. It may be more to your liking."

Without a word Kim raised his glass toward the other table and proceeded to go there, his entourage following in his footsteps.

"Black twenty-eight," the chairman called out.

The defense minister pushed twenty thousand dollars in chips toward the croupier, regarding him suspiciously. The croupier, his forehead dabbled with sweat, sent the roulette ball on its way around the wheel's rim. It fell into the slot at black twenty-eight.

Kim turned to his diminutive general in triumph. "Aha! You see? That is more like it, is it not?"

The general's dour expression softened into a tentative smile. The defense minister, no less amazed, sprawled his arms over the edge of the table and raked in the windfall.

Kim, lifting his chin, turned to inspect the faces of his soldiers. They smiled and broke into applause in unison. He took a swig of bourbon. "Red five."

The defense minister laid another twenty thousand dollars in chips on the table. The croupier, his demeanor somewhat calmer than before, launched the ball on its way.

Headed for black ten, it bounced out of that slot and obediently rolled over to red five.

Kim jerked his head back. "There, there you see!" He slapped his shocked defense minister on the back. The minister rushed up again to gather the booty, and the Great Chairman's pile of chips inched taller.

Benny, standing by with arms folded, signaled for a waiter to refill Kim's glass.

The chairman downed his whiskey in two gulps and held out his glass for more. "Black fifteen," he commanded.

The ball seemed sure to fall into red thirty-six but abruptly slowed and settled onto black fifteen. The icy stares of the soldiers melted into broad smiles.

Kim radiated with childlike joy. "This is more like it."

Emboldened, he attempted another ten spins of the wheel and won every one. His soldiers cheered at the miracle, slapping one another on the back, astounded at the Great Leader's feat.

Having mastered roulette, Kim cast his eyes across the casino in search of new worlds to conquer. Benny pointed to a blackjack table.

Everyone moved over in lockstep to it. Miraculously, the chairman won eight hands in a row.

Next Benny directed Kim to a slot machine, where the chairman's every pull of the handle rewarded him with a jackpot.

The jubilant defense minister, unable to contain himself any longer, gushed with patriotic fervor. "Clearly you have outwitted the greedy capitalists at their own games of thievery, oh Master of All He Attempts! Your boundless skill brings the most extreme joy to all your people!"

A photographer for the Pyongyang People's Press scooted forward and knelt down before the Dear Leader, snapping his picture in his moment of inexpressible glory.

Accepting the plaudits of his troops, the Victorious One turned to Benny, wobbling over to his host, his fourth glass of whiskey in hand.

"Would you like to try another game, Mr. Chairman?" Benny asked. "We have many more."

"Enough gambling for now, Mr. Pitypander. Before I get too drunk to stand, we have some business to discuss. Show me the plans for my new resort."

"Of course, Great Chairman. Right this way."

Benny led Kim to a room with easels holding the drawings of the Wonsan Pitypander Palace. The proposed hotel was to be magnificent, forty stories tall, modeled on the same building they were standing inside.

Benny presented the artwork with a flourish of his hand. "Your own gambling resort, Great Chairman, as you requested."

Kim bent forward, absorbing the fine details of the renderings. "Ah, most impressive."

Wielding a pointer, Benny identified the lobby, ballrooms, restaurants, shops, conference rooms, theaters, performance halls, atriums, dancing water fountains, and the enormous gambling floor.

"One hundred twenty-five thousand square feet, Great Chairman. Here you see a fully equipped, world-class casino, complete with every game we offer here in Macau. Bigger than anything they have in South Korea. Even bigger than the Happy Luck Casino in Seoul."

"Ah, even bigger than that? Yes, mine must be much bigger!" Kim turned to his defense minister. "That will bring us some foreign currency, will it not?"

Kim stepped closer to the sketches, his eyes fixed on the drawing depicting his bronze statue. The forty-foot figure's outstretched hands gripped two marble columns in a Samson-like pose, as if his likeness was holding up the building and removing it would pull the edifice down on his unworthy subjects' heads. "How many rooms will there be in the hotel?" the Great Chairman asked. "And what about security?"

Benny swelled with pride. Like all Pitypander hotels, the Wonsan Palace would be gargantuan, with the tightest security in the industry. "It will have three thousand rooms, Chairman Kim, each furnished with the latest in surveillance equipment, including face-recognizing cameras. Not so much as a fly will dare enter your resort without your knowledge and consent."

"Three thousand?" The smile left Kim's face. He crossed his arms, stamped his foot, and sneered. "I demand four thousand rooms, not one less."

Benny dropped his pointer on the floor. The plans were perfect to the last detail. He had hired the finest casino architects in the world and paid them three times their usual fee to finish the design in record time.

"Please understand, Great Chairman," Benny explained, his apprehension growing. "Your building site is small. Putting another thousand rooms on it would cost me three hundred million dollars. That would blow my budget."

"*Your* budget? You dare to set a budget for my palace?" Kim's eyes opened wide. "Insolence!"

The four-foot five-star general aimed his pistol at a chandelier and discharged three shots into it. Glass crystals rained down, clattering on the tile floor.

A jagged sliver landed on Benny's right shoe. He jumped back. "I, I guess we could build the hotel a little taller, Great Chairman. I'll have the plans revised. Four thousand rooms it is."

Next came the review of the partnership documents. Benny swallowed hard as the dictator's eyes stopped on the crucial page—the one about profit-sharing.

"Fifty percent?" Kim slammed his bourbon glass on the table. "You think I am a fool? You will have ten percent of the profits, not a single penny more."

"Ten percent?" Benny squealed like a stuck pig. "But, Great Leader, the Pitypander name alone is worth a fifty percent share. I'm putting up the capital. How can I make a decent return with only a ten percent share?"

"You bargain with me as if I were a fishmonger." Kim's eyes seethed. "Being allowed to build my pleasure palace is its own reward, is it not? I am contributing the people's labor. You are merely supplying capital. Is labor not superior to capital? Do you want to do business in my country or not?"

Benny took a step back. "But last time you were here, Great Chairman, I thought we agreed—"

"You thought?" Kim hurled his glass into the wall, the fragments scattering across the floor. "How much more thinking would you care to do, Mr. Pitypander?"

The four-foot five-star general thrust out his arm and pointed his pistol at Benny's temple.

Benny squeezed his eyes shut. Weren't his brains worth a few billion dollars? "Aaaah! I have finished thinking, Great Chairman," he shrieked. "Ten percent it is!"

Kim waved his hand. "Done. Make it so." He turned his back to Benny and folded his arms in disgust. "I grow weary of this tedious business."

Benny felt a bead of sweat dribbling down his cheek. "Uh, would you care to gamble some more, Dear Leader?"

Kim's mouth turned up in a wry smile. "I think I have won quite enough here for one day." He turned back around, raised his hands, and clapped them twice in the air. "It is time to see the leisure women."

"Oh, the women. Yes, the women." Benny had forgotten all about them. "They are waiting for us in the spa, Great Chairman. Right this way."

CHAPTER 21

A Soul Above Money

THE POWDER-BLUE BMW convertible parked in his parents' driveway caught Jack's eye as soon as he woke up and looked out the window. He got dressed and walked outside to take a better look.

According to a sticker on the car, it was equipped with a five-hundred-horsepower turbocharged engine, leather twenty-way power seats, and twelve-speaker surround-sound audio system. The roadster didn't belong to his parents. It couldn't belong to anyone in this middle-class neighborhood. Whose was it?

Jack walked around the side to take it in. Whoever had left it there wouldn't mind if he got in, just for second, would they? After all, it was parked in his family's driveway. He opened the door and sat in the front seat.

A phone rang inside the car. The sound was coming from the middle of the dashboard, where a green button marked TALK lit up. Jack touched it.

The screen turned on, showing a woman's smiling face.

"Surprise!" said the face.

"Governor, is that you?"

"So how do you like the car? Nifty, huh? The dealership told me it'll do zero to sixty in under four seconds."

Jack gripped the soft black leather on the steering wheel. It was like sitting in the cockpit of a jet fighter. There were more buttons, gauges, and controls than he had ever seen in a car. What did they all do?

"It's...it's awesome. But what's it doing here?"

The governor giggled. "It's a little token of my affection. I leased it for you. I'm so glad you like it. I didn't see any point in waiting for your birthday."

Jack noticed a small "Durango BMW Leasing" sticker affixed to the bottom corner of the windshield, with a time stamp indicating the car had been delivered an hour ago.

The convertible embraced Jack, coddling him in luxury. He ran his fingertips over the tan leather seats and caressed the buttons on the audio system. He jiggled the stick shift's rosewood handle. What a rush he would get from throwing this puppy into high gear and blowing the doors off every vehicle on the interstate.

Like it? He loved it.

The new-car smell teased Jack's nostrils. He pressed the button for the convertible top, and down it went, making a whirring sound, clicking into place like the tumblers of a lock.

The machine was a marvel of German engineering. But a token of her affection? Pitypander was acting weird again. A knot formed in Jack's stomach.

As he peered through the BMW's tinted windshield, imagining himself hurtling down the highway at Mach 2, his eyes landed on the ancient Honda Civic parked under his parents' carport. A tinge of guilt rose up in him, in revolt against his senses. The sixteenth-birthday gift from his parents—a hand-me-down—had served him faithfully, seeing him through high school and college. A patch for its torn seat and a new pair of front tires were all the old jalopy needed to get it through the next few months. Jack wanted a new car, but not one he'd have to explain to his family and friends, not one worth more than both his parents' salaries combined.

Jack squeezed the roadster's steering wheel and slapped it twice with the palm of his hand. "Nope. Can't do it."

"What's that?"

"Thank you, Governor, the car's great but I can't accept it. Wouldn't be right."

The smile on the dashboard screen turned into a frown. "Don't be silly. I want you to have it. It's for you. You'll enjoy it."

Jack hesitated. *Not so fast. Let's think about this.* Here was a golden opportunity for another interview. The police report he'd received yesterday had raised critical new questions about Collier. Gus had hired Jack because of his special access to this woman. It was his duty to use it.

Jack offered to drive the BMW back down to Durango Beach. They could discuss the gift at her mansion.

"That would be lovely, but I'm on Martha's Vineyard at our summer cottage," the governor replied. "I know, why don't you meet me here?" She gave Jack a choice: hitch a ride there on her Gulfstream, or wait until she returned to California—in three weeks. "I'd love to see you, Jack. Bring your bathing suit. The weather's perfect."

Three weeks? That was much too long. Gus's words echoed in Jack's head: "Are you gonna hit it hard this time? You promise you won't pull any punches with Pitypander?"

Martha's Vineyard it would be.

LYING BACK IN her Adirondack chair, Patty groaned at the extensive revisions Red Meat Speech Number Two would need.

She lifted her eyes from the page. What a shame to work on a political speech with the Pitypander compound at the height of its summer glory! The rose garden behind the old mansion was a profusion of red and yellow blossoms. Sailboats meandered aimlessly up and down the shore in a disorganized flotilla, driven by a lazy August breeze. Seagulls cawed in the cloudless sky, as if trying to call Patty away from the pressing work on her lap. She couldn't let them. Red Meat Speech Number Two must be ready for next week's Ladybug rally in St. Louis.

Number Two suffered from the same defect as her nine other stock speeches. It was far too easy on Diebold. Nigel advised she would lose ground in the polls if she didn't match her opponent's stepped-up attacks on her competence. The section of the address where she accused the president of harassing women lacked a knockout punch:

> I ask you, what part of 'no' don't men like P. Trayson
> Diebold understand? Why do we put up with a catcall-
> ing, hair-sniffing, girl-grabbing Republican like him in
> our White House?

Too mild and too vague, she realized. Diebold had committed flagrant acts of sexual misconduct. The speech didn't mention his sleazy affair with Dolly Newton, his secretary when he was a congressman. It ignored his rumored fling with Lindsey Copeland, the young aide he'd harassed during his first presidential campaign. If Diebold was slandering Patty as unfit, why hold back?

"No sense playing nice now," Nigel had cautioned. With autumn approaching, the long knives would be coming out from both campaigns.

Patty scribbled a note for her speechwriters: "Get tough. No more hinting. Be specific. Mention Newton and Copeland scandals explicitly. Go for the jugular."

A snipping noise came from the rose garden. Patty looked up to see a shirtless young man with short brown hair, standing amid the shrubs with pruning shears, lopping off dead branches. She guessed he was about eighteen.

Enough speechifying for one day, Patty decided. Ringing the bell on her side table, she summoned the maid for a lemonade on ice. When the drink arrived, she carried it to the rose garden and offered it to the youth. He took the glass with a grateful smile and gulped the beverage down.

Patty grasped a flower by the stem, careful to avoid its thorns. "My goodness, we do have a bumper crop this year, don't we?" Her eyes roved back and forth between the roses and the gardener's taut abdominal muscles. "I don't believe I've ever seen so many."

The teenager agreed there were a lot.

"I think I'll cut some for the front parlor," Patty said.

"I'll do it," he quickly replied.

"No, I'd like to do it. I need the exercise."

Gathering roses was exactly the kind of relaxing work she needed to take her mind off the campaign. Patty walked into the house, donned a straw hat, slipped on leather gloves, and set about working in her garden.

With so many flowers, where should she start? Patty picked a spot a few feet away from the bemused gardener. "Oh, don't mind me. Just keep doing what you're doing. I won't get in your way. I'll work over here."

The newest roses, having just broken open their buds and unfurled their petals, lasted longest in water, someone told her once. Patty hunted for the bud-breakers, her eyes sweeping back and forth every other minute across the garden, always returning to the youth. He seemed to take no notice of her. He must be shy.

"Goodness, aren't these marvelous?" Patty asked.

Silence.

"I said, aren't these marvelous?"

The bashful young gardener agreed they were, but kept his distance.

"Would you like another lemonade?" she asked.

"No, ma'am."

So it went: a snip here, another there, and another stolen glance at her gardener. Within ten minutes Patty had reaped enough fresh flowers to fill a dozen vases. In twenty minutes she had enough to supply every florist shop on Martha's Vineyard. Soon she had slaughtered half her garden.

"Sure you don't want another lemonade?"

"No, ma'am. I'm fine."

"Oh, well, suit yourself." Patty checked her watch. Jack was due soon anyway. Carrying a basket full of roses around the side of the mansion, she noticed a taxi stopped at the compound's gatehouse.

Jack was early.

THE YOUNG REPORTER was approaching the door when Patty, carrying her flower basket, intercepted him outside.

"Hello, Governor," he muttered.

Something was different about Jack today. He moved slowly, cautiously, with a businesslike seriousness in his face. She sensed he hadn't flown across the country for chitchat.

Patty led him to some chairs on the flagstone terrace, where they could watch the seagulls circling the beach. It was so romantic there. She wondered if Jack would think so.

Perhaps a drink would loosen Jack up. She asked the maid to bring her a mimosa with some cheese and crackers. She tried to interest Jack in something alcoholic, a beer at least, but he would only have a lemonade.

"Some cheese?"

He refused it, saying he was still observing his Vegan Vow. Fanny had not relaxed her iron grip on him.

"Oh, yes, I forgot. Well, I admire your fortitude." She bit into a slice of Brie de Meaux.

"Governor, I don't know if you've heard, but Rod Collier's dead."

Patty's hand flew to her chest. "Oh, no. That's awful. Oh, dear. How did it happen?"

Jack said he was still looking into it, there was something fishy about the details of the story, and maybe she would have some ideas that would point him in the right direction.

He reached into a folder for something—a death certificate. "It says here he died of pneumonia, but a friend of his told me Rod died in a car crash."

Patty shuddered. "A car crash? Oh, that's terrible. He was so young. His poor parents, they must be heartbroken."

Jack took out another document. "I was able to find this police report on the crash, but it doesn't say anything about Rod's death. I guess it's possible he hadn't died yet, but it doesn't mention any injuries either, even though his car flew off a cliff."

She looked away from him, toward the beach. "Oh, how sloppy of the police."

"Maybe," Jack said slowly, glancing at the report. "Or it could be there weren't any injuries. Suppose there wasn't anybody in the car? But that's impossible. How could a car have gone off a cliff with nobody inside?"

"Hmm, an interesting question. You've certainly done your homework. What do you think happened to Rod?"

Jack waited a few seconds before answering. "It's pretty weird. The guy's car crashes without anybody in it? It seems like some kind of setup. It makes me wonder if Rod Collier is really dead."

Jack stared hard, like he was X-raying her head. The reporter had never looked at her so intently before, much as she'd yearned for him to. Patty folded her hands together, as if in prayer. "Oh, I do hope you're right. It's always a tragedy whenever anyone young dies. Oh, his poor parents. How they must have suffered."

"Did you know any of this, about the accident or Rod's death?"

"Goodness, no." Patty fidgeted in her chair, rubbing her knee with her fingers. "I never heard about Rod again after the summer he worked in my office. I didn't have time to pay attention to what interns did."

"There's another weird thing in this accident report." Jack's eyes drilled into her again. "The car Rod totaled was a BMW roadster, leased from Durango BMW, the same model you leased for me."

Patty almost spilled her drink on herself. Was Jack saying what she thought he was? "Surely you can't be suggesting I had anything to do with his car."

Jack remained silent for a moment. "I didn't mean to insult you, Governor. I'm just after the truth. It's my job."

She squeezed her lips into a pout. "I thought you'd like a nice car to drive. The people at the dealership said a young man would like that one, so I leased it for you. Here I was trying to send you a little peace offering to make up for our little misunderstanding and you start thinking I'm up to no good."

Jack drew back. "Uh, I didn't mean—"

"I thought you might at least appreciate my little gesture."

"I do appreciate it, but I can't accept it. I'm a reporter. That would be a conflict of interest, can't you see?"

Patty scoffed. "Don't be a sap. You think you're the first reporter in the world ever to get a little gift from a politician?"

He shifted in his chair. "A BMW roadster is a huge gift."

"If you're afraid of ending up at the bottom of a cliff in a car wreck, simply say the word and I'll have the lease canceled."

"That's not what I meant. I wasn't accusing you of anything."

She folded her arms. "Okay, what did you mean? Why did you come here? To interrogate me?"

He hesitated for a moment. "I came to tell you I'd like you to take the car back. I can't accept it."

"Then don't."

"Sorry to bother you, Governor. I shouldn't have come. Goodbye."

With that, Jack put down his lemonade, stood up, and walked away.

Patty watched him plod down the long driveway toward the gatehouse, her eyes following his every step. She wanted to say something but no words came to mind—except the desperate, pleading ones she dared not utter.

What were the right words to get him back? Patty had no idea. Everything that was supposed to draw Jack closer to her seemed to repel him. What would he accept from her, if not her gifts?

Her situation seemed eerily reminiscent of something that had happened to Jenessa Fuller once. Patty tried to remember which book it was and concluded it must have been *The Lover's Quarrel*.

Then Jenessa appeared.

"Your approach isn't working. I thought for sure you'd realize that by now."

Jenessa was sitting in Jack's chair, wearing a jaunty summer hat as if on her way to Royal Ascot.

"Oh, no," Patty moaned. "Please go away. I'm too upset to speak to you."

"Darling, one telltale sign it's not working is he's run away again. Get a clue."

Patty sighed. "I suppose you have the answer as usual?"

Jenessa swatted at a black fly, which failed to notice her presence. "Are the black flies always this bad on Martha's Vineyard?"

"Not always," Patty replied. "Sometimes they're twice as bad. So you were going to tell me what I'm doing wrong with him?"

"Don't you see, no bribe is ever going to control Jack Snap. He's one of those noble, self-righteous types, much like my Alphonse in *The Lover's Quarrel*. He has a soul above money."

Patty wondered how that could be. "But he's broke. No one needs money more than Jack. He lives in Burbank."

"It was the same with Alphonse, if you recall."

Patty remembered the basic plot of *The Lover's Quarrel*, but had gone foggy on the details. "Alphonse lived in Burbank too?"

Jenessa's lip curled at the suggestion. "Don't be absurd. No man named Alphonse has ever lived in Burbank, or ever will. I mean when I tried to buy Alphonse off, he spurned my money. Take my word for it, bribery won't work on your Jack either. He's awed by your wealth, but not attracted to it. I'm sure you can grasp the difference."

Patty paused to think. "I suppose there is a difference between being awed and attracted, but it's too subtle for me to grasp."

"Then I'll spell it out for you," Jenessa said. "First Jack's a journalist and now he's a vegan. Most young men have voracious appetites, yet Jack prides himself on self-denial. He's a born ascetic. To make matters worse, he has integrity. Are you getting the picture now?"

"No, I don't get his generation, Jenessa. They're a complete mystery to me. What is it they want? What on earth is wrong with Jack?"

Jenessa burst out laughing. "Wrong with him? Nothing, my dear. He's perfect, as you can plainly see. Those bedroom eyes, the dazzling blond hair, those scrumptious muscles your lonely heart aches to squeeze—they have you firmly in their grip. But that's your problem, not his. It's not his fault you can't keep your eyes off him."

"I don't mean Jack's body. I mean, what's wrong with his head?"

"Why, everything is wrong with it, because it's as young as his body," Jenessa said. "It's a mess of untested beliefs about self-sacrifice, heroism, moral superiority, searching for meaning, making the world a better place—notions only time and the bitter experience of living one's life can expunge."

"But those are silly ideas he got from school. I have things of real value to offer him, in the real world. Things that can make Jack happy, successful, and rich."

Jenessa smiled, her eyes following the meandering stone wall enclosing the estate. "You used to be very much like him when you were his age. You were going to save the world too, before you met Benny, before you had all this, before you sullied yourself with politics and power."

Patty still was trying to save the world, in her own way. That was what the Pitypander campaign was all about.

She boiled with frustration. "For the life of me, I don't understand him. I can only give Jack the things I've gained over the years, not the things I've lost."

"What have you gained, my dear?"

Patty looked at the basket of cut roses she had left near the garden. "Money, power, and influence."

"Jack has rejected those things. They will never be enough to win his heart."

"Nonsense." Patty stood up. "Jack has his price, like anyone else. I just need to find out what it is." She retrieved her basket of roses and headed inside.

CHAPTER 22

A Better Offer

THE THREE PALM trees were in the right place: middle of the park, opposite the softball field, and about a hundred yards from the metal archway at the street. Jack stepped toward them, dodged two small boys flying by on scooters, and checked his watch.

"Mr. Snap, over here." A tall, thin man on a bench was waving at him. He stood up to shake Jack's hand. "Nigel Windborne, at your service."

Jack had never met Pitypander's campaign manager, though he had seen him many times—lurking behind the governor at rallies, whispering in her ear on the Empathy Express, milling around the hors d'oeuvres at the castle fundraiser. No matter the occasion, he was always dressed in a gray suit, white shirt, and polka-dot necktie, ready to do business. He didn't seem to have an "off" button. He never looked relaxed, and he laughed in a fake way, like he was putting on a show.

The long-limbed aide sat down first. "I'll get to the point, Mr. Snap. Governor Pitypander deeply regrets the misunderstanding between you two. She thought perhaps I, being a divorce attorney accustomed to negotiating delicate personal matters, might be well suited to intercede on her behalf. To smooth the waters, as it were. I do hope you don't mind my getting involved."

"No, it's all right. Go ahead."

"Very well." Nigel's lips turned upward in a professional smile. "The governor is anxious to restore an amicable relationship with you. She is most impressed with your journalistic skills and would like to know if you would be interested in a job opening. She's looking for a communications specialist for her campaign staff."

Jack nearly fell off the bench. "You're kidding. She's offering me a job?"

"That's right. You'd be handling her dealings with the press, working for Colleen Cook."

"Your communications director?" Jack had seen Colleen Cook running the campaign's press briefings. The scuttlebutt among the campaign reporters was that Cook had quit her network reporter job after being sexually assaulted by a producer and had joined Pitypander to help elect a feminist. She seemed nice enough.

"Correct. The post pays well into six figures and would give you instant exposure to every major news organization in the world. You could report to work at your earliest convenience—the sooner the better. Colleen has scads of work ready for you."

Jack's head was spinning. "My God."

"Assuming the governor wins in November, there would also be a place for you on the White House communications staff as a senior adviser. And, as a hiring bonus, she proposes paying off your student loans in full."

Jack's income would instantly quintuple. He would make top-level contacts in the press and Democratic Party. He might end up with a high-profile job at the White House. Doors would fling open to him for the rest of his life.

"And what do I have to do for this?"

Nigel smiled. "Not much, my good man. Just forget."

"Forget what?"

"About the little misunderstanding at Aspen, and about Rod Collier and all that rot."

Jack could move out of his parents' bungalow and rent a place of his own. He could buy a decent car. He could travel on his own dime. He would be freed from his crushing student debt.

All the former Eagle Scout from Burbank needed to do was to let go of a few things—starting with Rod Collier and ending with his self-respect. Pitypander's offer was crass but simple: his silence for a golden future.

"No dice," Jack answered without further hesitation. "I'm not interested."

"What do you mean you're not interested? You must be."

"I'm not for sale."

Nigel rolled his eyes. "Are you mad, young man? This is the chance of a lifetime. You could make huge strides in your career."

"I know."

"Is there something wrong with the offer? Something we can work together to improve, perhaps? An additional sum of money? A better car?"

Jack wouldn't even ask what sum of money the governor might be willing to pay. It was irrelevant. "No, it's not the terms of the offer. The offer is what's wrong with the offer. You're trying to bribe me again."

Nigel stood up. "Now see here, Snap, you're making a big mistake. This is not a bribe. It's a bona fide offer of employment. Governor Pitypander has only so much time and patience for dealing with you. I assure you she won't take this well."

Jack looked up at him with a defiant smile. "Her royal highness can take it however she likes. I'm still not for sale."

"Not for sale," Nigel muttered. "Extraordinary." He stood motionless for a moment, as if unsure what to do next. He pulled a business card from his coat pocket. "Well, if you change your mind, here's how to reach me."

"Not gonna happen."

"I shall let her know." Nigel spun around and walked away.

THE WISDOM, OR folly, of rejecting the governor's offer sank in as soon as Nigel left the park. Jack contemplated the steep price he'd paid and hoped his soul was worth the sacrifice. His integrity was becoming painfully expensive to maintain.

The Collier scandal must be big. Not that there was much to go on yet: The few facts Jack had gathered about Rod Collier's death amounted to little more than conflicting threads of information and supposition—not nearly enough to satisfy Gus..

The old editor wasn't going to wait much longer. As Gus reminded him weekly, the story was as perishable as a ripe banana. Its value depended on being published before the election, now only two months away. If Pitypander lost to Diebold, she would become an instant has-been on the national scene and her old scandal would fade, like her political career, into total irrelevance. Nobody would care what sins she'd committed as governor.

Jack pulled out his phone to check his messages. Among the usual intra-office emails was one with "Collier" in the subject line, from a sender he didn't recognize: jzcrazy898@mushmail.com. He clicked on it. All the email contained was an address:

Rod Collier
393-B South Locust Street
Los Angeles, CA

Jack fell back against the park bench, his eyes lighting up. This was a breakthrough—the first time he'd seen Rod Collier's name connected to any place outside Burbank.

He entered the address into the maps app on his phone. It was in an apartment complex in Lincoln Heights, less than an hour away.

Jack ran out of the park to the *Bee's* parking lot and jumped into his Civic. Driving down the interstate, he wondered why someone would send him an anonymous email with nothing but an address.

He exited the freeway at Lincoln Heights, made two turns, and saw a dented entrance sign marked "Altura Heights." Why had he been led here? The block of garden apartments behind the sign was a dilapidated jumble of stucco and fake half-timbering from the 1960s, flanked by a small parking lot with faded striping. Rusty air-conditioning units protruded through the walls, punctuated by satellite dishes. Jack parked on the street and ran up two flights of stairs to unit 393-B. He knocked on the door, but no one answered.

Racing downstairs, he followed a little green sign pointing to the apartment manager's office and knocked there. A middle-aged Hispanic woman with a mole on her cheek opened the door a few inches.

The apartment manager barred the doorway. "Yes, what do you want?"

Jack told her he was a reporter trying to find Rod Collier, a former resident of 393-B.

"He is not here," replied the woman.

"I know. But I thought you might know when he was here. Do you remember anything about him?"

She moved closer to the door, her dark brown eyes probing him. "Are you with the FBI too?"

"The FBI's been here?" Jack asked. "What did they look like? Was there a short fat man, with glasses and a big nose?"

"I don't know you," the woman replied. "I no talk about residents. Sorry." She slammed the door in his face.

Jack banged on it with his fist. "Please, lady, I need your help!"

She shouted through the door, "No, go away. Or I call the police."

Jack leaned against a concrete pillar outside, pondering his next move. His eyes fell upon a mail truck parked at the street. A mailman lugging a leather sack shuffled past him, heading to a group of metal mailboxes in the wall.

Mailboxes! They would have the names of the apartment building's residents on them.

When the mailman finished his deliveries and walked away, Jack moved in. Each mailbox was identified with a peel-and-stick label. The one for apartment 393-B was marked "Romero." Jack slid his fingernail under the sticker and peeled it back.

Underneath was another label, this one with two names written on it: Collier and Sylvester. A black line had been drawn through Collier, but the name was still legible.

Jack whooped with joy, as if he'd found buried treasure. Rod Collier had once lived in 393-B, and so had Vinny Sylvester!

Wait a minute. Vinny never mentioned living with Rod Collier.

In an instant, everything Vinny had told Jack became suspect. Had Vinny purposefully withheld critical information, or worse, steered him away from useful leads?

Jack ran back to his car and drove out of the parking lot. As he looked into his rearview mirror, he noticed he wasn't alone. A white SUV had pulled out behind him. It stayed in his mirror for several blocks, hanging a few car lengths back. It followed him onto the interstate.

Jack maneuvered to the freeway's right lane and slowed to fifty-five miles per hour, as traffic zoomed past at seventy-five. The SUV stuck with him, mile after mile, crawling behind at low speed. When Jack reached the Burbank exit, the SUV turned off the interstate with him, finally veering away only when he arrived at the *Bee*.

As the SUV roared by, Jack strained to see through its tinted glass. There was only one person inside—a man—and he wasn't Agent Seven.

CHAPTER 23

The Intimidation

"**HOW COULD HE** turn my offer down? It would change his whole life." Patty flung her newspaper on the restaurant floor. "You're a man. You must understand him. Tell me, how can we get through to him?"

"I haven't the foggiest," Nigel replied, reaching across the table for another tea bag. He picked up the pitcher of hot water, poured it into his cup, and stirred in some cream. "Snap insisted he can't be bought. It's most remarkable, even admirable, considering his meager prospects at his miserable little newspaper. He's as determined as ever, that much is clear. An hour after I met with him our man followed him to Collier's old flat in Lincoln Park."

"Lincoln Park? Oh, no!"

"He's getting too close for comfort."

The furrows in Patty's brow deepened. "Maybe Jack's holding out for more. What if we increase our offer?"

"Increase it to what? You've offered him the moon," Nigel said. "Also, I tried that straightaway. Snap was quite emphatic about his disinterest in being bribed. It's a matter of manly honor for him. He's a stubborn young fool on a moral crusade. That sort never learns."

Jenessa was right. Jack did have a soul above money. But did he have a soul above fear? Patty hadn't tested his courage.

Patty picked up her fork and slashed her omelet to pieces. Her father wouldn't have tolerated some kid endangering his political future. The Boston mobsters who had installed Luigi Ingratelli at city hall never showered gifts on anyone—they made simple physical threats a moron could understand. Lots of problems went away, Papa observed, if you led people to believe you were willing to smash their kneecaps. Whether you would actually do it or not was beside the point, because you never had to. Recalcitrant union leaders, unco-operative businessmen, and even principled newspaper reporters got the message. Most people were abject cowards.

"Rule by fear, Patty, my dear," she muttered.

"What's that?"

Patty sat back with a smile, picturing her father at the dinner table so many years ago. "Just a little nursery rhyme my papa taught me. He would pick up a napkin and pretend it was a puppet in his hand and point it at me. The puppet would say, 'Rule by fear, that's the ticket, Patty, my dear.' And we would all laugh, Mama, Marco, and me. We knew Papa would never actually break anyone's kneecaps, but the bad guys didn't."

Rule by fear? Why wouldn't a bluff work today? Weren't people still cowards? Weren't they cowards more than ever? "We could scare the bejesus out of Jack. We know people who can do that, don't we?"

Nigel raised a troubled eyebrow. "Certainly, but now you're talking violence. That would be wholly inappropriate for someone in your position. You're not a Boston mayor from fifty years ago, you're a presidential candidate. The risks would be huge."

"Soft violence is all I'm proposing." Patty chopped up her sausage. "Kinder, gentler violence. I don't want to hurt Jack—I just want to send him a message. Make him think twice about who he's messing with. Shake the principles out of him, that's all."

"How do you propose to do that without hurting him?" Nigel asked.

The same way Papa had done it.

Patty speared a piece of sausage with her fork, the corners of her mouth forming a malevolent grin. "We'll have some people grab him and then, in the nick of time, *bada bing bada boom*, a good Samaritan comes along and saves him. What luck! No harm to Jack, just a friendly wake-up call delivered with a personal touch. *Capiche?*"

She examined Nigel's face for some sign of agreement, but what she saw was fright.

He pushed back from the table and became still. "Uh, are you quite certain you want to toss a beamer at Snap? It's not good cricket. A lot of things could go wrong."

"Such as?"

"For starters, the police might get involved. You're not governor and they aren't under your thumb anymore, so you can't hush them up. Suppose they trace the plot back to you? We'd be finished. It's far too dangerous."

Was Nigel going wobbly on her? After whipping her into a frenzy about the importance of stopping Jack, her campaign manager had lost his nerve for taking concrete action. He hadn't come from a place where they knew how to play hardball. He was too civilized and effete.

"Tell them not to hurt Jack. Just scare him. That's all I'm asking. Deliver a gentle warning not to mess with Pitypander. A warning from the gods above, *capiche?*"

JACK'S EYELIDS CLOSED, his head falling toward his computer keyboard. He caught himself before he hit it, pulled himself back up, and looked at his watch. Ten o'clock. Another late night rummaging through police reports had turned up zilch.

The inconsistencies surrounding Rod Collier were piling up, one on top of the other. Neither of his supposed causes of death held up under scrutiny. And his life was just as big a mystery. His few friends at Burbank High could add nothing to Vinny Sylvester's account. Collier's family was also missing, gone without a trace, living somewhere on the East Coast—according to Vinny.

Everything the pizza cook had told him was suspect. He may have lied about the family's whereabouts, just as he omitted the fact he'd lived in the same apartment as Rod. Where was Vinny? He hadn't answered Jack's latest email asking for a follow-up interview.

Most ominously, several shady characters were now stalking Jack: Agent Seven, jzcrazy@mushmail.com, and whoever was in the white SUV. Jack had made himself a person of interest, like Agent Seven had said.

Leads were what he needed most urgently. His "facts" were shaky, and only new leads could make them stronger.

Jack's stomach growled, reminding him he hadn't had dinner. He looked around the newsroom and saw no one, not even the janitors. It was time to go home.

Halfway across the parking lot Jack heard footsteps. He stopped and glimpsed something rustling in the bushes. He pivoted toward it. In a split second two men in black ski masks lunged out of the shadows and were all over him, grabbing his arms and dragging him into the shrubbery.

A hand reached around to cover Jack's mouth. The man's body was short and chunky—that much Jack could see out of the corner of his eye.

"Shut up," the assailant whispered.

A more powerful hand gripped Jack's right arm and twisted hard. This man was a giant, six foot ten at least. Jack yelped in pain as the tendons in his elbow and shoulder crunched.

The hand on Jack's mouth slipped off for a second, allowing him to gasp for air. "What do you want? My wallet? Take it!"

The smaller man slapped him. "What did I tell you? Shut up!"

Blood gushed down Jack's upper lip. He could take the little guy on his left, but there was no escaping the hulk on his right. He stopped struggling.

"That's better," the smaller man said softly. "Okay, you wanna know what we want? You been looking for Rod Collier? We got some friendly advice for you. He's dead, okay? Leave him that way. You wanna be dead too? No? Okay, then we would strongly advise you—"

A gunshot rang out about twenty feet away.

Jack's arms dropped free. The two men scrambled through the bushes and out of sight. Jack wheeled around toward the gunman.

A middle-aged fat man with eyeglasses and a big nose stepped out of the darkness, displaying his FBI badge.

"So, kid, we meet again," the man said in a gravelly voice.

"Agent Seven! Am I glad to see you!"

The agent examined Jack's bloody nose. "Ah, look at you. I knew I should have shot you last time. Look at the trouble you're causing. Now I gotta save you from muggers, like a friggin' city cop."

"They weren't muggers." Jack wiped the blood off his face with his handkerchief. "They didn't want my wallet. They didn't even go for it."

Agent Seven looked toward the bushes. "Then who the hell were they?"

"You're asking me? You're the FBI. Why didn't you arrest them? You have a gun."

"Yeah, I got a gun. But like I said, I'm not a cop."

Jack wiped off more blood. "Too bad. I could have used one."

"Okay, kid, so if they weren't muggers, who would they be?"

"They were warning me." Jack raised his handkerchief to his nose and held it there.

"Who sent them? Pitypander?"

Jack didn't answer.

The agent let out a sigh. "Still won't talk, huh? Kid, you have a lot to learn about who your friends are. You're clamming up even after I saved you?"

"It's none of your business. You think I should be grateful you're tailing me everywhere I go?" Jack dabbed more blood from his nose.

"And if I wasn't, where would you be now? Kid, you're lucky to only get a nosebleed. Ah, look at you. What a mess. Here, take this." The G-man handed Jack his own handkerchief.

"Thanks." Jack pressed it against his nose.

"You know, it wouldn't kill you to show a little appreciation. At the rate you're going, it might kill you if you don't. I can't save you from yourself. I'm not your mommy."

"No, my mom would have shot 'em dead for sure."

Looking back across the parking lot, Agent Seven scratched his chin. "Well, whoever they were, they couldn't be North Korean. They were much too big, especially the tall one. He was a friggin' monster. He could have broke you in two."

Jack took a step back. "What did you say? Why the heck would they be North Korean?"

"Hmm, because that's what Kim Il Bong's bad boys tend to be." Agent Seven looked at his watch, as if counting how many seconds it would take for the information to sink in.

"Kim Il Bong? You're after North Korean agents? Why would they be coming after me? Are you nuts?"

"Nuts? I'm not the one taking on Pitypander, am I? What do you know about her and Kim Il Bong, kid?"

Jack, certain Agent Seven had gone insane, said nothing.

The G-man's eyes probed Jack's for a few seconds, as if trying to read his mind. "What the heck, maybe you don't know anything. Yeah, I think that's it. Forget it."

"Wait, tell me, what's Pitypander got to do with North Korea?"

"Never mind." Agent Seven turned to walk away. "Have a good night, kid. Keep the handkerchief. I'll put it on your bill." His dark blue jacket faded into the shadows.

North Koreans? Jack stuffed the bloody handkerchiefs into his pocket and drove home, more baffled than ever.

SETTLING INTO HER lounge chair, Patty read *The New York Times* article with a self-satisfied smile. With only two months until the election, she had made steady progress in the polls, drawing to within striking distance of Diebold.

Her television blitz of negative ads had neutralized his attacks on her fitness for office, exposing the incumbent's glass jaw on the red-hot issue of sexual assault. The unsavory image of the president's wanton hair-sniffing had irritated women, but Patty's most recent escalation—accusing Diebold of having affairs with his vulnerable young underlings—was driving them to her side.

Her next broadside would be even more incendiary. These ads, Nigel assured her, would depict the president as a serial sexual predator, fan the flames of resentment against his toxic masculinity, and clinch the female vote.

The maid entered the veranda with her Belgian waffles and coffee, laying the tray on the table beside her. Yawning, Patty reviewed her copy of Red Meat Speech Number Four, the talk she would give to the Seattle Ladybugs tomorrow. With its stirring rallying cry against the patriarchy, Number Four still roused her supporters to their feet.

Nigel soon spoiled her happy reverie, arriving with ill tidings of Jack's botched intimidation.

Patty put down her newspaper and looked at her campaign manager in confusion. Her ruse to scare Jack was too simple to have gone awry.

"A second good Samaritan? If it wasn't our good Samaritan who saved him, whose was it, in heaven's name?"

"We don't know," Nigel replied, all in a dither. "Snap was coming out of his office late at night and no sooner had our men grabbed him than some cheeky fellow fired a shot, swooped in, and ran them off. Our good Samaritan was waiting in the bushes, watching it all. He never had a chance to save Snap."

That wasn't the worst of it. The interloper might be from the Diebold campaign, which had every reason to recruit Jack to their side, Nigel warned. "If Diebold's people ever get their hooks into Snap, they'll take whatever he's got and hand it right over to the national press. We'll be finished."

Impossible. Patty knew the reporter far better than her aide did. "Jack wouldn't do that. He's worked much too hard on his story to give it up."

"Snap may not have a choice. Diebold's people could be putting a gun to his head as we speak."

Diebold's threats wouldn't work on Jack, Patty maintained. He wanted so badly to prove himself as a journalist. More importantly, Jack would never hurt her. It wasn't in his nature to be mean or vengeful. Jack was kind, brave, and reverent.

Patty's phone rang. It was Jack. Patty pushed the speakerphone button.

Jack came straight at her. "A couple of guys jumped me in the parking lot last night and told me to drop the Rod Collier story or else. Did you send them?"

Patty paused a moment, confused by Jack's hostile tone. This wasn't like him. He had always been so polite and deferential. "Jack, I'd never do a thing like that. You know how fond I am of you. Are you all right?"

"Yeah, except for a bloody nose. Some guy from the FBI ran them off. He asked me about some connection between you and Kim Il Bong. How do you know Kim Il Bong, Governor?"

Nigel fell limply into his chair, the color draining from his face.

"Er, I don't know him," Patty replied. "I have no idea what the FBI was talking about."

"Yeah, sure."

"Jack, I'm terribly concerned about your safety. Would you like for me to arrange to have a personal bodyguard sent to you? I'll be more than happy to pay for it. You'd be protected around the clock."

"Oh, yeah, complete protection, I'll bet. Yeah, sure."

Patty heard a click, followed by a dial tone. "Jack? Jack? Jack?"

Apparently Jack wasn't interested in being protected. Bewildered, she turned to Nigel. "Jack hung up on me. I think he's angry."

Nigel looked like he was about to have a seizure. "What the bloody hell did you expect? You tried to send Snap a message, and now he's sent you one."

"What's his message?" Patty asked, perplexed that she hadn't even understood there was one.

"That he's got the bloody FBI on his side, and he's not afraid of you."

That didn't make sense. Why would Jack be afraid of her when she had shown him nothing but the utmost kindness and affection? How could he be so ungrateful?

"What's this about the FBI connecting you to Kim Il Bong?" Nigel asked in desperation. "Oh, please tell me you've never met the man."

Unfortunately, she had. There was the time she had run into the little potentate in Davos, Switzerland, at the annual World Economic Forum, when she was governor. "That's what you do at Davos—hobnob with movers and shakers from around the world, rub shoulders with them, and be seen. But it was nothing. A handshake at most. Completely innocent."

"Would there be any record of it?"

"There might have been a photo-op." Patty put her finger to her cheek. "Yes, come to think of it, there almost certainly was. Davos is full of photo-ops. What's the use of hobnobbing with the swells if you can't prove you've done it?"

Nigel was stumped. "If that's all that happened, the FBI wouldn't be digging into your connection to Kim. They must have something on you more damaging than a group photo at Davos."

Patty gasped as a horrifying possibility presented itself. "Kim's connection—since it's not me, it must be Benny! That's it, Benny's doing a deal!"

CHAPTER 24

Family Assistance

THE BLARE OF horns honking filled Patty's ear as soon as Benny answered his phone. *New York. He's in New York today.* She laid her phone on the table and punched the speakerphone button so Nigel could listen.

"Benny, have you been doing a deal with Kim Il Bong of North Korea?" she asked, her voice quavering.

Street noise drowned out his answer. The only intelligible sound Patty heard was Benny's chauffeur barking, "Get out of the way, pal, I got the green light, beat it," followed by an obscenity and more honking.

"Benny! Are you there? Are you listening to me? What are you doing with Kim? Are you trying to sabotage my campaign?"

Five seconds passed. "Sabotage? Hell no, doll, you know I'm on your side."

"Oh, yeah? Then why is the FBI investigating me about Kim?"

Another honk. "What? The FBI? Oh, Christ!"

"Fess up, Benny. What have you been up to?"

"It wasn't my fault, doll. You gotta believe me," he answered.

"Fess up, I said."

Patty heard a long sigh. Benny told how Kim and his army had raided the Macau Palace.

Nigel jumped out of his chair. "They put a gun to his head? Why was he meeting Kim in the first place?"

Patty waved Nigel away and looked at him crossly.

"Who's that?" Benny asked. "Where are you? Who's listening to us?"

"It's just Nigel. I'm at home."

Benny was cursing under his breath. She heard the words "goddamn shyster lawyer" and hoped Nigel hadn't.

"It wasn't my idea. Honest. They broke in."

"A likely story," Nigel whispered. "The North Korean army just showed up."

"Sure, Benny. So tell me, how did this army get there?"

"On a train. The Chinese let them through," Benny said. "All I know is, the North Koreans barged in and before I knew it I was sitting in front of Kim with a machine gun up my nose. The little dude is calling the shots in this deal, not me."

Nigel mouthed the word "deal," his hands gripping the sides of his head like it was about to explode.

The remorseful tone of Benny's voice told Patty he was telling the truth. Crazy things like this actually happened in Benny's world of high rollers, celebrities, and big money. Anyone might show up at a Pitypander Palace—even Kim Il Bong.

"My God, Benny, you're doing a deal with him? What did you agree to?"

"To build Kim a big resort to earn him hard currency. I only get ten percent. It sucks, but what can I do?"

If that was the deal, the threat must have been serious. Benny never settled for a ten percent share of anything. He only cut partners into his deals when he had no alternative. Like when he'd married her.

So that was the secret to controlling Benny Pitypander: stick a gun up his nose. If only Patty had known this years ago, she would have armed herself right after their honeymoon.

Nigel reached inside his coat and pulled out a pen. He scrawled something on a piece of paper and handed it to her. It read "WHAT ELSE HAS HE DONE?"

"Is that all you've been up to, Benny? Have you been making any other deals designed to blow my campaign to smithereens?"

Silence.

"C'mon, Benny. Out with it. You know I'm gonna find out anyway."

"Okay, okay, we're in talks with a guy from Iran, and some other guy from Cuba."

"It's never just some guys with you. C'mon, spill your guts."

"Okay, the supreme leader of Iran and the president of Cuba. We're talking about building a couple of hotels for them, that's all."

That's all? North Korea, Iran, Cuba. Patty detected a pattern: While she was running herself ragged trying to become America's president, her egocentric husband was doing backroom deals with America's enemies, compromising her six ways to Sunday. Nigel collapsed in convulsions on the sofa.

"Will you do me a favor, Benny?" Patty asked softly.

"Sure, doll, anything for you."

She hollered into the phone at the top of her lungs, "COULD YOU STOP WITH YOUR FRIGGING DEAL-MAKING, AT LEAST UNTIL I'M ELECTED?"

A long pause followed. Asking Benny to cease doing deals was like asking him to quit eating lasagna. He would give it up for Lent, but not a day longer. Building his global empire was what Benny Pitypander lived for.

"Yeah, I suppose I could do that. Yeah, no problem," he said. "What choice do I have?"

It seemed there was a particle of love left in their marriage. Patty would take what she could get. "Thanks, Benny. That'll be a big help."

"By the way, babe, was that really your mother I saw this morning on TV, being dragged out of that Diebold rally?"

NIGEL RUSHED TO the television and clicked it on. The talking heads on cable news were discussing the incident. The chyron on the bottom of the screen shouted in bold letters:

ELDERLY PITYPANDER FANS DISRUPT
DIEBOLD RALLY

The clip had just started. President Diebold stood at a podium in his three-piece suit pounding away at Pitypander's general unfitness for office, her ignorance of foreign affairs, her history of destroying California's fiscal health, and her lunatic proposals for new taxes and regulations. Then he changed the subject from Pitypander's incompetence to her lack of character.

The president fingered his mustache. "Folks, you've seen what Governor Pitypander did to California. If we let that madwoman loose in the Washington swamp, imagine how she'll shake down giant international corporations and foreign governments. Patty Pitypander is the damnedest liar and thief who ever came down the pike!"

Four white-haired women sitting in the first row put on pink hats and stood up. Diebold, halting in mid-sentence, peered down at the little old ladies with a quizzical look.

Patty seized Nigel by the arm. "Oh my God, that's Mama! She's there with the Horizons House pickleball team! That's Thelma, and Maude, and Sally, and oh, no!"

Olympia stepped forward, shaking her finger at Diebold. "How dare you talk about my Patty that way! My daughter's no thief. You're the thief! Why, she'll be twice the president you could ever hope to be, you overgrown gasbag! How dare you say those things! Patty Pitypander for president!"

The other three women stepped forward, standing shoulder to shoulder, and shouted in unison, "Pitypander for president! Down with Diebold!"

The president's followers hurled a chorus of boos at them. Diebold winced at the spectacle of his supporters abusing the elderly, and raised his hands to stop them. "Please, folks, let's leave these old ladies alone."

The cacophony of boos only grew louder. Four uniformed men armed with truncheons and pistols dashed forward to quell the disturbance.

"Ma'am, please," said a security guard, a burly man with thick, hairy arms. "Please come with us."

Olympia scrunched her eyes up at the mountain of flesh towering over her. "No! I'm not leaving." She pointed an accusing finger at Diebold. "Not until that young man up there apologizes to my Patty for the nasty things he's said. He ought to be ashamed, the way he talks about her. My Luigi, God rest his soul, wouldn't stand for his lies and neither will I!"

Thelma locked arms with her compatriots. "We won't go either! We're not going anywhere. You just try to make us, sonny."

"You got to leave." The perplexed guard smiled sweetly. "Please, ladies?"

"No!" The Horizons House pickleball team would not budge, not for all the world.

The guards withdrew into a huddle. One of them pulled a walkie-talkie out of his vest, made a brief call, and signaled to the others to proceed. The big guard closed in, taking Olympia gently by her forearm. "Please, ma'am, you gotta go. Don't make me hurt you."

The camera zoomed in on Olympia. She reached for her purse and clubbed the guard over the head. "Take that, you big hairy ape! Grab an old woman, will you? Is that how your mother raised you? Not this old woman!"

"Ma'am! Don't do that!" He stepped back and reached instinctively for his taser.

"No, Larry, for God's sake, don't tase her!" shouted a guard. "You could kill her. She's Pitypander's mother!"

Larry hesitated. "For crying out loud." He slipped the taser back into his pocket. "Okay, then you tell me how the hell we're gonna get 'em out of here."

Olympia raised her purse again, ready to clobber Larry once more, but this time the guard blocked her swing with his forearms. She flailed at him, battering his beer belly with her fists. "I'll kick you in the nuts if I have to! Just watch me!"

"Ma'am! Stop it, please!" Larry caught her by the wrists.

Olympia fell limply into his arms, forcing the guard to lift her by her armpits. Her shoes scraped across the floor as he dragged her away, as boos from Diebold supporters cascaded down on her.

Olympia, undeterred, let out a shriek capable of cracking glass. "Pitypander for president! Down with Diebold! Bug, bug, bug, bug, bug!"

The camera zeroed in on the president, shrinking helplessly at the podium as the brawny guard manhandled his opponent's tiny octogenarian mother.

Patty hung her head in shame. How could her mother embarrass her on television like this? "Mama, your little girl can take care of herself. I'm all grown up."

She looked to her side. Nigel was doubled over with laughter.

Patty scowled. "What's wrong with you? Don't you see, Diebold will think I sent Mama to his rally on a kamikaze mission. He might do the same to me with his parents. Now I'll have to apologize for her disgraceful behavior. I don't know what's gotten into her."

"Are you daft? Let Diebold suffer," he replied with glee. "This is wonderful. You couldn't buy better advertising with a hundred million dollars. Diebold on camera, bashing the elderly—it's fabulous. Your mum's a political genius. She may have won you Florida!"

CHAPTER 25

Double Exposures

THE YOUTH, SIXTEEN and wiry, zoomed up and down the
big concrete bowl on his skateboard, awing the onlookers with
his tricks. He brushed the bangs out of his eyes with his hand and
soared high into the air over the rim in a double-twisting somersault,
coming down on his board as deftly as a cat jumping from a table.
The board seemed to stick to his feet like a magnet.

"Way to nail it, Randy," someone in the crowd yelled.

Some of the regulars at the Circle Beach skatepark, not much older
than this phenom, were world-class. Jack had heard they competed
for prizes worth tens of thousands of dollars, and probably made
more money than he did. You could earn a decent living riding a little
board with wheels on it, if you had the right stuff. The rule seemed
to apply to every human activity. Fun could be your work if you were
good enough at it.

Vinny's email had said to be at the skatepark at three. Jack checked
his watch. It was already ten past the hour.

"You think he knows something's up?" Fanny asked.

Jack slipped his arm around her. "All I said in my email was I have some new information about Rod Collier to ask you about. I didn't say what it is. Gosh, I hope he shows up."

Seconds later a bearded young man approached.

"Sorry I'm late. We had a rush of customers and I couldn't leave the kitchen until it was over." Vinny sat on the bench. "Who's she?"

"My girlfriend, Fanny Flowers. She works with me at the *Bee*. That's not a problem, is it?"

Vinny's shoulders stiffened. "I dunno. You didn't say anything about bringing somebody else here. Is she gonna keep quiet?"

"I already know the story," Fanny said. "I'm the one who told him about the Collier rumor."

The pizza cook stroked his beard and looked Fanny over. "All right, if she knows anyway, then I guess it's okay."

Jack opened his notepad and scribbled the date of the interview on it. "Uh, well, like I wrote in my email, I found some new information about Rod Collier. I think I know where he is."

Vinny's head jerked back. "What? He's alive?"

"I think so. I found out Rod lived in an apartment at 393-B South Locust Street over in Lincoln Park."

"He did? When?"

Jack looked hard at Vinny. "I thought maybe you could tell me. Your name is still on the mailbox there too. You didn't tell me you were roommates."

Vinny's eyes darted from side to side. "We weren't."

Jack absorbed Vinny's reaction for a few seconds. Maybe the pizza cook would come clean if Jack told him what he already knew. "No, you weren't roommates. The apartment manager wasn't much help, so I went back to the apartment and found your old next-door neighbors. They told me there was never more than one person in your apartment in the whole ten years they'd lived in the building."

Vinny stared off into space. "Uh-huh."

Jack continued. "So if you and Rod weren't roommates, it would take a heck of a coincidence for you both to live in the same apartment, one right after the other. There has to be another explanation."

Vinny squeezed his lips together, like he wasn't about to give the answer voluntarily.

Jack pulled out a page from his notes, with a photo of Rod Collier that Fanny had helped him find. "Does this look familiar?"

"No," Vinny replied.

"I think it looks a lot like you, but without the beard," Jack said.

Vinny rose to his feet. "I gotta go. My break is almost over."

Jack looked up at him. "You're Rod Collier, aren't you?"

Vinny stopped.

"There's no point in running anymore," Jack called after him. "Your cover's blown. Just tell us what happened to you."

Vinny did an about-face, standing motionless for a second, as if being pulled in opposite directions. He walked slowly back to the bench and sat down again, his face sullen. "I had to change my name and disappear. I was afraid."

"Of Governor Pitypander?" As creepy and pathetic as Pitypander was, Jack couldn't imagine being afraid of her.

Vinny sat up, his eyes bugging out. "Yeah, you bet. She's scary."

"And what about your death?" Jack asked.

"We faked it," Vinny replied.

"Who's we?"

"Her assistant, some English guy named Nigel. And some other guys who took orders from him. They helped me move to Lincoln Park and change my name. They even moved my parents to Fresno. They didn't want it to be easy for reporters to find me if Pitypander ever ran for president."

Jack showed Vinny the police report on the car crash. "So they staged this crash you were supposedly in with the BMW?"

Vinny sneered. "Yeah, but the idiots screwed up. The highway patrol couldn't borrow a dead body from the morgue in time, so they pushed the car off the cliff without one inside. That's why you don't see any pictures of my mangled corpse here."

"Then how did you end up dying of pneumonia?"

"After they messed up the fake crash, Pitypander's people had to make up something else, so they filled out a death certificate for me at the county coroner's office, and put down pneumonia as my cause of death."

"So you died twice," Jack said, nodding. "That was a pretty serious clue. Even I couldn't miss it."

"Nobody noticed it until you came along," Vinny said. "They warned me never to tell anybody about Pitypander, or they'd be back. But it was too late. I'd already told some guys at school."

The rumor about the affair had spread from there. It would have gone a lot further if Vinny weren't such a loner. Not many kids believed him. They thought he was a weirdo.

"If you went to that much trouble to disappear, why did you email me, Vinny?" Jack asked. "I never would have found you if you hadn't emailed me."

"I don't know. It was a stupid thing to do." Vinny looked down at his feet. "I saw your post asking about Rod Collier. With Pitypander running for president, I got scared some reporter would find me—but part of me hoped one would. The problem with disappearing is it's not a thing you can do on a lark and be done with. Staying disappeared is a life sentence."

"Were you also the one who sent me the email about your old apartment address?" Jack asked.

"What email?"

Jack took a hard look at Vinny. "You're not jzcrazy@mushmail.com?"

"No. That's not me. You already have my only email address."

So Jack did have a secret helper. Somebody else was out there who knew the Rod Collier story and wanted Jack to connect the dots.

There was no time to worry about that now. Jack must press further and dig into the sordid details of Vinny's affair with Pitypander, while he had the chance. He flipped the page in his notes. "So, like, what did she do to you, Vinny? I mean, when you were working in her office as an intern?"

Vinny squirmed. "Pitypander's a cougar. She seduced me."

"How?"

"Money and gifts, new clothes, the BMW. Hey, it was exciting at first. I was seventeen, dude. I thought why not, why fight it? Girls my own age thought I was gross. I could use a sugar mama. I never saw so much money in my life. It was just sex, right? I fell right into her trap. She bought me."

"That's disgusting," Fanny said, shaking her head. "A fifty-year-old woman."

"Yeah, it was pretty sick." Vinny's eyes filled with self-loathing. "I became her boy toy. Once she offered me a job as her pool boy. Another time she wanted me to run away with her. It started getting way too weird, like she was real lonely and living in some fantasy world and I was there to be the young stud she never had. When I stopped cooperating she realized she needed to cover her tracks fast. That's when her people showed up to help me disappear."

Jack had everything he needed now, except for one item: Vinny himself. "Are you willing to come forward with your story? I need a source."

Vinny recoiled. "Hell no, dude! Pitypander's running for president now. I'm in more danger than ever. If she gets elected, she could bring the whole U.S. government down on me—the FBI, the CIA, everybody. I don't want to die."

Jack slapped his forehead. "Jeez Louise, nobody's gonna die, Vinny. Pitypander was only the governor back then. They can't kill you for screwing a governor—especially a California governor."

"Oh, yeah? Like hell they can't! Somebody that powerful, they can kill anybody they want and get away with it. Forget it. I'm not messing with Pitypander!" Vinny jumped up and walked away.

UPON RETURNING TO the *Bee,* Jack noticed a piece of mail on his desk.

It was a manila envelope with a New York postmark but no return address. "Jack Snap, Burbank Bee" was handwritten on the front side. It hardly weighed an ounce, so it couldn't be a mail bomb. It looked safe to handle, so Jack opened it.

The only thing inside was a thumb drive, padded with bubble wrap. There was no note indicating why it had been sent. Jack stared at it for a moment. Then he stuck it into a port in his computer.

Two items came up in the file directory on his screen: a graphics file named "Pitypander.jpg" and an audio recording titled "Diebold. mp3." Jack opened the Pitypander file first.

A photograph of a swanky hotel entrance appeared. Statues of nymphs surrounded a water fountain in the foreground. In front of the hotel's doors, a small Asian man with a close-cropped haircut was stepping into a black limousine, surrounded by soldiers at attention, as a pot-bellied Westerner waved to him. A small sign in the lower left corner of the image bore the single word "Macau" below some Chinese characters.

The Westerner's owly brown eyes looked familiar. Jack zoomed in on the man's face. Startled, he reached for his phone and swiped through the photographs he'd taken at the Pitypander fundraiser at Aspen.

It was him all right—Benny Pitypander. The governor's billionaire husband had met with Kim Il Bong, totalitarian ruler of North Korea.

This was clear evidence of a scandal.

Where did this meeting occur? Jack typed "pitypander.com" into his browser and clicked his way through the website until he came upon a link to the Pitypander Palace in Macau. The hotel entrance on the website matched the one on Pitypander.jpg, complete with water fountain and nymph statues.

This was the Pitypander-North Korea connection Agent Seven had referred to, Jack realized.

Was this photograph related to the Diebold recording? Jack clicked on the audio file. He heard what sounded like a meeting. The voice of P. Trayson Diebold was unmistakable:

> "Ten cents on the dollar! How many federal properties can we put no-bid contracts on at that rate? How many cities?"
>
> "As many as we can re-categorize under the terms of your Clean Slate bill, Mr. President. We've identified two hundred billion dollars' worth of opportunities already."

The president was doing a private deal tied to his Clean Slate program. *Another scandal!*

Pitypander's husband was committing treason and Diebold was engaged in graft. The files seemed unrelated to each other, except they were both on the same thumb drive—and they had been delivered to Jack.

Who else had the files? Either story, if leaked to the national media, would be all over the news by now. No such thing had happened, so Jack could safely assume he was the sole recipient.

Who was the sender? Why had the files been sent to him? Was the sender expecting him to use them to smear Pitypander or Diebold? Or both?

The mysterious envelope had contained a kind of bomb after all—an information bomb. If it went off, it could reduce the election to a spectacle of tawdry scandals. How strange that someone would hand over such a potent weapon to a rookie reporter at *The Burbank Bee* instead of the grizzled scandalmongers at *The New York Times* or *The Washington Post*. The leaker had vested Jack with power and responsibility far, far above his pay grade.

And without any instructions.

The two scandals on the thumb drive were unlike the Collier affair. Jack had received these stories, but not earned them. They would win him no glory with Gus.

Gazing helplessly across the newsroom floor, Jack caught sight of his boss strolling toward his office with a cup of coffee. The crusty old editor would know exactly what to do with the thumb drive. Jack could wash his hands of it. He got up and started toward Gus's door.

Halfway there Jack stopped, turned around, and trudged back to his desk to reconsider.

Passing the buck to his boss was the coward's way out. Fate, for some perverse reason, had entrusted the thumb drive to him, and he was not one to shirk his responsibility. If the thing left his possession, one thing was certain: In today's partisan political climate, unscrupulous individuals driven by self-interest would abuse it. There was no telling what hell it might let loose on the country.

Jack had a duty to protect the public interest. Safeguarding these malign secrets, at least for a while until things became clearer, would be an act of civic virtue.

Besides, as long as he held the files, he had the option to change his mind and release them. Powerful people were after him. The information bomb might come in handy in his self-defense.

Keep them.

The reporter copied the files to his phone, slipped the thumb drive back into its envelope, and locked it inside his desk for safekeeping.

CHAPTER 26

The Love Letter

A S PATTY REGARDED herself in the mirror, a dismal thought struck her: Every day she lived past fifty-five would bring more gray hairs. She swept her hairbrush over her ear, hoping to bury the latest offenders under the dwindling mass of brown.

It didn't work. New gray hairs had a way of standing out, screaming a warning of advancing age at their owner. Once noticed, like age itself, they only accumulated. Should she ask her hairstylist to conceal them? No, it was too late for that. A significant change in her appearance would be seized upon by the press, with the unfair insinuation that she might be vain.

"Age is no excuse."

Patty turned around. Jenessa, wearing a chiffon robe, was leaning against the bathroom door, her hair rippling with a deep brown color betraying no marks of time.

"No excuse for you, maybe," Patty said. "You've been stuck at twenty-five for the past thirty years. What would you know about gray hairs?"

Jenessa sashayed into the bathroom. "It's men I know about, darling. There's no age limit for sexy."

Patty knew better than that. "Funny, that's not my experience with men. When I hit thirty-five Benny traded me in for two twenties and kept the change."

Jenessa stood beside her, taking a closer look at the problem. "A little gray here and there—no big deal. Jack isn't rejecting you because of your hair, although you could stand a new do. That mop makes you look like Mamie Eisenhower."

Patty laid the hairbrush down and leaned into the mirror. "If it's not my gray hair, then what? My wrinkles and jowls?" She put her fingers to her cheeks and pulled her skin tight. Her next Botox injection wasn't due for three months. Another facelift might leave her looking like a space alien, her plastic surgeon had warned.

"Nope, it's not the wrinkles."

Patty looked down. "My sagging chest? My huge rear end? My flabby thighs?"

One by one, Jenessa shook her head at all of Patty's misshapen body parts, indicating that her client had failed to understand the crux of her problem. "Your inadequacy isn't what you *aren't*. It's what you *don't*."

"What I don't? Oh, please, what is it I haven't done now?"

"You haven't been open and honest with Jack. You haven't bared your soul to him."

That didn't sound right. Hadn't Patty taken a great risk with Jack already? "I tried baring everything to him at Aspen. He shielded his eyes."

Jenessa folded her arms in exasperation. "Not your body, you twit. I'm talking about your soul. Honestly, I don't know why I try so hard with you. When it comes to men, you're as thick as a brick."

"Oh, why is it so important I bare my soul to him, Jenessa?"

The heroine sat down at Patty's makeup table and said in a soothing voice, "Because, my dear, he doesn't know you have one. You're so rich and powerful, so distant from Jack in every way, he can't see you as the vulnerable, emotional creature we both know you are. Patty

Ingratelli, the vibrant, idealistic, fiery young woman trapped inside you, is inconceivable to him. All he perceives is the cold, graying exterior of Governor Pitypander."

Patty grasped a handful of silver hair and sighed. "So it is an age problem."

"No, it is not an age problem!" Jenessa replied with a vehemence that took Patty aback. "It is merely a perceptual problem caused by the passage of time."

"What's the difference?"

"Oh, there's a great but subtle difference. One is reality, the other is the perception of reality."

"Sometimes I have trouble telling those two apart," Patty admitted.

"Obviously." Jenessa propped an elbow on the makeup table. "But you know perfectly well how to twist other people's perception of reality beyond recognition. What else is it you politicians do all day?"

"For one thing, we never bare our souls to anyone if we can help it," Patty replied. "Least of all reporters."

"You'll have to if you want Jack. Why should he open up to you if you don't open up to him?"

Patty picked up her hand mirror and inspected the back of her hairdo for split ends. "Open up? Jack won't even speak to me anymore."

"Which is why you must do something dramatic and unexpected— to smash his resistance." Jenessa swung her fist at the mirror as if to demonstrate. "Don't you remember how I got George Morley back in *Love's Third Encounter* after our little spat?"

Patty did remember. "You want me to write Jack an agonized love letter on perfumed stationery in this day and age? He's a Gen Z. They don't communicate that way."

"An agonized love letter, properly drafted, can pierce the coldest man's heart, whether sent by mail or email." Jenessa's voice resounded with the confidence she'd gained from long experience in piercing male hearts. "You must expose your vulnerability to him, no holds barred. You saw how well it worked for me."

It had worked well indeed. In *Love's Third Encounter,* Jenessa's letter to George had reformed his obstinate attitude to the heroine by melting his heart. The handsome rascal with the long sideburns was putty in Jenessa's hands after reading her heartrending epistle.

Patty put down her mirror and turned around. "Will you help me write it?"

"Of course, dear," Jenessa replied with an accommodating grin. "Why do you think I've come?"

Patty walked across the mansion to her office, started up her laptop computer and, with Jenessa at her elbow, tapped out an email:

> TO: jsnap@mushmail.com
> FROM: ppitypander@mushmail.com
> SUBJECT: Love
>
> My dearest Jack,
>
> Your frightening news about the recent assault on you outside the *Bee* has worried me so deeply I felt I just had to write. I know you believe I had something to do with it, and I don't blame you in the least for being suspicious. But I assure you the incident took me as much by surprise as it did you.
>
> Oh, Jack, how can I make you understand I would never do anything to harm you? If you only knew how concerned I am for your safety! I lie awake at night thinking how I might protect you from whoever it is has threatened you, to wrap you in my protective embrace. At least let me hire a private bodyguard to ensure your

safety. It would give me such peace of mind to know no violence can come to you.

My darling, I can contain my feelings for you no longer. The dam holding them back for so many months is at last bursting. I confess I knew we were fated to be together from the moment I laid eyes on you, the day you first interviewed me last year. Our time together since then has only made me more sure of it. Therefore, I must declare my undying love for you and my most fervent wish for us to be together forever. Yes, there is an age difference between us, I admit it, but we must not let a small thing like a number stand in the way of our true love for each other. Many couples have done it before us.

I want to run away with you, my love, if you will have me. My divorce from Benny will be easy enough to arrange, and my alimony from him will certainly guarantee the two of us will never want for anything. You will never have to work again a day in your life.

You may be asking yourself, what if I become president of the United States? Sure, I might be a little busy at first, but we can figure that out after my election in a few weeks. For now, it's enough for me to tell you of the love burning for you within my breast all these months and to hope you will welcome my reaching out to you in this way.

With deepest devotion,
Patty

She searched for any phrase or point Jack might not understand, reading the letter ten times. She must get it right. This might be her last chance to let him know how she felt.

"Oh, I hope I don't sound needy."

"Stop fussing over the damn thing. It's perfect, I tell you." Jenessa smiled with satisfaction. "Just send it."

What if Jack rejected her? What if the email fell into the wrong hands? "Send it!"

Patty's finger trembled over the mouse button. She took a deep breath and clicked it, hoping her heartfelt missive would streak like an arrow to Jack's heart, and not his spam folder.

PATTY COULD SCARCELY keep her mind on Red Meat Speech Number Five. She rose from her chair, threw open the curtains of her hotel suite, and looked out at the Philadelphia skyline.

Twenty stories below, amid the yellow and orange foliage on Independence Mall, crowds of tourists lined up to see the Liberty Bell. Patty wondered how many were her supporters. Some of them would focus on the grand history of the bell, others the big crack in it. If they would simply allow her to fix the crack, the bell would ring true once again—for everyone.

What had Americans become in two hundred and fifty years? Would they choose to run backward to the past with Diebold or stride bravely forward into the future with her? In two weeks Patty would know.

Her love letter to Jack kept intruding upon her thoughts. The speech to the local chapter of the International Union of Pipefitters would have to wait. Patty had other things to think about than offering free childcare, kindergarten, healthcare, college tuition, and senior care to America's union workers.

In *Love's Third Encounter,* George Morley had responded promptly with effusions of love upon receiving Jenessa Fuller's soul-baring letter. A fretful four days had passed since Patty had emailed hers to Jack.

She alternated between aching to have Jack and wondering what insanity had persuaded her to risk the presidency of the United States for a penniless cub reporter. It seemed Jack wasn't going to email or phone her. Something was wrong.

She called his number. His phone rang three times before he picked up.

"Jack, is that you?" she asked, her voice cracking.

"Yes, Governor."

"Did you get my email?"

Silence.

"Jack, are you there?"

She heard what sounded like a sigh. "Yes, I got your email."

"What did you think of it?"

Silence.

"Uh, I'm not running away with you, Governor. Sorry."

Somehow, in her heart, Patty already knew that. The letter was a long shot, no matter what Jenessa said, but if nothing else at least it proved Patty's love for him.

Maybe it was too much to ask Jack to abandon his life's dream of being a journalist for the more fulfilling love of a somewhat older woman. Perhaps her idea of divorcing Benny and eloping with him was rash. If it needed some fine-tuning, some thinking through, the two of them could work out a plan together, if only Jack would listen to her and be reasonable.

What about the other part of the letter, and the crucial question it posed?

Gathering her courage, Patty asked the question point-blank: "Do you love me, Jack?"

Silence.

"I'm gonna propose to Fanny as soon as I can afford a ring."

Propose? She should have seen it coming. His answer, though devastating, came with a silver lining: the ring. It would take months for poor Jack to save enough for a decent ring. That bought Patty some time. "Fanny Flowers, that's the vestal vegan you told me about?"

"Yeah, that's her. We're in love."

Impossible. Jack only imagined he was in love. He was chasing a fantasy. Why would he want some girl whose only ambitions for him were poverty and hunger pangs? Patty could spare him all this pointless self-flagellation and give him a life worth living, if only he would open his heart to the more mature love she offered him.

But once again, to her dismay, Jack had said no. Did "no" really mean "no"? Why did it have to?

Patty somehow mustered the good manners to hold her tongue. She mumbled her congratulations.

"By the way, Fanny and I found Rod Collier," Jack said bluntly.

"Oh? He's alive? How wonderful."

"Alive and well."

"Excellent. Then he must have told you that nasty old rumor about me was false."

"No, he told us how you seduced him and made him disappear for the rest of his life to protect your political career."

Patty was dumbstruck. First Jack had plunged a dagger into her heart and now, venting his anger, he was cruelly turning it inside her. How had Jack come to hate her so after everything she'd done for him?

She categorically denied the accusation. "Whoever you met lied to you. He's a fraud, set up by the Republicans to destroy my candidacy. You're being duped."

"He's no fraud," Jack said. "And that's not all. I have a photo of your husband meeting with Kim Il Bong in front of the Pitypander Palace in Macau."

Another brutal blow. Patty disavowed any connection to the North Korean. "It's fake news. Jack, somebody's using you to get at me."

"Sure. Well, thanks for the offer to make me your next victim, Governor, but I'm not gonna be your boy toy. And I won't be needing protection from you or your goons. You'll be needing protection from me."

Click.

"Jack? Jack?"

This wasn't possible. Just like that, Jack was gone.

CHAPTER 27

Scandal for Scandal

NIGEL STOOD AT the window of the hotel suite, looking like a sick dog. He swung around, his arms hanging listlessly at his sides. "If Snap publishes the Collier and Kim stories, it's game over."

Patty laid her chin on her chest, mystified that Jack could despise her so. God knows she had tried to reason with him. What could she offer the young reporter that he hadn't already refused? Now Jack was lost, and her campaign might be too.

Gloom darkened Nigel's face as he analyzed the likely reaction to the stories by various groups. "Diebold's people will have a field day, of course. They'll go straight for the gutter, painting you as a serial child molester and a traitor. I'd do the same in their place. Missing a chance like this would be political malpractice."

The media would grant the two scandals unequal attention. The Kim story was bad, but it was merely about selling out the country. Being salacious, the Collier affair had broad, earthy appeal and would generate higher ratings. Naturally, it would dominate the headlines. Reporters would hound Patty about it everywhere she went. She had tied the bell of sexual scandal to her own tail, and it would clang loudly behind her, drowning out her message entirely.

Patty stared vacantly across the room. Jack was too honest to be bribed and too brave to be scared—altogether too good for his own good. But what did it matter? Jack was gone. Her Adonis was in the clutches of that Fanny woman now.

Nigel made further dire predictions. "The first week Snap's stories come out, you'll be down ten points in the polls. Expect to be waylaid by a barrage of follow-up questions about your entire personal history, from potty training on. Nothing, not even your most trifling peccadillo, will be off-limits. False rumors will spring up out of nowhere and feed on themselves. One fire will ignite ten more. The truth will be irrelevant. Innuendo will rule the day."

"Oh, no."

They must limit the damage by any means necessary, Nigel concluded. "We have to destroy Snap's credibility."

"How?"

"The usual way: by launching a counter-narrative," he proposed. "We'll portray Snap's stories as an eleventh-hour Diebold tactic, a desperate attempt to prop up the president's poll numbers. You will accuse Snap of being a committed Diebold partisan—a paid right-wing hack, playing his part in a carefully orchestrated conspiracy to smear you. I'll ask Colleen to prepare a press statement and have it ready to go the minute Snap's stories break."

Patty quailed at his suggestion. She should personally destroy Jack's reputation, before he even had one? Wreck Jack's dream of making it as a journalist? The plan was too vicious. The embers of Patty's love still burned red-hot. She would always carry a torch for Jack.

A torch. Fire. Patty slapped her forehead. "That's it! I have a better idea. Fight fire with fire!"

"What are you talking about?"

"Fight a scandal with a scandal. What if Jack had a scandal to worry about? That might force him to bargain with us. We need leverage on him, you said."

Nigel sat down in the chair next to hers. "But what's his scandal? From everything I've seen, Snap's a goody two-shoes. Does he have any nasty habits I'm not aware of?"

"He does have one." Patty explained her idea.

Nigel leaned back and thought for a moment. "You know, it might just work, and I don't see much risk in it, given the circumstances," he said. "Let's try it."

When he had gone to make the necessary arrangements, Patty wrote Jack an email:

> TO: jsnap@mushmail.com
> FROM: ppitypander@mushmail.com
> SUBJECT: Charity Picnic
>
> Dearest Jack,
>
> I'm so sorry about the terrible difficulty we've had communicating lately. I'd like to propose a truce, if you would consider it, at least for one afternoon. It's for a good cause.
>
> I am sponsoring a fundraising picnic for one of my favorite local charities, the Children's Hospital of Los Angeles, in McIntire Park next Saturday at noon. It should be loads of fun for the children, with toys and games. Benny and I are major donors and they have asked me to speak, so I thought you may want to be there to cover my remarks for the *Bee*. We'd love to have you.
>
> All the best,
> Patty

JACK PUZZLED OVER the invitation. He detected none of the cajoling tone he'd come to expect from the governor. He could go to the picnic or not; it was up to him. Was it really possible Pitypander's attitude was improving?

The email hinted something important might happen at the picnic. If so, turning down the invitation would be a dereliction of duty. It was his job to cover Pitypander's campaign. He should put his anger aside and set out to attend the speech, in case the governor did say something newsworthy.

McIntire Park teemed with kids and parents. Jack followed the crowd to a clearing alongside a small lake, where Pitypander was shaking hands with the multitude.

She stepped up to the little stage and thanked everyone for coming. She noted that the Children's Hospital was among the first recipients of funding from the Pitypander Foundation. She and Benny were delighted to have played their part in funding the new cancer ward.

Heaping praise on the hospital for its history of serving the community's sick children, Pitypander basked in the glow of helping it do its essential work. She thanked the hospital administrators, told everyone to enjoy themselves, and waded into the crowd for more handshaking. But she said nothing newsworthy at all.

Jack shook his head in disappointment. He had come all this way for a five-minute speech about the hospital? Pitypander had wasted his time. As he turned to go, he noticed she was staring at him. Now he couldn't leave without at least saying hello. He stepped in front of her and forced a nervous smile. "Thank you for the invitation, Governor."

"Of course, Jack. Glad to see you made it. Let's bury the hatchet, shall we? Can we call a truce, at least for today?"

"Sure, why not? A truce."

She pointed to her left, where people were queuing up along a line of food trucks. "I was just on my way over there to have something to eat. Will you join me?"

Jack nodded.

As they approached the trucks, clouds of smoke billowed up into the air. The wind shifted, smacking Jack in the face with the aroma of beef cooking on a grill.

Next to the trucks, a white banner stretched between two trees. It read:

CHILDREN'S HOSPITAL BULL ROAST
SPONSORED BY
CALIFORNIA CATTLEMEN'S COOPERATIVE

Inside the windows of the trucks, buxom young women in cowgirl hats, wielding tongs, lifted T-bone steaks onto paper plates.

Jack stopped. "Oh, no," he muttered.

"Something wrong?" Pitypander asked, looking back at him.

"I shouldn't have come. I can't eat any of that. I shouldn't even be here. It's my Vegan Vow."

"That again? Jack, it's a picnic. You're supposed to enjoy yourself. Lighten up."

A sizzling sound filled his ears. A cowgirl, grasping a pair of tongs, flipped a steak and sent a plume of black smoke shooting above the trees. The smell almost knocked Jack down.

He salivated like a starving dog. "Oh, jeez, charbroiled sirloin. That smells so good. But I just can't."

Pitypander flicked her hand at him. "Oh, pish posh. These steaks are already cooked. They'll go into the trash if you don't eat them."

"Fanny would kill me if she saw me here. You don't understand, she's a serious vegan. These beef people are her mortal enemies. She'd chain herself to this food truck and scream at them to shut it down." Jack started to walk away.

"Don't be ridiculous," Patty said. "Fanny will understand. This is a benefit for sick children. Doesn't Fanny have a heart?"

The cowgirl smiled at him from the food truck. "What would you like, darlin'?"

His stomach growling, Jack turned toward the hollow-eyed children in line behind him, tugging at their parents' arms. Dozens of them, bald from cancer treatments, were waiting for him to move forward. He had never seen so many sick kids. Yes, Fanny had a heart, and it would melt at this sight.

"You're right. What's the point in going hungry?" Jack perked up. "It's lunchtime, let's eat." He bought a lunch ticket and asked for a twelve-ounce steak, a scoop of potato salad, and a handful of cheesy nachos. He smiled at Pitypander. "How could I not? It's for the kids."

They sat down at a picnic table. Jack ate like a lion devouring a wildebeest.

He returned to the food trucks for a second steak. Suddenly a cowgirl swooped down from a truck, threw her arm around him, and planted a big wet kiss on his cheek.

Startled, Jack jumped back. "Well, hey there." Looking over her shoulder, he saw a familiar-looking man a few steps away holding up a phone and taking their picture.

Seconds later Jack's phone hummed. He pulled it out to read the email:

> TO: jsnap@mushmail.com
> FROM: tpaddow@mushmail.com
> SUBJECT: Gotcha!

Photographs were attached at the bottom. The first showed him eating a steak. The next caught him kissing the cowgirl in front of the Cattlemen's banner. Other images had Jack chomping on hamburgers, macaroni, and nachos, his plate piled high. Jack took another look at the photographer. He was a Pitypander campaign staffer.

It was a trap.

He stormed over to Pitypander. "No way. You wouldn't do that to me, Governor, would you?"

She snickered. "Wouldn't I? You like scandals, Jack? Well, now you have your very own, charbroiled specially for you."

"Scandal? Me? What have I done?"

The governor put her finger to her chin. "I don't know, what have you done? Maybe you should ask your vegan girlfriend. Won't she think what you've done is a scandal? A crazy woman who would chain herself to a food truck?"

"Sure, I ate a steak, but there's no comparison between that and—"

Patty chuckled. "Oh, Jack, let me straighten you out. A scandal's importance is relative to what you have to lose. If your scandal, little as it may seem, can blow up your whole little world, then it's every bit as serious as mine."

"That's blackmail!"

She dismissed his protest with a sweep of her hand. "Blackmail—such a harsh word. I prefer to think of it as a fair trade. You forget about what you know, I forget about what I know, and that way we're even. *Capiche?*"

"It won't work. Fanny won't go crazy over a bunch of stupid photos."

"Are you sure? The Garden of Eden was lost by eating an apple. Fanny goes bananas over people eating steaks, didn't you say? And we both know it's not just these pictures. They're just a conversation starter. The real question is, does Fanny know about your parents?"

Jack pounded the table. "You leave them out of this!"

"I thought not. I'd love to leave them out of it. It's entirely up to you. It's your move."

"No deal." Jack jumped up. "Fanny will believe me. I know she will."

"YOU DIDN'T REALLY expect him to surrender to you right on the spot, did you?" the voice asked.

Patty looked up from her dinner. Sitting at the far end of her dining room table, partially obscured by the chrysanthemums in the silver centerpiece, was Jenessa in a white sequined gown, with a diamond tiara ensconced in her hair.

"I hoped he would," Patty said, "but I suppose you're going to tell me that wasn't realistic."

"No, darling, it wasn't." Jenessa reached a hand up to adjust her tiara as light from the chandelier glinted off it.

Patty craned her neck to see around the flowers. "Are you on your way to the Oscars? What are you doing sitting way down there?"

"I didn't want to startle you," Jenessa replied. "You're as jumpy as a frog as it is."

"I half expected you to show up this evening. Would you like something to eat?" Patty pointed to the serving dish. "The cook made enough boeuf Bourguignon for two, and it's getting cold."

"Thanks, but you know I don't eat," the heroine said. "It's a good thing, too. Heaven knows what a diet like yours would do to my figure. In thirty years I could end up looking like, well—"

"Me?"

"Yes, but I'm not here tonight to discuss your midriff bulge. We need to review your strategy with Jack. A minute ago you were brooding about his rejecting your blackmail attempt."

Patty, quaffing her cabernet, gave her visitor a wistful look. "The plan didn't work. If anything, it's stiffened his resolve."

"Hmm, I beg to differ," Jenessa said. "It was a very good idea, and well played. You've got him pretty much where you want him. He's anxious about losing his Fanny."

Patty wondered how Jack's latest display of stubbornness could have been anything other than what it seemed. "If Jack was worried, he didn't show it this afternoon."

"Wrong again," Jenessa replied. "He did show it, but you've never learned to read men like I have."

"I haven't had three hundred of them either."

Jenessa harrumphed. "You should be grateful to be getting the benefit of my extensive experience."

"I suppose you could call it that." Patty sliced up her asparagus vinaigrette and took a bite. "Not everyone would."

"Don't you see, dearest, if Jack had given in to you, he would have been admitting to himself he lacks faith in Fanny's love for him. Then he wouldn't very well be able to go forward with his plans to marry her, would he?"

Patty hadn't thought of that. Jack was simply protecting his own fantasy about his relationship with Fanny. "No, if you look at it from his point of view, I guess not."

"His point of view? See there, that's your problem in a nutshell." Jenessa wagged her finger. "If you knew the first thing about handling men, you would look at everything from their point of view. That's all they ever do."

Patty had to admit, that was certainly true of Benny. He was incapable of seeing things from her perspective. "All right, so what do I do next, coach?"

"Deliver the poison and give it time to work its magic, sweetness," Jenessa replied with an expert grin. "Fanny will fail Jack's loyalty test. She will overreact to his little indiscretion and try to use it as a club to gain even more power over him. That's when Jack will realize how controlling she is and how starving himself is only the beginning of what Fanny will demand of him if they get married. He'll naturally be frightened off by her, end their engagement, and reclaim his freedom, clearing the way for you."

Patty understood. It was a brilliant scheme, far cleverer than a bribe or threat—simply open Jack's eyes to Fanny's petty tyranny, as Jenessa had done with Bert Redstone when she exposed Honey Henderson's petulance in *Our Better Angels*.

Patty had been using the wrong approach, bludgeoning Jack with a sledgehammer when she should have been tricking Fanny into doing it for her. "Very good. I stand corrected about your experience. You do know your trade, you beautiful devil."

Jenessa's eyes sparkled as brightly as her tiara, as if acknowledging Patty's apology. "With that other woman gone, Jack will be yours to control once again. Now have those pictures sent to Fanny. There's no time to lose."

CHAPTER 28

Explaining

FANNY LOOMED OVER Jack's desk with her hands on her hips, her face in a frenzy. "Meat inspectors?"

Jack offered up a sheepish grin. "Uh-oh. I guess you got the email from Pitypander."

"Outside, now!" Fanny stomped away, heading straight for the elevator.

"I can explain." He jumped up from his desk and ran to catch up with her. "Stop!"

She stood in the elevator and pushed a button, closing the doors in his face. Jack hurried down the stairs and walked outside, where he found her fuming on the sidewalk. As she turned to walk away, he caught her elbow.

She swung around, yanked her arm out of his hand, and aimed an accusing finger. "Liar! You told me your parents were federal health safety administrators. No wonder you didn't want me to meet them."

His throat tightening, Jack choked on the justification for his evasiveness. "I was planning to tell you. It's—it's just, well, the right moment never came. I was afraid you wouldn't understand."

"Understand what, that they're killers? What else is there to understand?" Fanny turned to a woman strolling by. "Hey, lady, my boyfriend's parents are mass murderers! What do you think of that?"

The woman took one look at Fanny's crimson face and scurried across the street.

"So my parents work for the USDA," Jack said. "They protect the food supply. What's wrong with that?"

Fanny plunged her fingers into her hair. "What's wrong? Jack, meat inspectors are complicit in the massacre of millions of helpless animals. They're like the prison guards in a Nazi death camp. And you—you broke your solemn oath never to eat meat again. You're a turncoat to the cause!"

Jack explained how he'd been set up, how the picnic was staged to blackmail him into silence about Pitypander's scandal.

"No, Jack, you broke your Vegan Vow by yourself. Wait, you did have some help from that floozy, didn't you? A bimbo in a cowgirl hat offers you a steak and you instantly lose your self-control? Are you going to tell me that wasn't lipstick on your face?"

Jack threw his hands up. "Don't you get it? Pitypander framed me."

"Sure, blame it on her. Was it Pitypander who hid your parents from me? No, that was you. You're a lying meathead, from a family of unrepentant beefeaters!"

Jack rushed to his parents' defense. "That's enough. You think working in a meat processing plant is easy? You want people to get trichinosis and E. coli?"

"Yes, I hope they do. You meatheads should die horrible deaths, just like the poor animals killed to satisfy your cruel appetites—with the help of your meatpacking parents."

"Don't you badmouth my folks!"

Fanny turned her back on him. "You didn't tell me about them. You never were reformed. Some Boy Scout you are. You're nothing but a faker and a fraud."

Had she forgotten Jack's months of exemplary vegan behavior? No meat, no milk, no cheese, no pizza worth eating, no joy in life. What had it all been for, he wondered. "Hey, I took your vow, didn't I? I starved for you, I did everything you asked. I even protested with you in that stupid demonstration against chicken McNuggets."

"Stupid? Ah, so now the truth comes out. Your vegan virtue was nothing but an act. I hope you enjoyed your steaks, Mr. Snap. I never want to see your meat-chewing chops again." Fanny whirled around and stormed past him, heading back to the *Bee* building.

"Well, as a matter of fact, they were good steaks," Jack called after her. "The best I ever ate, doggone it."

JACK SAT ON a park bench, looking up at the sky, regrets churning through his head. How could he ever make amends with Fanny? Was there any hope for a habitual meat-eater and a militant vegan, or was the moral chasm separating them too wide?

"It's not that bad, kid. It never is."

The voice came from behind. Jack turned and saw a man in a blue suit, leaning his elbow against a palm tree.

"Agent Seven?"

Jack had never seen the G-man in broad daylight. Under the sun's glare he looked older and fatter, and his glasses even thicker.

The agent walked over and sat down next to him. "She'll come around if you give her a chance. What you need, kid, is an alibi."

Jack's eyes burned with indignation. The FBI man was eavesdropping on his conversations with his girlfriend. "Have you ever heard of privacy, mister?"

A wry smile appeared on Agent Seven's face. "Privacy, now there's an interesting concept. Like I told you before, kid, you're a person of interest. The bureau has a need to know. And when the bureau has a need to know, your right to privacy becomes, well, sort of academic."

"To heck with the bureau. I have rights like anybody else. Don't you need a warrant or something to spy on me?"

Agent Seven laughed. "Let's just say I have all the authorization I need. You should be real glad I do. I can save you from Pitypander." He reached inside his coat pocket and pulled out a digital recorder. "See this?"

"Yeah, so what?"

Agent Seven played a recording. It was Pitypander's voice:

> "You like scandals, Jack? Well, now you have your very own, charbroiled specially for you."
>
> "Scandal? Me? What have I done?"
>
> "I don't know, what have you done? Maybe you should ask your vegan girlfriend. Won't she think what you've done is a scandal?"

Agent Seven punched the recorder's "off" button. "What do you think of that?"

Jack was aghast. Now the FBI was recording his private conversations. Who was Agent Seven, and what was his mission?

"I think you shouldn't be bugging a reporter, much less a presidential candidate," Jack replied, with a mix of astonishment and dread. "Who the heck are you working for?"

"Wise up, kid." Agent Seven held the recorder between his thumb and forefinger. "This here will get you out of the doghouse with little Miss Vegan. With this you can prove Pitypander set a trap for you."

"First you're stalking me day and night, and now you're bribing me with an illegal recording?"

"Kid, it's not a bribe, it's a deal. You get this thing, and I get what you have on the high school boy. I also want everything you have on whatever's going on between Kim Il Bong and Pitypander."

"Oh, is that all? Some deal."

Agent Seven put his hand on Jack's shoulder. "Look, I'm trying to be your friend, kid. Things could get a lot harder for you. Like being indicted for obstruction of justice. You don't want that, do you?"

"Forget it. You can't pin anything like that on me and you know it."

"This is your last chance, kid. There's trouble waiting for you if you don't cooperate with us."

"Us? You mean Diebold, don't you? You're working for him, aren't you?"

Agent Seven didn't say a word.

"I know what I've done and what I haven't." Jack thrust his chest out. "I can play this game too. You guys are the ones in trouble."

"What do you mean?"

"I've got something on Diebold."

Agent Seven stiffened. His smirk disappeared. "Say what?"

Jack pulled out his phone, poked the screen, and played a few seconds of the Diebold recording he'd transferred from the thumb drive. "There's twenty minutes more of that on here. Whose recording do you think is worth more, mine about Diebold or yours about my eating a stupid steak?"

The agent's face grew pale. "Oh, that's not a good idea, kid. That's a confidential presidential conversation, probably top secret. How the hell did you get it?" He grabbed for Jack's phone. "Gimme that thing!"

Jack shoved him away. "Privacy—now there's an interesting concept. Funny thing about privacy laws, they don't apply to me because I'm a reporter, so when I need to know something, the president's right to privacy becomes, well, kind of academic. How do you like that?"

"Hand it over!"

"Not a chance." Jack dangled his finger over the screen. "You came here to make a deal? Here it is: Give me what I want and I won't email this recording of Diebold to Pitypander right now. I'll give you five seconds to think about it, mister. One...two...three—"

The agent threw his hands up. "Okay, kid, you win, don't send it!" He slapped his recorder into Jack's hand.

The reporter slipped it into his pocket and stood up. "Nice doing business with you, Agent Seven. Give my best to President Diebold, won't you?"

The G-man sighed. "That was a dumb move, kid. Believe me, a stunt like that will land you in big trouble."

CHAPTER 29

Retribution

P. **TRAYSON DIEBOLD** couldn't believe he was hearing about yet another scandal. His eyes, glazing over, wandered around the Oval Office and settled on the three heroes of industry immortalized on his credenza: his bronze busts of Cornelius Vanderbilt, Andrew Carnegie, and John D. Rockefeller.

Reminders of the Gilded Age never failed to lighten Diebold's blackest moods. Running the comparatively tiny federal government back then must have been an easy job, he mused. Even the scandals were better—mostly straightforward crimes like graft and bribery and only rarely the messy personal indiscretions of rival politicians. In the good old days, scandals didn't suck up so much of a president's attention. They weren't so hard to follow.

To be president today required a steel-trap mind for details, and Diebold was never surer he didn't have one than when his staff brought him a new scandal to worry about. The burden of keeping track of them all was overtaxing his memory. He rolled his leather chair forward to the edge of his desk as if it weren't his mind failing him but his hearing. He pretended to have misunderstood Attorney General Cooper.

"Do you mean to tell me this twenty-two-year-old, wet-behind-the-ears reporter for, for—?"

"*The Burbank Bee*, Mr. President. It's a little newspaper in Southern California. Snap started working there earlier this year, right out of college."

Jack Snap. Diebold examined the face smiling up at him from the FBI dossier. Snap didn't look like a national security threat. The fresh-faced young man with the scintillating grin could have passed for a high school senior. This was the fellow who had a recording of him discussing the Clean Slate contracts?

Diebold looked warily at his attorney general. "What in tarnation did he threaten to do with the recording?"

"He was about to send it to Pitypander," Cooper said. "He told our agent if we didn't hand over a recording to get him off the hook with his crazy vegan girlfriend about eating a steak that he'd email his recording of you to Pitypander right then."

The president rubbed his eyes. It must be the late hour. There were two recordings? "Run that by me again. This kid threatened to destroy me because he ate a steak?"

"No, sir. Snap's girlfriend went bonkers about him eating the steak, so he wanted our recording of Pitypander framing him with eating it so he could have an alibi for his girlfriend. To get our recording, he threatened to destroy you with his recording."

Diebold knew Pitypander was eccentric, but this was flat-out loony. Outing a vegan reporter for his dietary misdeeds? Nutty as it was, it might qualify as a scandal in its own right. "Is this steak-eating conspiracy something we can use against her?"

Cooper smiled. "If we had time, it would be fun to nail her with it, sir. But we have an urgent national security threat here— the recording of you. Snap can zap your conversation right to

Pitypander from his phone any time he likes. He's holding a loaded gun to your head."

Diebold noted the stark contradiction between what Cooper was telling him and the photo of the wide-eyed young man in the dossier. Snap didn't look the least bit nefarious. Also, if Pitypander was framing Snap, why was he on her side? The kid should be a staunch Diebold ally.

"Snap's neutral, or at least pretending to be." Cooper explained how the Collier rumor had led the FBI to monitor the young reporter. "We think Snap's got a boatload of dirt on her. We've been trying to get hold of it for months."

"What the dickens do you think he means to do with it?" Diebold asked.

"We have no idea, sir. Snap's a loose cannon. He's hungry, out to make a name for himself, looking to make a big score—Pitypander, you, or anybody else he can nail with a scandal. That's what makes him so dangerous. It's why we need to keep him quiet."

"You mean, bribe him? Okay, so bribe him," said Diebold.

"We tried that. Bribes won't work on this guy. Our agent says Snap's a straight arrow—the stubborn, self-righteous type. Impossible to control."

Diebold's forehead twitched. Every problem they brought him was impossible to control, or it wouldn't have landed on his desk. Now a baby-faced reporter threatened to torpedo his administration.

With only weeks until the election, the Democrats were likely to spring a new scandal on him any day now—an October surprise. If Pitypander got control of Snap before he did, she'd use whatever dirt he had.

"Dang it, Coop, this crap just gets deeper and deeper. Can't you give me some decent options?"

"Our agent had an idea, Mr. President," the attorney general replied. "Both of Snap's parents are federal employees, working for Agriculture, so we have some influence on him there. If we put the squeeze on them, Snap might get the message and fall in line. If anybody's gonna control Snap, it better be us."

"And if that doesn't work, what will you do with the Snaps?" Diebold stopped right there. "Wait, no, on second thought, don't tell me. I don't want to know."

"No, sir, you don't. If you'll authorize an action, we'll take care of the details."

"An action? Damn." Diebold rubbed his eyes again. It sounded like an impeachable offense—but no worse than the one the young reporter might reveal. "Okay, go ahead. Just you be sure to keep my fingerprints off this thing, you hear?"

JACK LOOKED UP from his computer and saw Gus Masterson waddling his way to summon the reporter to his office.

The big door banged shut behind them. Gus sat down behind the mountains of paper on his desk and asked for a progress report on the Collier story.

Jack fidgeted, looking glumly at his notebook. "Nothing's changed, sir."

"Rod, or Vinny, or whatever he calls himself now, he still won't go public with his accusation against Pitypander?" Gus asked.

"No, not the last time I got in touch with him," Jack replied.

"When was that?"

Jack cast his eyes at the floor. "A few weeks ago."

Gus nearly jumped out of his chair. "What? After all you went through to find him, you let your only source get out of touch? For a story as important as this?"

He hadn't let Vinny get out of touch. The pizza cook simply hadn't answered any more emails. When Jack returned to Circle Beach in search of him, the cashier at Jumpin' Johnny's said Vinny had quit his job without giving notice.

"I think we scared him away," Jack said. "He must have freaked out, thinking about what might happen to him if Pitypander got elected. He knew we could find him there, so he quit his job to throw us off his trail."

"And you never found out where he lives?"

"No, sir. He never would say. He's gone underground again."

Gus drummed his fingers on his desk and looked into space. "God, that's a helluva shame. A blockbuster story like that, going to waste so close to a presidential election."

Jack bowed his head, not sure what Gus wanted him to do.

"All we need is for Vinny to come forward and we'd have the story of the year. When will we get a chance like this again?" Gus looked at his wall of plaques and awards, his eyes resting on his Pulitzer prize.

The old man's words hung in the air, heavy with the implication that Jack hadn't done everything possible to find Vinny, as if a show of disappointment would light a fire under the young reporter.

Jack searched his mentor's eyes for guidance. "It wouldn't be right to publish a story like that without having Vinny as a source, would it, sir?" He waited for Gus to affirm that they must uphold journalistic standards at all costs.

Gus sat back, laid his hands behind his head, and let out a guilt-inducing sigh. "It wouldn't be ideal. But under the circumstances we might have to."

Jack leaned forward like he hadn't heard the old editor right. "But, sir, how would I write my article on Vinny without Vinny in it?"

Gus looked up at the ceiling. "You could give Vinny a pseudonym in your story and say he didn't want to come forward because of likely damage to his future. Everyone would understand that. We would be protecting his anonymity. That's appropriate in a situation with a vulnerable young victim and a powerful sexual predator like Pitypander."

Jack felt a pang in his stomach. "But, sir, we don't have Vinny's permission to do that. And even if we did, without Vinny coming forward it would be my word against Pitypander's."

"You won't be standing alone," Gus assured him, pledging to back his reporter a hundred percent. "It'll be the *Bee's* word against Pitypander's. That means it'll be my word. As your editor, I'll be taking the heat with you. I'll stake my reputation on it. And we'll have one helluva story."

Stunned, Jack studied the old man's face. It couldn't be that simple. If they could publish the Collier story without the victim's participation or consent, Jack's months of exhaustive research had been a colossal waste of time. He could have saved himself the hassle and just made the whole thing up. Who needed real sources? Scandals could be pure fiction. Given the hyper-partisan political atmosphere of the country, many would be.

Why the sudden lowering of Gus's standards? A sickening possibility slithered into Jack's mind.

Maybe Gus was looking at the end of his career. Before packing it in, he wanted one last hurrah, one more brass plaque. He was willing to cut every corner to get it, even sacrifice his young reporter's credibility. For Gus there would be no long-term consequences for a false scandal story.

"Go with what you have," Gus ordered. "Get on it right away. We're running out of time. I want your story on my desk in three days."

"Three days, yes, sir." Jack wandered back to his desk, carrying the shattered remnants of his respect for Gus's journalistic integrity.

He sat down and stared at his keyboard. He would have to write the piece—that was his duty. He resolved to write it without straying an inch from the truth, sticking to facts he was absolutely sure of. But which were those?

He tapped out a title for the piece: "Pitypander's Lost Intern." He stared at the keyboard some more. His phone rang before he finished a single paragraph.

"Mom? I'm at the office. Can't talk. I'm busy."

Mimi Snap apologized for bothering Jack at work, but wanted him to know she and his father wouldn't be home that night. They had been arrested by the FBI at the meat-processing plant and were on their way to federal prison.

"Tainted meat samples? They can't jail you for that, Mom. What the heck did they find in them?"

"Strychnine," his mother said.

CHAPTER 30

A Price to Pay

PATTY PICKED HER way through the chaparral, stepping down the path to the big round boulder on the beach where she often went to sit and think. As she watched the waves roll in, seagulls circling overhead cackled and took turns diving for fish.

A gust of wind came up and nearly blew Patty's hat off her head, but she reached up and caught it in time. She heard more cackling. The seagulls were surely laughing at her, and just as surely she deserved it.

The young man she'd sought so desperately to control now held her fate in his hands. Jack, with his misguided virtues, could single-handedly destroy her dreams at his whim. She wondered what Fanny had made of his meat-eating transgressions and his slaughterhouse parents. Had Patty's plot to drive a wedge between them succeeded?

The leash tugged at Patty's hand. The corgis were growling at the sandy slope above.

"Cain, Abel, stop that." She yanked them back.

Glancing at the hillside, Patty was surprised to see Jack being escorted by a Secret Service agent, their feet tumbling down the narrow footpath.

"Hello, Governor," Jack said. "They told me I could find you here. I gotta talk to you. It's super important."

What could have brought Jack here in such an awful rush? Had he finally come to his senses? Patty felt her heart palpitating.

Determined not to betray her joy, she molded her lips into a frigid smile. "Of course, Jack. How wonderful to see you." Patty waved off the Secret Service man, who turned and climbed back up the hill to watch over them.

The person standing before her wasn't the same Jack as before. His carefree exuberance was gone, and his lustrous blue eyes had lost their youthful innocence. His brow folded with worry as he informed her his parents had been jailed for poisoning the food supply.

Strychnine! Patty's jaw fell open. Little Mimi and her roly-poly husband, Bob, were accused by the Feds of attempted mass murder? The obvious absurdity of the charges proved Diebold's arrogance and ruthlessness. What a despicable tactic, using poor Jack's parents as pawns to control him. On the other hand, the president's ploy had worked better than anything she'd tried. Patty wondered why she hadn't thought of it first.

Jack's eyes were so soulful, so full of filial devotion. If only he could show her a fraction of the affection he held for his parents. But that might require his seeing her as being their age, which would spoil everything.

"That's horrible," Patty said. "Are you thinking someone is behind the arrest, someone political, I mean?"

Jack told her about his most recent confrontation with the mysterious FBI agent.

"And do you actually have damaging information about Diebold?" He refused to say.

She read the truth in those noble eyes of his. Jack clearly had serious dirt on Diebold, enough to do massive damage to the president's campaign. Otherwise Diebold wouldn't have taken such a grave risk attacking a reporter's family. Even a rookie reporter could be dangerous.

Jack's situation was even more astonishing than hers. Despite his utter lack of guile and worldly experience, through no fault of his own, this artless young man who couldn't tell a lie had acquired the power to decide who should be president of the United States. For a fleeting moment the natural order of mankind had turned upside down and virtue had the upper hand over vice. The meek had inherited the earth. But the meek, being meek, didn't have the slightest idea what to do with it.

Patty did, and her unbounded confidence gave her a rush of satisfaction. Jack was hers, and he had come to her on bended knee. She looked into his supplicating eyes as he pleaded with her to save his parents. What a strange reversal of fortune: she had the worst man in the world to thank for subduing the best.

First, they must clear the air. Patty shot an angry stare at Jack. "I don't know what I can do for you. Last time we spoke you wanted to make war on me. Are you ready for a truce?"

"If it will help my folks," Jack replied.

"What do you want me to do?"

"You're a friend of my mother. You could get my mom and dad out of jail."

"How would I do that?"

"Call Diebold. Make him a deal or something."

Jack's appeal to her was as desperate as it was naïve. She was the only influential person he knew well enough to ask for a favor. He thought she had special powers. Maybe she should pretend to, if only for the satisfaction of twisting the knife in him.

"Did you want to make a deal with me when I asked you to stop threatening me with made-up scandals?" Patty asked.

Silence.

"Jack, you're acting like it's up to me. You're holding all the cards. That makes you the one who's responsible, not me."

Jack bit his lip. "I'm responsible?"

"Of course you are. If Diebold wins the election because of you, you'll be to blame for what happens to them. If I'm not in the White House, I won't be able to help them, will I?"

It was all up to Jack. He must decide whether his parents were prosecuted, or ever worked again, or spent the rest of their lives in jail.

He looked like she had dropped a ton of bricks on him. Crushed under the load, he bent over and laid his head in his hands. "Maybe we could make a different kind of deal."

"What would that be?"

He grimaced. "You still like young guys, right?"

For a second she thought she must have misheard him. Was Jack really offering her his body in exchange for his parents' freedom? Patty drew back, her heart racing. The incomparable Jack Snap was asking if she wanted him! Was this a trick question?

She glanced to her right. Perched on the big boulder next to them was a young brunette in a black sleeveless evening gown.

Jenessa shook her head furiously. "No! That's cheating. He has to want you on his own. If you win the game this way, it will only leave you empty and transform your love into guilt. We have standards, darling. You don't want to get Jack under duress!"

"I don't?" Patty looked at the apparition in confusion, but there was no mistake. Jenessa vehemently disapproved.

Jack looked bewildered. "You don't want me?"

Patty turned to Jenessa again. Surely there must be exceptions in such special cases as this.

But Jenessa, who knew everything there was to know about love, was pointing both her thumbs down.

"No, I don't." Patty pulled herself upright, nearly choking on her words. "That's right, I don't."

Jack was slack-jawed. "But, all this time, with what happened at Aspen and your letter, I thought—"

Patty touched him gently on the hand. "I got a little carried away a couple of times when I'd had a little too much wine. I'm fond of you, Jack. Yes, very fond, but that's all. Sorry, but I don't have any influence with Diebold, especially now. I don't see how I can help your poor parents."

Jack said he understood. His head hanging low, he trudged away through the sand, as Patty's eyes followed him up the footpath.

It would have been so glorious, a night with Jack Snap, one worthy of a million Jenessa Fuller novels. But it was not to be. Some boundaries must not be crossed, even for love—no, especially for love. After all, Patty had a conscience. She had standards.

Patty sat a moment in contemplation, thinking of the exorbitant price she'd paid for her standards. Exactly how high must they be? She turned to ask Jenessa, but the heroine had gone.

JACK STARED AT his computer screen for a solid hour, unable to type a word.

He got a second cup of coffee, walked around the office floor, looked out the window, got a third cup, re-read his notes, stretched, and got a fourth cup. He pounded his forehead with his fist. Still, not a single sentence came out.

The doubt sown by the governor's refusal held Jack's conscience firmly in its grip. Maybe Pitypander was just a huge flirt and the moves she'd been putting on him were meant in jest. She had rejected him flat out—that much he knew. Would a cougar do that?

If Pitypander were not a cougar, he had been grossly unfair to her and writing the Collier exposé would be unconscionable. It would be a partisan hit job—not only unsourced, but far worse: untrue. If he wrote the story, he would destroy Pitypander and elect Diebold, his parents' jailer.

Therefore it was his solemn duty to kill it.

He drew in a deep breath, walked over to Gus Masterson's office, and knocked on the door.

Gus spun around from his computer and smiled up at him. "Jack, how's the story going? Can't wait to see it."

Jack closed the door behind him and sat down. "Sir, I can't do it. I can't be part of smearing Governor Pitypander. The facts aren't there to support the story."

Gus pulled off his reading glasses. "What do you mean? We've already been over this. Collier confessed to you in person. We don't need him to be the source anymore. You're the source now, and I'm gonna back you to the hilt, like I promised."

"No, sir, it's not that. I've got some new information. I'm not sure Pitypander's guilty."

The old editor's brown eyes bored into him like lasers. "How do you know? What's the information?"

Jack looked away. "Uh, I can't tell you. I've got some doubts, that's all."

Gus leaned across his desk and displayed his dreaded Masterson scowl. "Ah, you have doubts. Well, that's different." He waited a few seconds before unloading. "What the hell? You mean to tell me after all the time and money we spent having you chase this goddamned story, you want to kill it? Why? Did you find Collier?"

"No, sir. He's still missing." Jack's shoulders tensed up. "It's like, well, I've learned some new stuff about Governor Pitypander."

"Stuff? What stuff?"

"Stuff that's made me think she might not have done exactly what Collier said she did. I don't feel good about the story anymore. It's not solid enough, with Collier not willing to come forward to back it up."

"Damn!" Gus slammed his fist on his desk.

Jack cowered in his chair. "I'm sorry, sir."

"So am I." Gus pointed his finger at him. "Jack, look here. It's not your job as a junior reporter to decide whether a story's solid enough. That's my call. Mine, you got that? I'm the boss and I'm telling you to write your damn story. At least tell me what this 'stuff' is all about."

Jack looked down at his shoes. "Can't do it, sir. It wouldn't be right."

"Wouldn't be right? To hell with that! We've got a blockbuster story here, boy! The kind a reporter gets once in twenty years, if he's lucky." Gus stood up and leaned his body over his desk. "Is that your final word?"

"Yes, sir."

Gus chewed his lip. "Then here's mine." He pointed to the door. "I can't work with a reporter who can't produce a story and won't take orders. There's the exit, son. Go clean out your desk. You're fired."

ALL THE MEMENTOS of Jack's brief career as a newspaperman easily fit inside one cardboard box. In it he lovingly placed the tee shirt he'd worn at the *Bee's* softball games, his reporter's notebooks, his emergency necktie, and his journalism style book.

Pulling out his desk drawers to make sure he'd left nothing behind, he noticed the one that locked. Inside was the digital recorder he had blackmailed Agent Seven into giving up.

He heard a sigh, looked up, and saw Fanny.

Her eyelids were puffy, but the anger was gone from her face. "I heard about what happened. I came to say goodbye."

Jack picked the recorder out of the drawer. "That's funny, I was just thinking of you. I was going to play this for you but never got the chance. Not that it would have mattered."

"What is it?"

Jack punched a button on the recorder and replayed his conversation with Patty at the picnic:

"Blackmail—such a harsh word. I prefer to think of it as a fair trade. You forget about what you know, I forget about what I know, and that way we're even. *Capiche*?"

"It won't work. Fanny won't go crazy over a bunch of stupid photos."

"Boy, was I wrong about that," Jack said.

Fanny touched her hand to her cheek. "How did you get that recording?"

"The FBI."

She gasped. "The FBI? What have you been—"

"They've been stalking me for months, trying to get the Collier story from me. They were even recording the picnic. I was going to show you this to prove Pitypander framed me."

"Jack, why didn't you tell anybody the FBI was after you?"

He dropped the recorder into the box. "And lose my big chance for a scoop? No way. Gus would have pulled me off the story for sure. I figured I could handle it myself. Now my parents are in jail, all because of me. But I guess you'd say that's what a bunch of meatheads had coming to them."

"Jack, I'm sorry. I didn't mean it."

"Yeah, sure, a little late for that." Jack picked up the box and walked to the elevator. "Goodbye."

She followed him out to the parking lot. "Jack! I didn't mean it!"

He ignored her and kept going. Jack was almost at his Honda Civic when he saw four men in blue FBI uniforms coming toward him.

"Stop right there, kid." Agent Seven pulled a pair of handcuffs out of his jacket and locked them around Jack's wrists. "You're coming with us."

CHAPTER 31

Saving Jack

P ATTY SAT IN her living room, brooding over whether she should have consented to meet Fanny Flowers, even briefly. The encounter was bound to be unpleasant.

Nonetheless, the urgent tone of Fanny's email, with its subject line "PLEASE HELP JACK" in red letters, had enflamed Patty's curiosity, overriding her misgivings. Something terrible had happened to warrant Fanny's desperate appeal.

The meeting offered another benefit as well: At last Patty would get to know her rival. Who was this dark enchantress who had cast such a spell over Jack that he had refused coq au vin, Provençal stuffed squid, and Patty herself, all in a single day at Pitypander Castle?

There was a knock at the door. When the butler entered the room with Fanny Flowers, Patty fell back against her chair. The imagined sorceress was Gidget in a blue skirt and white blouse.

"Governor Pitypander." The young woman shook Patty's hand perfunctorily, her voice frosty and businesslike.

So this smallish thing, incapable of registering much more than a hundred pounds on a bathroom scale, was the vaunted Fanny Flowers, the apple of Jack's eye? She didn't have much of a figure, and her face was much too angular to be considered pretty. Patty could stop worrying that Jack was a breast man. She took some comfort in that.

If not Fanny's body, then what was it that caught Jack's fancy? The sassy face suggested it was her personality. That was it: Fanny was a dominatrix, a predator, a minx who took advantage of guileless young men with no idea they were being manipulated.

The young blonde scanned the vast living room, her eye drawn first to the Picassos and Dalís above one of the sofas. Gazing up at the ceiling, she tapped a marble column with her knuckles, like an inspector ensuring it was the real thing and not some movie-set foam prop.

"Wow," Fanny said, taking in the size of the place.

Wow? There had to be more to the little vixen than this. Jack wouldn't have fallen for an empty-headed boob. This must be a show, a front intended to lower Patty's guard. She didn't buy it for a second.

Patty motioned toward a sofa. "So tell me about Jack. What seems to be his problem now?"

"He's in jail."

"What, in jail? Jack?"

Fanny explained that the reporter had not only lost his job but had been arrested by the FBI on trumped-up charges of endangering national security. Jack had told her he had information on a scandal involving the president and some federal contracts, but would not elaborate.

"Well, a little jail time might do Jack some good." Patty checked Fanny's face for her reaction. "Maybe that will teach him not to chase false rumors."

Fanny bridled at the provocation. "Jack wasn't chasing false rumors. I know about the Collier story. I met Rod Collier myself. He wasn't lying."

"Oh, is that so?" Patty lay back against the sofa cushion. "How do you know?"

"I can tell a liar when I see one."

Patty lifted her chin. "Are you calling me a liar, young lady?"

Fanny locked eyes with her. "Yes, I am. And much worse."

"That's outrageous. Did you drive down here from Burbank to insult me?"

A defiant smile appeared on the young reporter's face. "No, I came to make a deal with you. I know enough to write the Collier story myself. I can finish what Jack started, or you can help free Jack and his parents."

Patty snickered. "Nice try. You're bluffing, sweetie. If you write the Collier article, Diebold gets elected and keeps the Snaps in jail for years. It'll be your fault. Why would you want to hurt Jack?"

Fanny hissed with indignation. "You know damn well I don't want to hurt him. And that's another thing. Why did you want to break us up?"

"I don't know what you're talking about."

"Another lie!" Fanny shouted. "Don't pretend you weren't the one who had the photos from the picnic sent to me. Jack showed me the proof. Why did you do it?"

"Nonsense. You drove Jack away yourself and now you regret it. You need me to help you get him back."

That volley hit the mark. Fanny bent forward, dejected. "I did drive him away, it's true. I tried to change Jack. Now all I want is Jack exactly like he was the day we met."

Patty sniffed at her. "It's too late. He's seen you for what you are: a domineering, conniving strumpet who insists on controlling everything in his life, including what the poor boy eats."

"Domineering? Conniving? That makes two of us, then."

"Fine," Patty replied with a wave of her hand. "If I can't have Jack, nobody can."

Fanny gasped. "Oh my God, it's true. You admit it. You *are* a cougar."

Patty jumped up. "I am not! How dare you! Get out of my house this second, you hussy!"

"Gladly!" Fanny stormed to the door. "What a sick, pathetic woman you are! You're totally insane!"

"Out of my house or I'll call the Secret Service and have you arrested!"

Fanny stomped out. Patty slammed the door after her, turned around, and leaned back against it, breathing hard.

"Ahem," said someone in the living room. "Is it over? Is it safe to come out now?"

Patty turned to her right. Jenessa was peeking out from behind the drapes.

"Yes, the battle is over." Patty's bottom lip quivered with rage. "But I'm not sure who won."

Jenessa walked to the sofa and sat down. "So that's the other woman. How interesting."

Patty sat beside her. "Yes, that's her. Can you believe the nerve of that young tramp, coming here to threaten me, after what I've done for Jack?"

Jenessa pulled a nail file out of her purse and began running it over her fingertips. "Not very impressive, is she? I'm glad to know she's all we're up against. You're lucky not to be facing stiffer competition. She's not nearly as busty as I would have expected. A man of Jack's caliber is worthy of a D cup at least."

"My thoughts exactly. She isn't good enough for him, not by half. She doesn't deserve him."

"But she did make one good point about Jack, dearest." Jenessa dropped her nail file into her purse. "He's in a terrible fix and you ought to help him if you can. There's nothing sadder than a broken boyfriend."

Patty scratched her head. "I can't believe Diebold threw Jack in jail. He must be extremely worried about whatever it is Jack has on him. Something about federal contracts, she said. I wonder what it is."

Jenessa advised a merciful approach. "Never mind what that woman wants, it's in your interest to save Jack too. Love is cruel enough for the damage it does to a man's heart, my dear—we mustn't leave a trail of complete destruction in our wake."

A trail of destruction. Jack was behind bars, vulnerable, surrounded by hardened criminals. Awful things might happen to him while the guards' backs were turned. He would be preyed upon, molested in the dark of night—by strangers.

Poor, defenseless Jack.

Patty flew into a panic. With Jack's parents in jail, she really was his only hope. "You're right. I must rescue him from Diebold, right away."

THE CLOCK ON the wall ticked off the minutes. How much longer would this take, Patty wondered. She tried to focus on what Nigel was saying at the morning's briefing, but her mind kept returning to Jack. What perils was he facing in the federal penitentiary? Patty waited for a convenient pause in the meeting—and waited.

Her campaign chairman droned on about how the latest round of aggressive ads targeting Diebold's misogyny had erased the president's lead. Women who had never considered themselves feminists were flocking to the Pitypander Nation. All well and good, Patty thought, but what about Jack?

With a click of the remote, Nigel summoned four incriminating images of Diebold onto the television screen: sniffing his secretary Dolly Newton's hair, resting his hand on the shoulder of campaign aide Lindsey Copeland, vetoing a bill to fund free childcare, and sitting in a room with his all-male cabinet. "This November," a female voice-over intoned, "let's break up the old boys' club. Enough with sexual predators. Put Pitypander in the White House."

Sexual predators! Jack was locked up in a place infested with them! Patty could hold back no longer. "I want to call Diebold."

Nigel looked at her like she was cuckoo. "What? Call Diebold a week before your last debate? Why?"

She told him the terrible news about Jack.

Nigel saw nothing terrible about it. He simply smirked. "I'd say that's a fitting end for Snap. Diebold did your work for you. It serves the young blighter right, doesn't it?"

"But we have to get Jack out of jail. It's dangerous there."

Nigel was unmoved. "What the bloody hell! Leave Snap right where he is. The fool brought it on himself, skulking about, prying into your business. I say we let the ingrate rot in jail!"

There was a more practical reason to save Jack, she argued: he had the goods on Diebold. "Nigel, don't you see, Jack's gotten hold of something big—so big Diebold risked jailing him to cover it up. If I can free Jack, maybe he'll tell us about Diebold's scandal."

"You're depending on Snap's gratitude to help us? When has that ever worked? Despite everything you've offered him, all he's ever done is hound you."

"We have to try."

Nigel saw it was no use resisting her. A call to the president was arranged. An hour later, Patty's phone rang. She depressed the speakerphone button.

"I'll be damned. It's the Diva of the Downtrodden," said the president. "You're the last person on earth I expected to hear from. What do you think you're doing, Governor? First your ads turn me into a pervert, then you slime me with that tired old crap about Newton and Copeland. Next I guess you'll be painting me as a pervert in a raincoat. You think I'm gonna just sit back and let you smear me, lady?"

"Those aren't smears, Mr. President. The videos speak for themselves. They're perfectly fair."

Diebold continued his tirade. "That was on top of the BS you were spewing at our last debate—your horse crap about my plan to starve little children and shut down their schools. That's a total distortion of my Clean Slate program and you know it."

"Mr. President, I was calling you about something else, if you'll allow—"

"You think you're going to raise my negatives? Wait until you see what I'm about to do to yours. I'm gonna blow you out of the water."

Patty finally managed to bring up the issue of the Snaps. "I'm only asking you to let them go. This election is between you and me. Let's leave these little people out of it. There's no reason for us to ruin their lives."

"I don't know about any Snap family, Governor, but when I'm done with you, your reputation will be in so many tiny pieces you'll need a vacuum cleaner to suck them off the floor. Does Rod Collier ring a bell? How about Kim Il Bong? Huh? You think you're gonna play rough with me and get away with it?"

If Diebold wasn't going to listen, it was pointless to continue. Nigel motioned to her to end the call. Patty thanked the president for his time and politely hung up.

Nigel, ashen-faced, sank into a funk. "Diebold knows about Collier and Kim! He's going to dump it all on you at the debate! My God!"

Patty looked at her campaign manager with dismay. Nigel was a brilliant strategist, but when things got tough, his nerve deserted him. The more Patty dealt with Diebold, the less he frightened her and the madder she got. The SOB was going to sling a lot of dirt at her? So what? *Bring it on.*

Patty remembered how her father's face used to fill with rage when the opposition at city hall smeared him. Bullies, he called them. She could still hear Papa's booming voice, lecturing his two little children at the dinner table that they must never be afraid to face bullies down, on the school playground or anywhere else: "The harder they come, the faster they flees. Catch a mouse in a trap and a rat in his sleaze."

Out-slimed by P. Trayson Diebold and his Texas mob? Luigi Ingratelli's daughter scorned the thought. The president was a dirty, lying rat, and if more sleaze would catch him, she knew just where to get it.

CHAPTER 32

The Dirtmaster

THE WORLD'S ELITES were the same everywhere. All of them rose to the top and stayed there by developing extensive networks of other elites.

The Casino King knew that better than anyone. He made it his business to know where the world's movers and shakers went to have fun. Anywhere there was a Pitypander resort or one could be built profitably, Benny cultivated relationships with the top government insiders and fix-it artists who served and protected the ruling class. His shadowy contacts had the connections that really won elections. Patty needed that network.

Benny had gone somewhere in Europe a few days ago to do some deal. He answered Patty's call on the third ring.

"Thank goodness I caught you," Patty said with relief. "Where are you?"

In the background, she heard the murmur of multiple conversations. People were speaking French.

"I'm still at the Palace in Monte Carlo, having a late lunch, but I'll be on my way back to the States soon," Benny replied. "What's the problem, doll? You sound out of breath."

"Listen, Benny, we're having a major crisis here. Diebold's about to dump a lot more dirt on me than we thought. I need your help, before our final debate."

Benny sighed so loud she could hear him through the phone. "I warned you about Diebold, didn't I? I told you the SOB would come after you with both barrels by the time this damn election was over."

Diebold was targeting Benny as well, Patty informed her husband, for his deal with Kim. U.S. intelligence agencies almost certainly had him under surveillance.

"Holy crap."

"Benny, we have to expect the worst, both of us. We need some serious dirt."

"How would I have dirt on Diebold? I don't even know the guy. Never met him in my life."

"Hasn't Diebold ever been to one of your hotels or casinos?"

"Probably, at one time or another," Benny replied. "Diebold's the high-roller type. He wouldn't be in Vegas to see the Blue Man Group. Diebold's a player if there ever was one."

Patty suggested searching the Pitypander Resorts reservation systems for Diebold's name. "Maybe there's something on Diebold stored on your cameras. Maybe you have him naked on video with a call girl? Hopefully something worse."

"Yeah, babe, but even if we found something, I couldn't give it to you. It would ruin my business if people thought visiting a Pitypander Palace could be used against them. You know, 'What happens in Vegas, stays in Vegas'? I can't mess with Diebold. If you lose, that mother would eat me for breakfast."

Benny still wasn't getting it. "It's too late, Benny. You can't afford for me to lose," Patty said. "If I lose, you lose. Diebold can already indict you. There are federal laws against trading with North Korea, not to mention treason. You could be looking at ten years in the slammer."

"I don't wanna be involved in this. I never did."

"Too late, Benny. You're in it up to your eyeballs. Are you with me or not?"

"Yeah, I'm with you, babe." His voice trailed off into a low grumble. "God, why did you have to run in the first place? I told you not to. Now you're taking me down with you. It's all that damn shyster lawyer's fault."

Patty ignored his grousing. "No time for that. You know a lot of special people, Benny. Do you know anybody who could help us? Like maybe the people who put you in touch with Kim?"

"That was just one guy. He's a business consultant who finds things for a fee. I don't think you want to talk to him."

"What's his name?"

"Krok."

"Has he got the right connections?"

"Yeah, he's all about connections. But he's pretty slimy."

"Slimy? That's perfect. Can you put me in touch with him, Benny?"

AT THE APPOINTED time, precisely eight o'clock, Patty heard a faint tap on the door of her hotel suite. She opened it, motioned to the man standing outside, and closed it quickly behind him.

Gorok Krok was exactly as Benny had described him: a heavy-set fellow with an ill-fitting blond wig, bushy eyebrows, and shifty brown eyes.

"Mr. Krok, thank you for coming on such short notice. I hope you didn't have any trouble with the Secret Service. I told them to let you through."

"It was no *trawble*, Mrs. Pitypander," Krok said in a thick foreign accent. He handed her the business card for Krok Business Services, Pudding Lane, London.

Patty pointed to a pair of wing chairs. "Please have a seat. Did my husband tell you what this is about?"

"No." Krok sat down, his eyes scanning the walls and ceiling, as if he expected to see something looking back at him. "He says only that you have big problem and to come at once."

"It is extremely urgent. But first, before we discuss anything, I must have your promise of total secrecy."

"Yes, of course." Krok lowered his voice. "I will keep secret. Krok always will keep secret for any client."

"Good." Patty scrutinized his business card again, thinking it odd there was no street number in the address. "My husband tells me you have contacts around the world and can find anything or anybody. He says you run a kind of search firm, or some such thing."

"Yes, that is correct. We find what you look for."

"Anything I look for? Do you mean you look for people or things?"

"Yes." Krok opened his briefcase and handed her a short list of the sorts of cases clients had requested Krok Business Services to investigate: marital infidelity, missing persons, corrupt acts of business partners, stolen art treasures, and any other type of annoying personal problem a billionaire might have. "What is it you seek, Mrs. Pitypander?"

"A scandal, Mr. Krok." Patty held her voice to barely above a whisper. "A big scandal. Right away."

"Scandals? Yes, I look for scandals for you. Whose scandals, if I may ask?"

"President Diebold's."

"President Diebold!" Krok's eyes grew big.

"Yes, the election is only days away and I'm afraid what we have on him now won't pass muster. We need something far more serious."

Krok leaned away from her. "President Diebold? Hmm." He scratched his head. "President of United States. Interfering in American election. I don't know—"

"I'm in a terrible hurry, Mr. Krok. I need the scandal by Monday." Patty reached into her purse and pulled out her to-do list. "Oh, I almost forgot. I'll need concrete proof of it too, like a photograph or recording, something I can show people. About three hundred and thirty million people."

Krok's head was reeling. "All that, by Monday? So soon?"

"Yes, is that a problem? Are you too busy to do it? I know this is awfully short notice."

"That is not it, Mrs. Pitypander. There is little time, but I can do it. I have many connections. Krok can do the impossible. We find big scandal for you."

"Good."

"But there is one thing you must agree to," Krok said with a disconcerting gleam in his eyes.

"What?"

"There is big danger for Krok in this, you know this, yes?"

Krok was implying it would be expensive. Patty had assumed so. She braced herself, concerned she was about to hear an amount so astronomical it would blow her campaign budget, or worse, force her to go crawling to Benny for money. "How much do you charge?"

A sly grin appeared on Krok's face. "For investigations of such people as President Diebold, my fee is not money, Mrs. Pitypander. That would be dangerous for both of us. Money is easy to trace."

"What is your fee, Mr. Krok? Just tell me."

Krok looked around the room and whispered, "That you will join the Krok Club."

"The Krok Club?" Patty whispered back. "What is that?"

"It is group of special people like yourself. It means when Krok calls you at the White House, you will answer my call. This is how you will pay me."

Krok was building some sort of network of elites to facilitate his business. So he was a lobbyist—nothing wrong with that. Washington was chock-full of them. Krok's services weren't going to cost a penny. She wouldn't have to ask Benny for anything.

"It's a deal, Mr. Krok."

★ ★ ★

GOROK KROK TURNED both locks on the door of his hotel room and closed the curtains. He ran his debugging device around the room and stood in the corner with his back to the wall.

Holding his phone close to his body, he punched in his fifteen-digit security code. A text message from Lieutenant Colonel Laprinsky was waiting for him.

"Requesting status update," Laprinsky's dispatch read. "Have you delivered all information to both candidates?"

Krok typed in his answer. "All Pitypander material delivered to Diebold FBI contact, but Diebold material has not reached Pitypander. She has hired me to find scandal for her. Should I cooperate and give Diebold material to her?"

A minute later Laprinsky's reply appeared: "Why does she not already have Diebold material? What happened to thumb drive? Did you not deliver it to young reporter?"

Krok gnashed his teeth. It was so unfair. He had sent the thumb drive with time to spare, but now he would be the one blamed for jeopardizing the whole operation. "Yes, I delivered it, but the idiot did not leak the information. He is in jail and is unable to leak anything to anybody now."

A minute later the order from Laprinsky appeared. "Urgent that you get Diebold material to Pitypander immediately. No time left for intermediaries. Work directly with her."

"Acknowledged," Krok answered. "Any further instructions?"

"Destroy evidence and return for debriefing."

Debriefing? That didn't sound good. What disciplinary action would they take? A slap on the wrist? A shot in the back of the head?

A nerve agent slipped into his tea? What did Bludinov usually order to be done to screw-ups?

"Will do," he typed, his hand trembling over the keys.

"One thing more, Gorok," Laprinsky's final message read. "Next time, pick experienced reporter."

CHAPTER 33

The Great Debate

HER HEART AFLUTTER, Patty watched from a wing of the concert hall as the moderator walked to center stage. She stole a sidelong glance. Thirty feet away, fondling his gold watch, stood P. Trayson Diebold.

The moderator announced the event in a voice strong and clear. "Ladies and gentlemen, welcome to the Milwaukee Center for the Performing Arts and the final debate of this presidential election." He introduced the two combatants, triggering rounds of applause.

Patty sucked in a deep breath, dialed her smile to its highest setting, and stepped into the spotlight, meeting Diebold in the middle of the platform. He was carrying an inch-thick folder with the presidential seal at his side. She swallowed hard. Every sin she had ever committed must be in that folder. Fighting off the Texan's disdainful smirk, she stood her ground and pumped his hand.

Squeezing her own folder all the harder, she walked to the opposite lectern and pulled out a pen and sheet of paper to jot down notes.

After reviewing the debate rules, the moderator turned to Diebold. "Mr. President, the first question concerns foreign policy. In the wake of continuing missile tests by North Korea and the bellicose rhetoric of its leader Kim Il Bong, how do you propose to deal with the growing nuclear threat posed by that country?"

Diebold grasped his microphone, his eyes sober and grave. His administration had closely monitored the development of North Korea's intercontinental ballistic missile program, he reported, and thanks to his efforts, America's nuclear deterrent was ready to handle any threat the regime might pose. "However, the American people need to know that, even as I've been protecting our country from the North Koreans, Governor Pitypander and her husband have been trading with them. That's treason, ladies and gentlemen."

Patty swung around to face him. "Treason? That's outrageous. I demand you retract that statement immediately!"

"Governor, please," said the moderator. "You'll get your chance. Let the president continue."

Diebold cleared his throat. "The NSA, CIA, and FBI have informed me the Pitypanders have held secret meetings with the North Koreans, making deals with one of America's chief enemies. I have official proof of their treachery here in my hand."

Diebold held up a photograph showing four laughing, glassy-eyed people in a big hot tub, raising wineglasses in a toast.

A hush came over the audience.

Kim Il Bong was splashing in the froth of the hot tub, his head turned in a grin at the other man, a fat Westerner with black hair. Bare-breasted Asian women clung to both men's shoulders. Patty shuddered.

Diebold pointed to the Westerner. "That man you see there is none other than Benito Pitypander, Governor Pitypander's husband, owner of Pitypander Resorts. He's meeting in Macau with Kim Il Bong, celebrating their joint venture to build and operate a casino complex in North Korea. The Pitypanders will get a cut of the profits. Ten percent, I understand."

Patty's hand shot up. "I object! This is slander."

The moderator hammered down his gavel. "Please, Governor Pitypander. You'll have your chance to rebut. Go on, Mr. President."

Diebold held up a second photograph. "This next one is a satellite image of the Pitypander construction site in Wonsan, North Korea. You can see the earthmoving equipment. The Pitypanders have already broken ground for the foundation. They plan to call it the Wonsan Pitypander Palace. Isn't that nice? It will be part of the Pitypanders' global business empire."

Diebold pulled out a third photograph, this one of Patty shaking hands with Kim. "Here you see Governor Pitypander herself with her old pal Kim Il Bong, living it up with the elite in Davos, Switzerland. This photo is several years old. The governor and Kim have been buddies a long time. The governor, you understand, is in the pocket of Kim Il Bong."

Veins bulged from Patty's neck. "That's a bald-faced lie!"

"A lie?" Diebold waved the three photographs at the audience. "Folks, these billionaires are selling out America to the North Koreans. If the Pitypanders are doing this as private citizens, imagine how they'll sell you out when they're in the White House."

Patty pounded her lectern. "I demand to respond!"

The moderator rubbed his forehead. "Go ahead, Governor, but please, no more outbursts."

Patty glowered at Diebold. "The president knows full well this meeting between my husband and Kim was a setup by the North Koreans to sabotage my campaign. My husband was forced into this real estate deal."

"Forced?" Diebold held up the photograph of Benny and Kim cavorting with the women in the hot tub. "Is that a glass of champagne in her husband's hand? Is it California or French champagne, I wonder. Folks, does it look to you like Mr. Pitypander is being forced?"

"He was being held at gunpoint by the North Korean army!"

Diebold grinned. "Ah, at gunpoint, you say? On the south coast of China? Please tell us, Governor, how did this supposed army get through China? By spaceship?"

The moderator belatedly intervened. "Mr. President, please, it's her turn."

Patty clutched her microphone, her voice rising to just below a shriek. "This is an outrage! I had nothing to do with that North Korean deal and you know it. My husband was taken advantage of. And that photograph of me at Davos is from a chance encounter that happened years ago. I don't know Kim."

Diebold rocked back on his heels, snickering. "Sure, sure."

She reached inside her folder and pulled out a document. "As for selling out America, President Diebold is scheming to sell America itself—to himself. I hold in my hand a ten-page transcript of a recorded conversation between the president and his business cronies. They're discussing how to buy up federal properties at ten cents on the dollar as soon as the president passes his fraudulent Clean Slate program."

Diebold laughed her off. "You're delusional!"

Patty continued. "His program is designed to result in a fire sale of government land and buildings. The best properties will be re-categorized to make them off-limits to other bidders. He and his oligarch pals will scoop up those properties for practically nothing and become instant billionaires." Patty read a sample of the transcript:

> "Ten cents on the dollar! How many federal properties can we put no-bid contracts on at that rate?"
>
> "As many as we can re-categorize under the terms of your Clean Slate bill, Mr. President. We've identified two hundred billion dollars' worth of opportunities already."
>
> "How many are in the consortium with us?"
>
> "Five. We've already lined up all the capital we'll need."

"And you're sure this will be legal?"

"It will be when your bill goes through."

Patty held up the transcript, wielding it like a club. "A consortium to buy up federal property on the cheap. This, my fellow Americans, is the whole intent of the president's Clean Slate program, buried inside his thousand-page bill. It's nothing short of grand theft—a gigantic self-dealing scheme to enrich my opponent at your expense. President Diebold doesn't give a damn about your personal freedom or your taxes and never did. He's a sham from his mustache to his spats. He should be impeached immediately."

"I demand a chance to respond!"

The moderator sighed. "Go ahead, Mr. President."

Diebold shook his finger at Patty. "You have no business impugning my reputation, Governor. Not when you've been busy servicing high school boys."

"What! How dare you!"

"I'll show you how I dare." The president reached into his folder, pulled out a photograph, and held it up for the cameras. It was a teenage boy with a purple spiky mohawk. "Folks, this boy's name is Rod Collier. When he was a summer intern in the governor's office a few years ago, Governor Pitypander seduced him. That's right, folks, seduced him—a teenager in high school, when she was fifty!"

Patty snarled at him. "That's a lie!"

Diebold looked straight into the camera. "America, the sad truth is, Governor Pitypander is a cougar, a damned reprobate, a pervert of the first order. She was corrupting this teenage boy in her back office while pretending to represent the people of California. She accuses me of victimizing women while she lures young men to her billionaire's boudoir with her power and money. Then, with her husband's vast gambling fortune behind her, she has the brass to accuse me of trying to get rich. She's nothing but a flaming hypocrite."

"I categorically deny it!"

Diebold rocked back on his heels and laughed. "You can't deny it, lady."

Patty shook her finger at him. "I do deny it! This is just another one of your smear tactics, ginned up by your campaign to divert attention from your shameless sexual assaults on women. Where is your proof?"

Diebold looked down at the podium, grim-faced. "The boy can't speak for himself, and you know damn well why. Because he's dead."

"Yes, Mr. President," Patty confirmed. "Sad to say, Rod Collier is dead, the poor boy. Which means you have no proof."

"Just because he happens to be dead doesn't mean—"

"No, I'm not dead!"

All eyes turned toward the third row of the auditorium. There, a bearded young man was standing up from his seat, waving his arms frantically.

"I'm Rod Collier!" he said, his voice ringing across the concert hall. "What the president told you was true. Except I'm not dead! The governor made me disappear. It was a cover-up—to protect her so she could run for president! I'm not dead! I'm not!"

Patty's mouth fell open. "I don't believe this." She turned to Diebold. "Have you no shame, Mr. President? You hired an actor to pose as Rod Collier? Incredible!"

The moderator pointed at the intruder. "Whoever he is, he's not allowed to disrupt this debate. Security! Get him out!"

Three security guards rushed to the young man's side. They pulled him out of the audience and dragged him toward an exit.

"I'm Rod Collier! It's true, it's all true what the president said!" His voice trailed away as he disappeared through a doorway.

A furor arose in the audience, as thousands of conversations broke out among the stunned spectators.

The moderator banged his gavel. "Please, let's have some order, here. Please, everyone, please quiet down. Go on, Governor. Finish your rebuttal."

Patty's eyes overflowed with rage. "I don't know who that young impostor brought here by the president was, but the real Rod Collier died tragically some time ago. That's the only thing the president said that is true. However, there is another young man about the same age as Rod Collier who has been outrageously mistreated by the president. His name is Jack Snap, and he's very much alive."

"Ridiculous." Diebold turned to the audience. "She's trying to change the subject. America, isn't this woman the damnedest liar you've ever seen?"

Patty held up a photograph of Jack for the camera. "President Diebold, look at that face. That's Jack Snap, the face of innocence. Jack was an aspiring young reporter barely out of college who was only trying to do his job the best he could. He had hopes and dreams, and yes, Jack had his whole life ahead of him. But then, when he discovered your Clean Slate conspiracy, you had him and his parents Bob and Mimi imprisoned to cover up your crime. The poor Snaps—father, mother, and son—are rotting in your federal dungeon as we speak. You should be ashamed, Mr. President!"

Diebold, his face reddening, slammed a fist on his lectern. "You're crazy! I've never heard of these people."

"More lies!" Patty stared straight into the cameras, shaking her head. "My fellow Americans, Percival Diebold, or P. Trayson as he fancies himself, pretends to be for protecting your freedom, but he's harassing a young reporter for the crime of doing his job. Isn't that the purest form of tyranny? Mr. President, isn't it bad enough you're plotting to plunder America's treasure? Now you're attacking our sacred First Amendment rights. Mr. President, I demand—no, America demands that you free Jack Snap and his parents this instant!"

A woman in the audience pulled out a pink hat, put it on her head, and stood up. "Yes, free him!"

A chorus of women around her did the same, shouting in unison, "Free Jack Snap! Free Jack Snap!"

It took five minutes for the moderator to quiet them down.

CHAPTER 34

The Election

BY NINE P.M., as election returns from more eastern states poured in, the wrinkles on Patty's forehead had bunched up like an accordion.

She glanced sideways at Benny, and he grasped her hand. He hadn't done that since his father's funeral. *My God, he's as worried as I am.*

Nigel displayed an intrepid smile, making a futile effort to calm the campaign staff. Their eyes were riveted with his on the ballroom's massive television screen, their career hopes yo-yoing with the vote totals as the lead shifted back and forth.

Patty's inner circle of political operatives downed chardonnay and munched on shrimp hors d'oeuvres, engaging in whispered conversations about their personal ambitions for jobs in the new Pitypander administration. They could feel the tectonic plates of the universe shifting under their feet, but couldn't tell which way.

Florida was all Nigel would talk about. Unable to contain his anxiety any longer, he pointed at the screen. "Something's amiss in South Florida. Those numbers haven't budged in thirty minutes. That's impossible. They should have changed by now."

A red banner appeared, announcing the breaking news that Montana had gone for Diebold.

Nigel shrugged the state off. "Montana, oh, who gives a damn? We were never going to convince those gun-toting rednecks anyway. Tell us about Florida."

NBC anchor John Hedges called upon the gray-haired colleague sitting beside him. "George Garbo, what impact do you think the scandals revealed at last week's debate have had on these results?"

Garbo, the peacock network's sage political observer, opined that the turnout had been massively depressed by scandal. "John, the mud-slinging has clearly taken its toll. By my count at least forty million voters were so turned off by the debate they stayed home. That has to be holding down the Pitypander vote, especially in the big cities."

Nigel laid his hands on his hips. "A voter boycott, isn't that lovely? And whose fault is that? Oh, yes, I remember. Some rotter had to spoil everything and do a real estate deal with Kim Il Bong."

Benny gave him a black look. "Oh, yeah? Well, a half-decent campaign manager would've shot a million holes in Diebold's Clean Slate program. You never could figure out a good comeback, so people bought his dopey idea. What did you expect, harebrain?"

"Knuckle-draggers and simpletons bought it, maybe." Nigel peered down his nose at the billionaire. "Speaking of which, weren't you a Diebold supporter yourself less than a year ago?"

Benny slapped his wineglass on a table, ready to duke it out. "Yeah, until some shyster lawyer came along and convinced my wife to run for president. If you hadn't, the whole Kim thing wouldn't have happened and I wouldn't be in this fix. Now I could be headed for jail, thanks to you."

"Fancy that. So I suppose it's my fault you were caught in a bloody hot tub tippling with an international pariah?"

"Yeah, that's right, pal." Benny aimed his finger at Nigel. "You roped us both into this. This whole disaster's your fault."

"Stop it, both of you." Patty pointed at the television. "Look there."

Another red banner had appeared on the screen, reading "Illinois called for Pitypander, Arizona for Diebold."

The lines on Nigel's face eased a bit. "Ah, there we are, back on top. But what the deuce is going on in Florida?"

The news anchor put his hand to his earpiece. "We're getting word that a problem has developed in Broward County, Florida. It seems the vote count has been delayed by irregularities involving absentee ballots. For more on this we're going to our reporter Denise Harrison."

"Oh my stars, not Broward County again," Nigel said, shaking his head in disbelief. "Can't they ever do anything right? That does it—I'm calling our lawyers." He pulled his phone out of his coat pocket and stepped away.

A blonde woman on the television was holding a microphone. "John, behind me a scene of utter chaos is unfolding. The Broward election supervisor, Susan Winks, has invalidated absentee ballots cast by military personnel on the grounds that their votes arrived after the deadline. Diebold's lawyers have vigorously protested her action. They are also pointing to a highly unusual pattern of undervoting at the top of the ballot."

Harrison explained that undervoting usually occurred at the bottom of a ballot, where local candidates were listed. Either someone was selectively deleting votes for president or the voters were so appalled by both Diebold and Pitypander they couldn't bring themselves to check the box for either.

Harrison thrust her microphone into the face of a pudgy middle-aged woman in a pink hat. "Mrs. Winks, the Diebold campaign has charged that you are a militant Ladybug trying to throw the election to Governor Pitypander by deleting Diebold votes and presenting them as undervoted ballots. Do you have any comment?"

The election supervisor brushed off the allegation. "They're a bunch of Diebold's misogynists, Denise. We'll be done with the count by morning. There's nothing out of the ordinary going on here."

The camera panned the room where election volunteers were sorting ballots. Patty's eyes zeroed in on one of the volunteers, an elderly woman with white hair.

Olympia Ingratelli dropped an armful of ballots to wave at the camera, as paper fluttered to the floor.

Patty's hand flew to her heart. "Mama!" She pointed at the screen. "That's my mama there! What's she doing counting ballots?"

Patty recalled her mother mentioning she'd been volunteering for the county. She must have offered to help with the election. Was Mama monkeying around with the vote count?

Of course she was. Isn't that what Papa would have wanted? Some help for their little girl?

"Please, Mama," Patty begged, as if her mother could hear her through the television. "Please, for once in your life, don't help me! This could screw up everything!"

Olympia shook her fist at the camera. "Pitypander for president! Go Patty, go!"

The camera returned to the reporter. "As you can see, things are in their usual state of total disarray here in Broward County. That's all we have for now, John. Back to you."

The stalemate in Florida continued for hours, as charges and counter-charges of voter fraud flew back and forth between the Diebold and Pitypander camps. By two o'clock, Benny gave out. Patty looked down at his body sprawled across a chair, snoring loudly. *Poor dear, the spirit is willing, but the flesh is weak.*

The next thing Patty knew she was feeling a light touch on her shoulder.

"Patty, wake up."

She opened an eyelid. Nigel was looking down on her, beaming from ear to ear. The television was still blaring in the background. The last thing she remembered it was four o'clock and Florida was still mired in chaos.

Patty sprang from the sofa. "Broward! What's happened in Broward? What time is it?"

"It's six o'clock," Nigel said with a chirp. "It's too soon to say, but it appears you may have been elected president of the United States."

PATTY SAT IN her living room by the phone, bent over, her chin propped up on her hands like she was waiting for a baby to be born.

At last the phone rang. It was the head attorney for the Democratic Party's legal team.

Patty put her hand to her cheek. "Diebold's going to concede? He's not going to fight us tooth and nail in court? Really?"

Nigel jumped to his feet and pumped his fist. "Aha! I told you so!"

Diebold's lawyers had convinced him he couldn't win, her lawyer explained. Her margin in Broward County was just big enough to tip Florida her way—by three thousand votes.

"We did it, Patty! We did it!" Nigel danced a jig with her on the carpet.

Their attention turned to the television, and the haggard face of P. Trayson Diebold. In a strained voice the defeated incumbent took his parting shot at Patty.

"My fellow Americans," he said with foreboding, "the reins of our government will soon pass into the hands of a woman thoroughly unfit for high office, a woman of the lowest character whose unfounded attacks on me have seen no equal in our time, a woman who has misrepresented my privileged conversations to frame me with a crime I did not commit. It is with a heavy heart that I—"

Patty hit the mute button. "I can't take any more of his insults. He didn't even have the class to call and congratulate me. Then he does this."

Nigel guessed at the reason. "Being beaten by two electoral votes probably didn't sit well."

"Do you think he would feel better if I had trounced him?"

"Yes, because a narrow loss will torment him forever, like when you lost California to Fist. It's the close ones and endless thoughts of what could have been that tear you up."

Nigel speculated that Diebold had other reasons for throwing in the towel. With his get-rich-quick conspiracy unmasked, he'd lost his last reason to be president. Why put up with the Washington swamp another four years if he couldn't use it to cash in? By conceding, Diebold would avoid certain impeachment for his self-dealing scheme. He could retire to his Texas ranch in peace.

Nigel understood Diebold to a T. Her trusted adviser, with his keen insights into the elusive logic of other people's motives, would make a fine chief of staff. He'd watch her back.

They heard a trumpet blast coming from outside the house. Patty rushed to the window. Down on the beach, a hundred women in pink hats were gathered on the sand. One held a sign reading "Patty, you did it! Bug, bug, bug, bug, bug!"

"It's the Ladybugs! They've come to celebrate with us!" Patty waved at them.

"I hear they're out hunting for Rod Collier," Nigel said. "He won't bother us again. Not with all those women after him."

Minutes later Patty's telephone rang again. It was her social secretary with a call on the line.

"Kim Il Bong? Are you sure it's not a prank?" Patty turned to Nigel. "Should I take it?"

"Kim Il Bong! How is that possible?" Nigel thought for a second. "Well, you can't very well refuse his call. You'll cause an international incident."

"All right, put him on," Patty said.

"Hello, is this President Patty?"

"This is President-*elect* Pitypander," she replied. "Is this Chairman Kim?"

"Yes, hello, President-elect Pitypander, is Benny there?"

It was as if Kim was asking if Benny could come out and play. Patty looked to Nigel for guidance, but he was equally mystified and only shrugged. "No, uh, Benny is in Las Vegas today. Can I help you?"

"Ah, well, I heard the good news on television. I am calling to congratulate you both."

"Thank you, Chairman Kim. I'll let Benny know."

"We had a good time in Macau," Kim said. "I look forward to a happy time again with him. The Wonsan casino will be ready for visitors next year. Tell Benny to come. You come too."

Visit Kim's new casino with Benny? As president of the United States? What an absurd idea.

No, on second thought, it was a stroke of genius, Patty realized. The Wonsan incident could be pitched to the press as a diplomatic break-through. By his farsighted act of goodwill in building Kim his own resort, Benny had cleared away decades of hostility between the United States and North Korea. The Pitypanders deserved the Nobel Peace Prize.

The media just might buy it. Patty thanked Chairman Kim for his kind offer of a state visit to Wonsan and promised to consider it.

"President Patty! What a cheeky fellow," Nigel remarked when the call ended. "How did he get your phone number?"

"Good question." Patty scratched her head. "Wait, I know. Mr. Krok must have given it to him."

Nigel stroked his chin. "Mr. Krok again? That dodgy fellow seems to be in the middle of everything. By the way, I've been meaning to ask, how was he able to get the proof of Diebold's Clean Slate scandal to you so quickly?"

"He said he has lots of connections."

"I'm sure he does. But he couldn't have pulled off the research alone, not that fast. He'd need a large organization."

Patty cocked her head. "Whose large organization?"

Nigel's eyes turned toward the ceiling, as if he'd been struck by a bolt of insight. "Who's notorious for disrupting other countries' elections?"

"Viktor Bludinov? You think Krok is—"

"Well, he's no Hungarian. Not with that name."

Patty thought back. The Clement scandal. The Kim scandal. Supplying dirt on Diebold. Could Gorok Krok have been involved in all of it?

A shiver ran down Patty's spine. Krok was a Russian agent. And she was the newest member of the Krok Club.

Nigel had been right all along. Connections did win elections.

CHAPTER 35

The Farewell

PATTY PROPPED HER feet up on the ottoman and looked out
from her beloved veranda. The waves, crashing one after another
against the rocks, swirled up into a mist, leaving no trace of themselves.
In the end, did the waves win the struggle, or the rocks? Most likely
the rocks, she guessed. History taught that every relentless force, even
hers, was doomed to be swallowed up by inertia.

There was plenty of that where she was going, and it would resist
her with all it had. For at least four years, maybe eight, she wouldn't
know a single moment of such peace as this. To restore herself, she
resolved to return home frequently. The Durango Beach mansion
would be her western White House, her escape from the myriad
derangements of the capital. Here the seagulls would fly overhead,
the gray rushes would sway in the ocean breeze, the sea figs would
push up through the sand in spring, and whatever Washington did
to her, these signposts of sanity would reset her compass and make
her whole again.

She found her broad-brimmed hat in the closet and grabbed the
leash, setting out for the beach with Cain and Abel. They yapped and

panted ahead of her as she picked her way down the hillside to her favorite spot in front of the cove, where she noticed a figure to her right.

It was Jack Snap, sitting on a boulder. The dogs ran up to him.

"Hello, Governor," he said with a big grin. "I thought you might come by sooner or later."

Patty could hardly contain her delight. "Jack! How did you get out of jail?"

He reached down and rubbed Cain's head. "Diebold let me and my parents out yesterday. I came to thank you."

Jack told her how the debate had brought instant national attention to his plight. At Patty's request, the Ladybugs staged "Free the Snaps" protests in cities around the country. The imprisonment of the Snap family became a cause célèbre for the Democrats and a pointless embarrassment for the lame-duck Diebold administration.

Her effort to spring Jack succeeded. The women of America rose up in protest after seeing Jack on television. That face had to be freed.

He looked well considering what he'd been through. Patty was just glad he was out of any danger of being preyed upon.

"Fanny told me you lost your job at the *Bee*."

"Yeah, she's about to lose hers too." Jack gave a shrug, as if he'd gotten over it already. "The *Bee* is shutting down."

The elderly owner of the *Bee* had died a week ago, and his heirs had no interest in keeping the money-losing paper alive. The employees were in shock, except for Gus Masterson, who'd known for months the end was coming but hadn't told his reporters for fear of losing his staff prematurely. Gus had wanted just one more big scoop before calling it a career, but never got it.

"What will you do now?" Patty asked.

Leaning his arms back against the rock, he gazed at the horizon. "I'd like to try something else."

"Another newspaper job?"

"No, another career." His face was marked by disappointment. "I thought I could take pride in being a reporter, even if it didn't pay. You were right—I did come along too late. Journalism's dying, the honest kind I wanted to do."

Jack had soured on being a reporter after less than a year? Patty didn't think all reporters were bad—just all of them but Jack.

A wave of guilt washed over Patty for the role she'd played in killing Jack's dream. Journalism, what was left of it, desperately needed young people like him to restore integrity to the profession, to save it from its growing obsession with scandals.

Maybe she could rescue him from his disillusionment. "Jack, if you'd like, I could help get you another job. We could use a man of your talents in the White House. Would you like a job in my communications department?"

Jack shook his head. "Thanks, Governor, but Fanny and I, well, no offense but we're done with journalism and politics. As soon as we're married, we're gonna make a new start. Fanny wants to get back to nature. We're thinking about doing organic farming. There's a commune she heard about near Coachella."

Married? Farming? A commune?

No, this was impossible. First Fanny had made Jack a vegan, and now she was turning him into a hippy? Patty bit her tongue. "Oh, you want to be a farmer. That's nice. Well, your parents were farmers once. What kinds of food will you raise?"

"Fanny's thinking artichokes."

"Artichokes?"

Jack's face lit up. "One of her vegan friends at the commune told her about them. Did you know artichokes are full of antioxidants, even more than red wine and chocolate? They prevent cancer and heart disease. They're full of good stuff. And we're gonna raise them the right way—without pesticides."

There it was again, the fire in Jack's eyes, the same youthful ardor he had shown a year earlier for investigative journalism. Only now it was for Fanny's organic artichokes.

"Anyway, Governor, I wanted to thank you for going to bat for me and my folks. I figured this would be my last chance to see you."

"My pleasure," Patty said. "And if the artichoke commune doesn't pan out, please do drop me a line. I can always use a man like you."

She didn't mean that the way it sounded. She hoped he understood.

"Will do." He paused a moment. "Uh, I also came by to ask you one last question, off the record, of course."

"Yes?"

"That was the real Rod Collier at the debate, wasn't it?"

A gust of wind lifted a lock of his tousled blond hair. Patty peered into his marvelous blue eyes. She could trust Jack with the truth. "Yes, you got the story, Jack. You're a fine reporter. Never forget that."

He beamed at her. That was the thing he had come for.

She looked down at her feet. "I hope Rod's going to be okay."

"I think he will be." Jack lowered himself from the boulder down onto the sand, smiled once more, and strolled away.

Cain and Abel jumped up to run after him, but Patty pulled back on their leashes. She leaned her arm on the boulder and looked out at the breakers.

"Don't make such a long face."

Patty wheeled around.

Jenessa was standing on the beach in a lavender windbreaker, her hands stuffed into her pockets. "You had to let him go. You had no choice. He's taken."

"If he wants to devote his life to artichokes, how can I stop him?" Patty asked helplessly.

"Exactly right. You can't." Jenessa did a mocking imitation of Patty's downcast face. "Once they discover artichokes, there's no bringing them back to Burbank."

Patty tossed her head. "I don't care for your sarcasm right now."

Jenessa smirked. "My dear, we both know perfectly well it's not artichokes that are bothering you."

"Oh, what is it, then?"

"Come on. It's Fanny Flowers of course. You've been beaten by a militant vegan who looks like a refugee from *Beach Blanket Bingo*. That's got to hurt."

Jealousy. Humiliation. Was that all she was feeling?

"No, it's that I completely misjudged Jack," Patty lamented. "I thought he was ambitious, and I wanted to help him. He told me he wanted journalism, that it was his passion. Now he says vegetables are his thing. It just goes to show I didn't—"

"You really didn't know Jack."

"Not at all. Not biblically, not emotionally, not spiritually, not on any level, not ever. I didn't know Jack," Patty admitted. "Oh, what's wrong with me?"

Jenessa sat beside Patty and slung her arm around her. "There, there, I tried to help you, darling, but let's face it, you're not cut out to be a predator."

Patty fell back in confusion. "I'm not?"

Jenessa shook her head. "If you were, you wouldn't have let Jack get away, no matter what I said. Even Fanny is more of a predator than you. She has Jack wrapped around her little finger, wanting to raise artichokes, while you—well, you have no clue what he wants."

"Then why did you try to coach me?"

"So you could see the truth for yourself. You're not cougar material. You're just lonely."

Patty could never be like Jenessa, not in real life. She looked down at Jack's footprints in the sand, already being eroded by the breeze. "So I'm not going to get any better at this. Time's up. I'm too old to catch any of them." She slapped herself on the thigh. "That's it—no more young men for me."

Jenessa clutched at her heart. "No more young men? Oh, I don't like the sound of that. I was looking forward to being your Secretary of Love." She zipped up her jacket and turned to go. "Fantasies are one thing you must never give up, Patty Pitypander. Young men never change. Why should your fantasies about them?"

"Young men may not change in your world, Jenessa, but look what's happened to them in mine. They don't make 'em like they used to."

"No?" Jenessa craned her head around, looking up the hillside toward the mansion.

Patty followed Jenessa's eyes. Atop the cliff, as if on a pedestal, stood a young marine smartly clad in a white cap, black coat with brass buttons, and white trousers. A member of the guard detail assigned to protect the incoming president, he was tall, broad-shouldered, and stood ramrod-erect as he watched over the beach. This was the second time this morning he caught her eye.

He had to be at least eighteen. He was legal.

"You like that one, don't you?" Jenessa asked.

"Yes, of course." Patty's eyes widened. "Look at his face. Look at those shoulders. Why, he's stunning, don't you think?"

"Then go for him, Madam President," said her imaginary friend. "What have you got to lose?"

ACKNOWLEDGMENTS

I WOULD LIKE to thank several people for giving me invaluable ideas in the early stages of writing and editing *The Cougar Candidate*, including beta readers David Ordoobadi, Bob Bear, Gary Aichele, Pam Humphrey, Lisa Howeler, Natalie Freese, and Megan Jackson. Thanks also to copy editor Ryan Chapman, who gave me suggestions for improvements in the text. Designer Peri Gabriel did an outstanding job on the cover. Special thanks to Kitty Werner of RSBPress for re-introducing me to the amazingly complicated business of book publishing.

THE AUTHOR

WILL WORSLEY grew up near Alexandria, Virginia, and earned degrees in English and business administration at the University of Virginia. As a staff writer and text editor at Time-Life Books, he wrote and edited articles on a wide variety of non-fiction topics. Many years later, as a money manager overseeing portfolios for several large institutions, he got the idea for his first novel, *Investing in Vain*, a satire about politically correct investing which was published in 2017. He lives in Northern Virginia.

A REQUEST FROM THE AUTHOR

THANKS SO MUCH for reading *The Cougar Candidate*. I hope you liked it. Patty and I would love for you to leave a review (as you've seen, she's going to need all the help she can get). Your review can be anonymous, and it only takes a couple of minutes. Here are some links to get you started:

Amazon.com
Goodreads.com
Barnesandnoble.com

To receive an occasional email about my upcoming releases, please join my mailing list at

willworsley.com.

You can also follow me on Facebook at

facebook.com/willworsleyauthor.

Will Worsley